UNCHARTED TERRITORY

for Robin and Rand
Thank you for
building community
where you are.

Ron Richin

Uncharted Territory

is a coming-of-age novel, written for young adults and adults who enjoy a triumph of life over fear.

Jack is a high school track star and a mountain climber – skills he shares with his famous, but demanding father.

In his junior year, a climb with his father on Mount Tecumseh in the Oregon Cascades becomes a disaster, almost killing Jack and threatening to destroy his family.

While recovering, Jack must develop the courage to confront his emotionally remote father and forge a deeper relationship.

Uncharted Territory

A Novel
by
Rae Richen

Back Beat Publications
an imprint of Lloyd Court Press

Published in the United States of America by

Back Beat Publications,
an imprint of
Lloyd Court Press
P.O. Box 12262,
Portland, OR 97212-4039

www.raerichen.com
www.lloydcourtpress.org
503-284-8532

Cover art by Owyn Richen
Book design by Diane Wagner
Chapter silhouettes by Carol Sands

Book group reading guide by Back Beat Publications

ISBN 978-0-9832242-0-4

First Edition

For Woody, Margaret, Jim and Owyn,
who shared the trails, the campfires and the stories

Acknowledgements

The family of any author deserves kudos for cheering, reading, criticizing, feeding and maintaining its storyteller. Woody Richen does all of these and more for me, plus he tells me when the story has gone astray. What a guy.

My children offered golden nuggets when they were most needed. Margaret asked for my manuscripts to help her through a tough year in a hardass teaching job. Margaret, my hope to give you strength was the reason I wrote those stories. Your request was the best pay. Jim promised, "Mom, I'll read you when you come out in paperback." Jim, your challenge has been met. Now, my entertaining young story teller, write some of your own tales. Owyn asked to read this manuscript, then three days later called to say, "After twenty pages, I forgot this was you and just wanted to know what was going to happen next." Owyn, I cut the first twenty pages and got on with the tale. Thanks for the great critique.

Writing colleagues deserve thanks for refusing to let me get away with maundering and wandering. Thank you to Bonnie Bean Graham, Marlene Howard, Sue Bronson, Carole Miller, Marlynn Roberts, Martha Miller, Judy O'Neill, Myrla Magness, Linda Leslie, Eric Witchey, Diane Wagner, Mitch Luckett and Ken Byers. You each give insight, tools, encouragement and needed kicks in the rear to keep me moving forward on my storytelling quest.

Dr. Amy Lawrence gave the author good advice on hospital procedures and safety methods. Master Sergeant Scott Light read the climbing chapters and gave advice regarding modern climbing processes. He also took the author on a tour of the operations of the Air Force Reserves 304th Rescue Squadron Pararescue Team. Any errors in the story regarding these topics are the fault of the author and not of these two generous people.

"Of courage undaunted; posesssing a firmness and perserverance of purpose which nothing but impossibilities could divert from its direction . . ."

— President Thomas Jefferson, writing of the character of Captain Meriwether Lewis.

"The object of your mission is to explore the Missouri river, & such principal streams of it, as, by it's course & communication with the waters of the Pacific Ocean, may offer the most direct & practicable water communication across this continent . . ."

— President Thomas Jefferson, instructions for Captain Meriwether Lewis and Captain William Clark for the exploration of the uncharted territories of the Louisiana Purchase.

UNCHARTED TERRITORY

CHAPTER 1

A Cooper's Hawk circled. Voles shivered in fear. Pheasants scurried to hide – food in the bottomland near the wide rush of water.

The hawk fixed an unblinking stare toward the northern side of the raging river, the shore that basked in the heat of autumn sun. Hills and farms stretched away from her flight toward dark forests and three snow-covered peaks.

She glanced at the river's southern shore where enormous basalt cliffs shadowed iron rails, a wide ribbon of concrete and the water's edge. The hawk rode warm air, gliding past the southern black walls where they thrust close to the water, a tall tower of rock.

In the morning, she had watched three human figures climb that tower. On this, her third down-river flight, she glanced at the humans. On the west face of a three-hundred-foot wall, they descended – two roped together, the third, the one with the long black hair, climbed alone. The hawk considered possibilities. Too big to eat. Too fettered to fly. Humans where they did not belong.

She soared down-river in search of smaller game.

"Off the rope," Berto Diestra called.

Eighty feet above Berto, Jack Huntington sat on a narrow rock ledge. He rested, planning how to descend safely. Today he, Berto and Kristi Labbé had scaled the western cliff of Crown Point to celebrate his seventeenth birthday. From the high pinnacle, they'd gazed over the vast width of the Columbia River, and out at the long, dark reach of cliffs. After lunch, they began the climb down to the river bottom, the railroad tracks and the dusty parking space that held Berto's Chevy truck.

Now, two hours into their descent, Jack dreaded this pitch: eighty feet to go, the equivalent of eight stories of tall building. He rubbed hard on his left leg and tried to will away the aching cramp that threatened to make this climb a one-legger.

He had experience with this Cramp-Beast. He knew he needed to force it loose, so he stalled and stretched his leg. The muscles tightened.

Below him, Berto stood on solid ground in the gravelly dust and hot sun. He took off his climbing helmet and wiped his face. His dark tan and his thick waves of brown hair were filled with the grime of a good climb. Berto looked like a football player, but he was a lot more interested in climbing than butting heads.

Jack shifted painfully on his seat, and glanced across the cliff face to check Kristi's progress. Kristi Labbé climbed solo on the way down – a practice she'd started last year. Her black hair swung behind her. Her strong arms were muscle and slenderness. Her long legs stretched toward new footholds.

Jack knew his dad would be proud of her. Kristi loved risk – like his father, their climbing teacher. Jack couldn't keep her from risk. He could only be here in case something happened. A lot of help he'd be – the guy with the bum leg.

He pushed his own wild hair back under his climbing helmet, and tried to breathe away his leg cramp. *In through the nose. Out through the mouth,* the trick Mom had taught him.

And he forced himself to focus on beauty instead of his betraying body. He watched a hawk swing around in a circle near the top of Crown Point. The bird seemed to glare at him before it swooped off.

Jack's gaze followed the hawk down the Columbia River Gorge. Miles farther west, a barge chugged upstream, threading its way among red and blue sailboards and pods of fishing boats. The afternoon sun lit the crests of heavy waves and the edges of the cliffs. Jack kept breathing and thought about that time two hundred years before, when the first white men came down this river – a wild ride.

Breathe in through the nose . . .

Jack had read stories of the tribes standing on shore, watching, waiting to save the idiots in the clumsy canoes.

Out through the mouth . . .

"Stop daydreaming," Berto yelled. "You climb like an old lady."

Jack gasped at a deep cramp. Angered by his leg, he yelled at Berto, "I got a grandma could climb faster than you."

"Your grandma was good, all right." Berto's voice lost its brassy edge. "Clip into the rope and rappel, man. I'm hungry"

"Berto, you're always hungry."

"Yup," Berto said. "You fall, I'll raid your pack for your power bars."

Jack tried to laugh, but his leg hurt too much.

"What's up?" Berto called.

"Muscle cramp," Jack answered.

"Drink water," Berto said.

Jack raised his water bottle. He upended it and drained the last two drops into his throat. He stretched his heel toward the river, then checked the two anchors they'd put into the cliff wall – on the north, a tie-off around a large boulder, and, a few feet further south, a metal anchor-chock spiked into the rock. Jack's rope ran through the chock's nylon loop.

He checked his rappel rope and its braking device on his body harness. He turned his butt sideways to the cliff and willed himself to go. He gripped his anchored rope and reached with his foot for the wall below.

His foot found the wall. A shock ran down his thigh, into his calf. He kicked out. His hip slid on the rock ledge. He felt a slab near his left foot crack and loosen.

"Edge! You're on the edge," Berto yelled.

"Falling rock," Kristi called.

Jack yanked his rope to a halt. His legs flailed over emptiness. He held onto the rope with his braking hand and slid his other hand up the rope above his head. He drew his knees toward his chest, and pulled more of his body onto the ledge.

Below he heard the crash of heavy basalt, but there was no way to see where it landed. Through red stabs of pain, he made himself study his safety anchors. The rope around the boulder held.

"Berto's hit," Kristi yelled.

Stunned, Jack knew he had to get to safety so he could rappel to his friend.

"Can you get to him?" Kristi called.

"Yes," Jack called, but his voice didn't carry because a ripping spasm seared up his back. In spite of pain, he focused on his second anchor point, the metal chock Berto had wedged into the rock wall fifteen minutes ago. That safety rope hung slack. The chock had moved.

And if it moved once, it would move again. Jack's throat dried. He focused on the other rope, now his only anchor. He inched his way upward, trying not to think. But an image intruded – Berto bleeding.

Jack's knotted foot hammered. He crawled onto the ledge in stupid pain as his leg muscle tightened again, a powerful torque of rubber band. Berto needed him, yet moments passed before he could force himself to sit up. He looked down. Berto sprawled on the talus slope of broken rock fanning from the cliff base toward the trees. His climbing helmet lay ten feet from his head.

Eighty feet, Jack thought. I have to do it with one leg. But I must have two good anchors.

"Jack, what gives?" Kristi yelled.

"I'm coming," he shouted.

From his belt, he yanked a spring-loaded cam to replace the loose anchor. As he reached for it, he stopped. The crack had widened. The face of the rock had moved. If he pulled out the chock, more rock would sheer off and fall on Berto. Jack pulled out his Buck knife and sliced through the loop of nylon so future climbers wouldn't mistake it for a usable anchor.

Pulling a bolt from his belt, he limped along the foot-wide ledge. Away from the loose slab, he screw-drivered a hole in the rock with the awl-like tool on his knife. Moaning against pain, he used the knife's handle to twist the bolt through the outer rock and deep into the cliff face.

Desperate, he pulled a sling through the new anchor and attached his rope for a smooth rappel. He glanced up at the three hundred feet of basalt they'd climbed that morning. Two hours ago, near the top of Crown Point, they'd celebrated a day when no cramps struck Jack.

He took a deep breath of cool air and rock moss. Below, Berto moaned and rolled to his side. Jack checked that he was not directly above Berto – almost fifteen feet between his path and Berto's prostrate body.

"I'm on my way," he called to Kristi. She climbed, reckless and fast, but still a long way above him. He turned away from thoughts of her danger, and prepared to rappel down the cliff by putting his back to the river, the yellowing cottonwoods and red sumac trees in the bottom land. Jack banged on his thigh once more with both hands, then grabbed his rope and backed off the ledge.

Loosening the rope through his brake hand, he walked down the rock-face. At each step, he pushed hard against his foot. Inside his climbing shoe, the foot had frozen in its drawn-tight position, but lightening jolts into his leg told him he was not going numb. That meant he could still tell the leg what to do.

Gritting his teeth, he controlled his descent. He worked his rope. He hoped speed would get him to the ground before pain blotted out thought. His vision darkened at the edges. A bad sign. He blinked, and let the rope out faster. Friction burned through the palms of his gloves. He hopped down the rock-face on his good foot. Overbalanced, he whacked into the cliff wall. His helmet jarred against rock. The smell of burnt glove leather rose as he pulled taut against the braking tube.

Jack's mind narrowed until he saw only his braking hand, the rope-brake device, and the woven pattern of rope strands. He elbowed away from the wall, letting out the brake, moving faster. He tried to control his speed, but his hand wouldn't pull up on the rope. Thrusting his good leg out, he kept his body away from the cliff. He could barely see as far as the rock face.

He knew he would soon black out.

"Pull up," Kristi hollered. "Pull up!" But he couldn't pull hard enough, so he took a look at Berto's position and dropped the last fifteen feet.

Instinct, and years of jumping high hurdles, made him push away from the cliff and further to the north of Berto. He tucked and rolled over sharp rocks. His body slammed to a halt in the shade of the overhanging cliff, twenty feet from his friend.

Every bone cried out at him. He wished never again to move, but he rolled toward Berto.

CHAPTER 2

Jack stared at blood on Berto's forehead. His friend's eyes were open, but not focused.

Off in the distance, Kristi thumped to the ground. He heard the gritty rub of her climbing shoes on rock as she ran toward them. She fell next to Berto, grabbed his wrist and whispered. "Numb brains, don't you two die on me."

"You care, Babe?" Berto whispered. Relieved, Jack tried to smile, but couldn't.

"Hush up, Buzzard Bait," Kristi said. She whirled from Berto, glanced at Jack's eyes, touched his arms and shoulders, and then searched with her fingers along the bones in his neck. "You feel anything?" She asked.

He stared up at her black hair, her blue eyes and the sharp, worried angle of her brows. For her sake he should breathe again. With the first shallow pant, his whole back cramped.

"Ah!" he cried out.

"Oh!" Kristi shouted. "You can talk."

"Yes, dammit."

"Lie still," Berto said as he slowly pushed upright. "We'll get help. You could have a broken neck."

"And what were you doing with your helmet off?" Kristi demanded of Berto.

"A fly got in my ear." He shucked off his backpack, closed his eyes and rubbed his forehead.

"Snake's sake! Sit down, Bert." Kristi said. At that moment, she sounded just like her tempestuous mother, back before she got sick. Jack would have laughed, if he could.

"Jesus María," Berto muttered, digging in his pack. "Ahhh. Here's my cell phone."

A call for an ambulance, hospital, and Dad – Jack didn't want Dad to know. He rolled onto his back. It hurt like heck, but he could move. "I'm not getting in an ambulance."

"Can't hear you," Berto said. "My head's still ringing."

"Empty rooms echo long." Kristi said.

"All right. All right," Berto said. "We're all doomed: Kris climbs solo; I take off my helmet; Jack climbs with no legs . . .."

"Look," Jack said, "I can wiggle all my fingers." He tried not to wince.

Berto leaned toward him, phone in his hand.

"Put the phone away and help me up," Jack said. "I'll be fine."

Kristi said, "Prove it. Get yourself up."

Berto raised his eyebrows. "The lady speaks."

So Jack rolled to his side again. Holding onto all but one groan, he pushed to a sitting position. His foot cramp tightened.

"Aiee!" He untied his shoe as fast as clumsy fingers allowed, whipped it off and massaged the arch muscle, hard and deep. His toes seemed frozen at a right angle to his sole.

Berto lumbered to stand. He slumped against the cliff and rubbed his sleeve over his cut forehead, smearing blood into his hair. He paid no attention to the red on his sleeve, but started reeling in Jack's rope.

Jack rubbed his foot and watched Berto for signs of concussion. He seemed okay, but Dad had created stoics of all his climbing students. If they hurt, they rarely said so. They all acted like Dad, clones of Mallory Huntington.

He exchanged a glance with Kristi. She raised her eyebrows, rolled her eyes and took over wrapping up the rope.

Jack pressed both thumbs into his sole. He thought he'd licked this muscle problem using Doc Bradley's suggestion – loads of saltine crackers before climbs, and lots of the old *agua*. But his foot threatened to burst at the arch.

Kristi stopped wrapping the rope. In the sudden silence, Jack glanced up. His friends stared at him.

"What?" Jack asked.

"That rash you claim is fiberglass splinters . . ." Kristi began.

Jack stared at his reddened knuckles. "What else could it be?"

"You finished building that basement room six weeks ago," she said. "As far as I know, after it gets in your skin, fiberglass doesn't climb from your hands to your arms."

Jack stared at his arms. The rash had traveled.

"It ain't no fiberglass rash, Buddy," Berto said. "Plus, you been over six-foot tall for a year now, haven't you?"

"So?"

"So, if you stopped growing a whole year ago, how come Doc Bradley still claims these cramps are growing pains?"

"No clue."

"You got that right," Kristi said. "Doc Bradley has no clue."

Berto chimed in, "Look, Jack, your cramp – the one that started during the hurdle race last spring, that didn't let up for two days."

"What's your point?"

"That's not growing pains in my mom's book," Berto said.

"Dang! Is your mom in on this, too?"

"You eat at our house. A lot," Berto said. "She's taken our pottery to her university chem lab for heavy-metals analysis. First the orange juice pitcher, now the bean stew pot . . ."

"Why would she do that? You're not getting sick."

"She says I could be getting it, too. Maybe that's why my grades are suffering."

Both Kristi and Jack snorted over that one. Jack stood up, trying to ignore the thought of Berto's mom worrying. He tromped hard on his foot, raising dust from gritty rock. Pain shot up his leg. He gripped his thigh. He raised his left leg and pushed his sole against the cliff face. The heat of rock warmed his foot. While he inhaled the sharp tang of hot basalt, Jack worked at his foot muscle.

His dad always said you had to teach a muscle you were in charge. This was one stubborn muscle.

Berto whistled. "Brother, you could put your boot on backward and that foot wouldn't know the difference."

"It's gonna let up," Jack insisted.

"Man, you gotta ask for another doc."

Jack pretended not to hear. No way could he ask Dad to go around Doc Bradley. Bradley was his father's climbing buddy. They ran marathons together, and the Hood-to-Coast relay.

After a moment, Kristi shook her head, as if in disgust, and then said, "Mind if I break out the trail mix?"

"You been hoarding that stuff?" Jack asked.

"All for you, Jacko. I think you need some chocolate and raisins. Gotta counteract the complete box of Saltine Crackers you inhaled on the way here."

Jack let go of his foot and reached out, but Kristi pulled the bag away. "Not with that cheesy hand, my friend."

Jack looked at his right hand, and his sweaty foot. "Right," he said, and used his left hand instead, spilling mix near his empty boots. The stuff tasted great. He rocked forward onto his toes, testing.

Berto pulled pairs of hiking boots out of their packs and dropped Jack's in the dirt next to his empty climbing shoe.

"Tell you what," Berto said. "I'll put the boot on you, but not tie it so you can get it off fast."

Good old Berto had read his mind. Jack nodded and grabbed another mouthful of trail mix.

"Look, Jack," Berto said as he bent over the shoe. "Doctor Bradley is your dad's friend."

"So?" Jack lifted his foot.

"So, he's gonna say what makes his pal happy. Anything to please your old dad, the Great Athlete." Berto shoved Jack's foot into the boot's open mouth

Jack waited for more, but Berto and Kristi said nothing. And that left Jack to fill the void with thoughts. Moments later, he said, "Dad pays the bills. I'll have to take it up with him."

Kristi's eyebrows rose. "That'll be a steep climb with no safety rope."

She said nothing else. Jack tried to imagine talking to Dad about a new doctor.

After a few moments, Berto nodded toward the Chevy truck. "If you need to lean on me, just holler."

They still had to hike down the rocky talus slope, through cottonwoods and sumac, and across the railroad tracks to Berto's ancient Chevy. Jack glanced at the nasty bump on Berto's head, then stared off through the sumacs toward the battered truck. It was going to be a long trek.

"I can make it," he said.

Kristi's blue eyes glared at him down her straight nose. He'd often tried to paint her image – steel backbone and warm skin. His brush found her indefinable.

Kristi turned her back on him. She offered Berto her arm, which he accepted, pretending his was a gallant gesture and not a need to lean on someone until his brains unscrambled. Kristi started down the talus slope, kicking away loose rock. Jack knew she was trying to make his solo hike easier.

As his friends walked in front of his gimpy stride, Jack imagined Berto's mother in her chem lab, analyzing a shard of bean-stew pot. She and his own mom always worried about other people. Some folks, like Kristi's mother, were so deep in their own torment they had no clue anyone else might be hurting. Others, like Dad, urged you to ignore pain and keep climbing.

Dad's method worked, mostly.

Chapter 3

The next morning, Jack followed his father to the basement. "I've gotta work on the model for my industrial design class," he explained.

Dad hauled his mountain tent out of storage, getting ready for his climb of Denali – an assignment from *World Climber* magazine.

Jack strode past the washer and dryer, stepped over a pile of his not so pleasant track clothes and stopped at the woodworking bench. He plugged in his soldering gun, cleared his throat and forced himself to talk. "Yesterday's cramps were bad."

Dad's eyes widened, staring at him.

Fear, Jack thought. Then he got real. *Dad has no fear.*

"Doc Bradley gave you a clean bill of health," Dad said.

Jack lowered his soldering gun to the workbench and said, "I need another opinion." It came out too soft.

"Come on, Jack. Are you saying Bradley's no good?"

"No." His voice gained strength. "I'm saying Bradley looked at my foot and my legs in his way. I want someone to look in a new way."

His father went back to untying the tent, allowing his graying black ponytail to hide his face.

Jack expected a rebuff. Silence irritated.

Dad leaned the tent bag on the workbench, next to Jack's half-finished boat.

"Watch that," Jack said. "I'm not done fitting the iron frame together."

"Oh, sorry." His dad pulled the bag away from the model, then glanced at Jack's project. "Kind of a fat boat, isn't it?"

"A copy of a boat Lewis and Clark took with them up the Missouri," Jack said. "At least this design is as close as I can come from the descriptions."

"Yeah? Ugly as sin."

Jack waggled his eyebrows. "Sometimes ugly works," he said.

"Not often," Dad chuckled.

Jack tried to laugh with him. It was an old debate between them, Dad's idea that beauty always meant 'better'. The discussion usually involved the state of Jack's room.

At that moment, Dad reached for Jack's free hand. He rubbed at the knuckles with a thumb and asked, "That from solder burns or wood splinters?"

"I think it's the fiberglass insulation." Jack said, looking at it as others would – red and raw.

Dad frowned. "I told you to keep your gloves on."

"I must have had the gloves off sometime, but I sure don't remember it." He'd been the one cutting insulation when they built these basement rooms, Mom's art room and the woodworking room

"Did you tell Doc Bradley?"

Jack nodded. "He said it would come out when I swim with the team."

"It's around your soldering goggles, too," Dad announced.

Goggle eyes and raw hands – girls would walk away in droves. "Look." Jack rolled up one sleeve. "It's spreading up my arm. Does fiberglass do that?"

Dad stared at the red lines on Jack's forearm. His eyebrows rose. He blinked several times, then glanced up into Jack's face. For a moment,

Jack sensed unbearable tension, but a second later, his father returned to fiddling with the tent bag.

"If Bradley thinks it'll disappear, it will," Dad said.

Once again, he'd steered their talk away from a second opinion. Dad hated doctors' offices. Last year, he offered bucket-loads of reasons for not checking out a lump on his elbow. Mom finally took Dad on a sightseeing ride, supposedly to see the building projects where she was the architect. She ended the ride at Doc Bradley's office where they drained off fluid caught in some part of the joint. As the elbow healed, Jack had razzed Dad about fear of doctors, but the joke had provoked only a long silent stare.

He steeled himself for another go at Dad. "I could get an opinion from Bradley's partner, Dr. Edwards."

Dad shook his head. "That man couldn't climb out of his rocking chair."

"Bradley trusts Edwards enough to be his partner."

"Edwards has never been under the kind of physical stress that makes a guy feel like quitting."

Hot shock flooded Jack. "I'm not quitting!"

"I've seen guys cook up all kinds of illnesses to avoid doing the tough thing. Take your Uncle Jackson . . ."

The edges of Jack's vision darkened. "We're not talking about Uncle Jackson," he said.

His father pointed at Jack's chest. "Jackson cooked up an excuse to quit. And he did it at the worst possible time."

Jack pushed against his father's accusing finger. "I'm not cooking this up."

"Guys like that fail at everything they try."

Jack hissed. "Uncle Jackson has a great life."

His father shook his head as if Jack knew nothing. Ticked off, Jack leaned over the table. "You're not hearing me, Dad. I like climbing. I want to climb. But I can't trust my legs."

Dad's Adam's apple went down and up twice before he spoke. "I hear you good. You had a scare in the high hurdles in front of hundreds of people."

"Damn right."

"If you look for it to happen, it will happen again."

"Dad," Jack said, "I have to find the cause of these cramps."

With deliberate slowness, his father placed the peg bag on the washing machine. He pushed stray black and gray curls from his face. "You think more doctors will give us the answer?"

"I want to climb. I want to run, and swim. I want to, but I can't."

Dad raised his hands as if in surrender. "All right. All right."

Jack sensed he was backing off only to take new evasive maneuvers.

"How's this," Dad said. "We get a battery of tests done – whatever the insurance will cover. Does that suit you?"

Jack waited for the 'However' he knew was coming.

"And," Dad said, "when nothing shows up, you get back into action. Move beyond that incident with the hurdles."

"Something will show up," Jack said. He unplugged the soldering iron, shoved around the tent mess and started up the stairs. "I'll call Doctor Edwards myself."

CHAPTER 4

Dr. Edwards obviously had pull with specialists. He made appointments for Jack. For five days, Jack endured x-rays, got wired to machines, imaged, poked and tested to boredom by a series of doctors. On Tuesday, Dad's brother, Uncle Jackson, appeared at the hospital just as the family arrived before one of Jack's test.

"What are you doing here?" Dad growled when they met in the hallway.

Uncle Jackson ignored Dad. He merely studied Jack for a moment. Jack smiled at him.

Uncle Jackson nodded, turned and walked toward the far door of the hospital.

"Mallory, leave off," Mom said. "Your brother cares about Jack."

Dad glared at Mom. "I don't like his influence on our son."

Mom stared at Dad in silence. To break the unbearable moment, Jack took her arm and steered her and Dad toward the doctor's office. Before he entered the office, Jack watched his uncle at the far end of the hall. Uncle Jackson turned, waved and then pushed open the doorway to the parking lot.

Later that day, the doctors took a small piece of Jack's thigh muscle for a biopsy. When he came out of the anesthetic, bandages surrounded his leg and covered an inch-long incision.

He stared at the walls in the recovery room. *All these tests. Edwards looks for an enzyme imbalance – does that mean 'something really screwy'?*

Jack thought about every muscle disease he'd ever heard of. Some struck great athletes. Disease took from them what they most loved to do. Jack's scalp tightened.

When they released him from recovery he got dressed in regular clothes. A nurse ushered Jack into a small meeting room. Mom and Dad were there. Bradley was delayed, so Edwards spoke to them alone. He looked at Jack as he explained things.

"We've eliminated a lot of possibilities. No torn muscles, no infections, no tumors, good blood reports, so far."

"Whew!" Jack blew out, surprising himself.

Edwards smiled at him. "We're relieved, too."

Mom's hand reached for Jack's. Hers was warm and wet with sweat.

"When that muscle biopsy comes back," Edwards said, "we'll see what kind of answers we get from it and one more blood report. I'm looking for an enzyme called CPK that's produced when muscles are injured."

Jack knew about injuries. You get over injuries – rest, ice, heat and you're back on the field, running with the rest of the guys.

Edwards interrupted Jack's thoughts. "If there's an unusual amount of that enzyme, we'll start searching for the cause."

"What if you find nothing?" his father asked.

"Then we haven't looked in the right places, Mr. Huntington. You don't often see a guy's legs tighten and his foot fold over the way Jack's did yesterday on the stair-master. Muscles do that because something is wrong."

Dr. Edwards did not mince words with his father.

"What about my rash?" Jack asked, staring at his reddened hands.

"We're not sure how the rash is related, but we've sent the photos of your hands to other labs for identification. We'll work hard to figure out what's going on, Jack."

After the meeting, Mom hugged Jack quickly before she went into the ladies' room. He figured she was going to wipe the tears from her face and put on new lipstick. He was so relieved he wanted to cry, too, or at least sit down. Jack opted for sitting. Dad stood, fiddling with his key chain.

As Jack collapsed into a waiting room chair, Dr. Bradley arrived and called Dad into the meeting room to plan a run together, or that's what he said. Jack overheard the words 'small strokes', and then 'Multiple Sclerosis'. He had the impression Bradley was telling his father these could not be the cause of the problems, but Jack no longer put any trust in Bradley's assurances.

Doctor Edwards would have talked to Jack instead of whispering to Dad. Back when Mom was so sick after baby Kaitlyn was born too soon, Mom's doctor had talked directly to Jack about what happened. But not Bradley. He'd pretended the baby's death meant nothing to Jack.

Jack strode out into the hall, his anger at Bradley renewed. His head whirled from fury, or maybe from anesthetic. Pacing the hall, Jack wondered why Bradley acted secretive. Jack knew he wasn't having strokes – that was for old people. But what if he did have something like Multiple Sclerosis? What then?

He leaned his head against the wall and closed his eyes. The click of Mom's heels came toward him. He glanced at her freshened face and the concern in her soft green eyes and decided not to tell her what Bradley was doing in the other room.

"Honey," she said, "that anesthetic must be getting to you. Let's go home."

. . .

Early the next morning, there was a tentative knock on his bedroom door. Jack woke with a groan. He'd slept sixteen hours and still felt the effect of something in his head. The knock came again. Dad would have just opened the door.

"I'm awake, Mom."

As she worked her way around his piles of books, he noticed she was carrying a metal box.

"What's that?"

She laid her free hand on his forehead, and smiled as if satisfied with his temperature. Then she set the box beside him. It made a deep dent in his quilt.

He scooted up in bed and blinked dizzy whirling out of his head before lifting the box onto his lap. "Fishing tackle?"

"No worms and no flies," she said.

He flipped the heavy latch and lifted the lid. Inside, a shelf swiveled up with the rising lid. The shelf held small tubes. He lifted the first tube and read the label: *Cerulean Blue*. Watercolor paints: burnt sienna, yellow ochre, thalo green.

Staring at the smooth labels, he found himself unable to think. To keep from hugging her like a little kid, he joked. "Geez! Colorful!"

"Now you don't have to come clear down to my basement room to paint."

He smiled up at her. "Tell the truth, Mom. You don't like the way I squeeze the tubes."

She laughed. "The toothpaste and the paints would last longer if you squeezed from the bottom."

From behind her back, she pulled out a package of d'Arches' best watercolor paper.

"Whoa!" Jack stared at the big tablet. "Quite an investment."

"I figured you could use some fun after all those tests."

Jack fingered the paints, thinking of all the wild places he wanted to capture on paper. Then in the bottom of the metal box, he saw a fine sable brush and a wide camelhair brush.

He pulled the camel brush out. "This is great, Mom."

Her smile widened into a grin. For a moment, he thought maybe she was going to hug him, but she just messed his hair and said, "You're welcome."

And then she trod lightly around his stuff again, saying, "Breakfast is on."

As soon as she closed his door, he climbed out of bed, and made a few practice strokes on the paper tablet. He imagined the cliffs above White River Glacier appearing on his page – blue, peach and gray-white in the morning sun.

Then he stopped and looked at all she'd brought him. He dropped his new brush on the bedcovers.

Is this Mom's way of saying I won't climb or run? I might as well paint?

Air whooshed out of his lungs. He leaned into his fists on the bed. He wasn't crying. He was adjusting. Facing reality. Bradley had told Dad something. Dad told Mom. They were figuring out the best way to tell him. Mom's way was to start by encouraging his painting.

Dad called, "Get yourself down here, son. Your mother's stupendous pancakes are going to waste."

Jack dropped to his knees, his head on the rumpled covers. *Just a moment. A moment to think.*

"Jack? You hear?"

He pushed himself up, breathing in and out fast as he wiped his nose on his pajama sleeve.

"I hear you, Dad."

Then he flipped the bedcovers over the pillow, grabbed the paint-brush and thrust it back in the fishing-tackle box. He stashed the paint tools under his bed, in case Berto or Dad came in. At the mirror near the door, he tried to make his face look calm. Then he forced himself to walk downstairs without limping.

As he sank into his chair, he saw Mom give Dad a significant glance, but neither of them said anything.

Mom dished up pancakes and eggs. "Why don't you stay home today? Let's be sure the medicine isn't making your head light."

"Alison?" Dad said.

Mom ignored Dad. "I want to be sure your system's clear before you go to gym class or do after-school track workouts."

Dad growled, but didn't say more. Babying him was so unlike Mom that Jack grew more certain his parents weren't telling him the truth. He started to blurt out the questions pounding in his head. *Tell me what Bradley said. What's the matter with me?*

But he didn't want the answer. So he moved his pancakes around on his plate until Mom said, "Might as well go back to bed."

He stayed in his room, but not in bed. He set up to do his homework. Instead, he slipped a piece of watercolor paper onto his desk and began painting Mount Hood. He practiced controlling the brush strokes and listened to the silences downstairs between his parents. They left the kitchen table without talking and went to work in their separate home-offices. The house seemed to be waiting for news, the way it had when Dad last climbed Mt. Rainier and disappeared in a blizzard for three days.

Several times, Dad or Mom came to check on him. He kept expecting the next piece of his health news to be dropped by one of them, but they were sadly quiet. Jack had put each of his finished paintings on the closet floor to dry, but on one visit, Dad noticed the paint and the brushes in a glass of water. He frowned.

"Don't you have a paper you should be writing?"

"I'm writing down ideas for it as I read."

"First things first, fellow. You've missed a lot of school."

A few minutes later, Jack heard his folks arguing in whispers downstairs. Once his mother's voice rose. "He needs alternatives."

Why? He wanted to shout, but he didn't. He remembered a day when he was about eight. He'd been playing with Mom's paints at the kitchen table. Dad had come in and made some comment about how watercolor paints were all pastel and ladylike. Since then, Jack had always waited to use the paints after Dad left the house. But he got such a kick from watching trees and fish appear on his page that he'd never stopped painting.

Around noon, he heard Dad coming upstairs. Jack had already put away his paints and gone back to work on his school papers.

Dad poked his head in. "Your meds worn off yet?"

"I think so."

"Bet you could go to school tomorrow."

"Yup."

"Your mother is making us a good lunch. Let's go."

That afternoon, Jack slept. He dreamed he teetered on the ledge near the middle of the Crown Point climb. He was strapped into a wheelchair made from his bicycle – two thin tires with a racer seat precariously welded between them. His crazy chair rolled toward the edge of the cliff. Jack made a grab for the chock he'd left in the basalt, but it came out and brought half the cliff-face with it. The heavy rock smacked into him again and again as they tumbled down a long, unending dive.

He woke on the floor of his room, shaking.

CHAPTER 5

He made it to a half day of school on Thursday – the wrong half to see Kristi. According to her friends, Kristi's mom was sick again. Kristi had been called home.

Jack caught up with Berto right after calculus. Berto's bandage was gone. The cut on his forehead still shone ugly red, but it was closed.

"That's looking better," Jack said.

Berto ran his hand across it. "Rubbing it with vitamin E. It'll fade," he said. "You don't look too bad."

Jack gave a wry laugh. "You mean I look as bad as I feel?"

"Yup. Like last week's pancake – soggy around the edges. They do that biopsy yet?"

"Yeah. No report though." Jack said. "Bert, don't spread that around. I don't want Kristi to worry."

Berto glanced away. Jack followed his gaze to a knot of girls down the hall, mostly Kristi's friends. "Yeah," Berto said, "she's got plenty to worry about."

"What do you mean?"

"It's a real pain, always having to clean up after your mom. This morning Kris seemed like . . . real worn down."

"God, I'm gonna take Mrs. Labbé to a hospital and lock her in."

"Right, Jacko. You whip them all into shape. Maybe impose an exercise program on the old lady."

"As if . . . Hey, Bert, can you take over Kristi's job? Help me with the Mountaineering Club this afternoon?"

Berto shook his head. "Nope. I got a part in the play."

Jack blurted, "Twelve freshmen and sophomores by myself?" Then he realized what Berto had said. "You tried out for the play?"

"Yes, amigo. I'm Captain Von Trapp, the pater familias of stage and screen."

"Von Trapp. That's a lot of singing, isn't it?"

Berto puffed out his chest. "All these years belting out hymns in Jesús El Salvador Baptist Church gave me great lung power, Jacko."

"Naw!" Jack laughed. "It was the high altitude climbing."

"Oh, sure! Climbing does it." On the instant, he opened his arms and sang out, *"Climb every mountain, ford every stream."*

Everyone in the hall stopped to watch Berto turn into a short, dark-haired imitation of an elderly nun. He waved his strong arms, filling the air with images of conquered mountains and rivers, singing about following dreams. Sugar-movie stuff. When he finished, the center-hall crowd broke into equal cheers and jeers.

Jack exclaimed in a circus-announcer voice, "See and hear Berto Extroverto in our very next theatrical production – 'The Sound of Mu-zak.' Tickets available at the Outhouse near the track."

The crowd laughed, with good-natured hisses thrown in.

Berto bowed deeply, turned to Jack and winked. "Thus soars my reputation as a suave idiot."

"A lead part!" Jack said. "That's great."

Berto grinned. The bell rang for the next class. They headed for U.S. history. Toward the end of that class, Mrs. Thompson made a long-term assignment that set the whole room groaning. They had to choose two partners, write a paper and do an oral presentation.

"During the 1840s and 1850s," Mrs. Thompson said, "thousands of European-Americans endured a six-month journey to carve out a new life here in Oregon. In your reading, find examples of people who made that journey. What drove them to risk the unknown? What tools did they develop to survive?"

Jack knew what drove people to take risk. He'd been into risk all his life. Without facing the unknown, he'd never discover how much strength was in him. And facing challenges always brought the promise of a fresh view of the world. From the top of a cliff or a mountain, life became new. And he always went home to capture that vision in pencil or paint.

Berto broke into his thoughts. "It's a group report," he said. "We can do it together."

Jack nodded. "Let's put Kristi on the team, too."

After signing up, they started out the classroom door with Berto grumbling. "Risks? It was my great-great grandfather Diestra who took all the risks. He settled California when only the black robes and the native tribes roamed the hills – way before the eighteen hundreds. Then you 'English' came out hunting gold, and took over Hacienda Diestra."

Jack poked Berto in the shoulder. "Listen to you. I bet when your great-great-grandfather started running cattle and sheep, the Yaqui and the Apaché were pissed. He fenced in their hunting grounds."

Berto snorted. "Now you sound like Kristi."

"Somebody has to stick up for her dad's folks when she isn't around."

They pushed through the crowd of students in central hall and moved toward their next classes. Stopping near the choir room, Berto said, "For a settler's tool, I'm gonna write about the miner's pick – short and to the point. An essay on the pick can unearth all kinds of mayhem and risk: gunfights, land grabbing, claim jumping . . . " He grinned. "I feel an essay coming on, 'The Unsettling of the West'. Think Mrs. Thompson will like it?"

Jack waved away doubts. "She'll be shocked and in awe."

Berto was well into the mood now. "And Kristi's essay can be 'How the U.S Government Unsettled Native Americans'."

"And then," Jack said, "I can bring on the most unsettling tool – Mr. Nobel's famous invention."

Berto's brows rose. "Ah, dynamite. The tool that really opened things up."

. . .

Late that afternoon, at the climbing wall of the Recreational Equipment store, Jack encouraged Mountain Club members to test themselves up a few feet and back down. Then he showed them how to wrap the belaying ropes around their hips and practice using a brake hand and a friction device to stop a climber's fall. Teaching these yahoos alone was hard work, but fun. At first, he worried about having a leg cramp, but his left foot only tightened a few times. By the time the members had learned how to use their fingers and toes to hold onto small cracks in the rock, Jack was on top of things. He was convinced his legs were better than usual.

On the way home, while the mother who was the van driver maneuvered the late afternoon interstate traffic, Jack's foot started to cramp again. He whipped off his boot and pushed against the seat in front of him. When the pain slowed, he could talk, so he asked the next project leaders to bring climbing safety devices to the club meeting two weeks away.

The cramp returned. To distract himself, he counted cars in the next freeway lane while pushing on his foot. Behind him, he heard a girl named Lila whisper loudly to her seatmate.

"You notice Kristi Labbé isn't here. She's sick at least once a week. I bet she's hung over."

The other girl said, "Why would anybody drink in the middle of the week? There's no parties."

"Her mother is from some cold Scandinavian country. Probably depressing. I bet they drink all winter."

"But Kristi's never drunk, not even at parties," the other girl said.

"Alcoholism runs in families, you know," Lila said.

Lila's bubble voice grated and Jack's anger seemed to make his whole leg cramp.

Enough, he thought and turned to glare at her. "Lila, does diarrhea of the mouth run in families, too?"

The shocked quiet in the van warned him. He'd let pain make him stupid. His verbal jab had forced attention to Lila's dumb talk. Now the story of their argument would be all over school. And every time it was told, the story would start with Lila's statement about Kristi and alcohol.

CHAPTER 6

While lying on his bed, Jack called Kristi's house and heard her phone get knocked off the cradle. For several seconds, only giggling came through the earpiece. The voice could have been Kristi's, but she didn't seem to hear him yell her name. And then, someone hung the phone up.

Lila's nasty comment came into his head. Berto had said Kristi seemed real worn down. Jack tried to ignore the question forming in his mind. Kristi would never drink.

He dialed again. The line was busy. For a charge of seventy-five cents, the phone company promised to let him know when the line was free. He punched the number and then sat, attempting to read as he waited. That didn't work, so he went through his growing file of river paintings. He emptied out a bottom drawer to store them. While he organized them, he watched the face of the phone. An hour later, it became clear Kristi wasn't going to be available.

. . .

He had all his paintings out on the bed when Dad came in, without knocking as usual. Jack stood quickly between the bed and the door, but Dad saw what he had there anyway.

"You helping Mom frame her paintings?" he asked.

Jack glanced at them. They weren't so good you could mistake them for Mom's. He decided to brave it. "No, Dad, these are mine."

"Yeah? How come so much yellow and pink in the sky?"

"Must be yellow and pink in the sky sometimes."

Dad grinned at him, and pointed at a forest scene with a wild-colored horizon. "At sunset, maybe. But you've left a logger still topping that tree at dusk."

"Maybe he's up there watching the sunset," Jack cracked.

Dad laughed. "Not likely. But how about we watch sunset over at the track?"

Kristi's phone wouldn't ring. Jack knew that. "Sure, coach. You need to be schooled in the one hundred meters or what?"

"You're on. I'll ask your Mom to hold dinner and come with us."

. . .

At the end of their mile warm-up, Jack felt better than he had in a long time. The peach sun had set, but lights from the tennis courts lit the track, too. Up at the courts, Mom banged ninety-mile-an-hour serves into a backboard and then volleyed against herself at a good clip.

Dad bent over and touched the ground. Jack pulled his right leg up to stretch his thigh and back muscles.

"You been doing your stretches before climbing and track workouts?" Dad asked.

"Coach Cotton won't let a guy just run onto the field."

Dad frowned.

"I'm better this week, Dad."

His father glanced up. A crooked smile lit his face. "Great! Let's get to the start line."

They pretended to get into the blocks, knuckles on the asphalt.

"Mom's next serve is the starter's gun," Jack suggested.

"Right. When it hits the back board."

Out of the corner of his eye, Jack could see Mom toss her ball. Her racquet arced. Jack crouched with his father. At the pock sound of her racket's connection with the ball, they both leaned forward.

The ball smacked into the backboard and they were off. Heads forward and waist-high at first, in three strides they straightened and gave their legs and arms full play. Jack could feel the heat of his father's sweat and knew they ran neck and neck.

The first thing his father had taught him was to feel where the others were and never look. "Looking over your shoulder slows you down."

Jack concentrated on forward motion of the cleanest, most efficient kind. Arms, head, chest, legs, all moving forward at a pace he rarely achieved when he ran with other high school athletes.

He leaned across the finish line inches ahead of his father. They both ran on several yards, slowing down and then walking. When Jack regained his breath, he turned and saw that Dad fiddled with his stopwatch.

"Thirteen seconds and four tenths. A little slow for you." Dad kept futzing with the watch, but Jack could see the twitch of smile at the corners of his mouth.

"A little fast for you though, old fella?" Jack said.

Dad laughed.

Jack decided now was a good time to say what he felt. "Thanks for postponing your Denali trip to come to the doctor's tests last week."

Dad glanced away. "Got to get my best climbers back out on the mountains as soon as possible."

"Yeah? Want a two hundred meter challenge?" Jack jibed him.

"Not so fast, gentlemen." Mom surprised them both. "Our dinner will be shoe leather if we don't rescue it from the warming oven."

Dad swung his arm over Mom's shoulder and hugged her. "How's the rocket serve?" he asked.

"Not as accurate in this cold as in the heat of summer." Mom nuzzled Dad's neck. Jack looked around to be sure they were alone out here.

"We should get out to the court more often," Dad said.

Mom laughed. "You'd play tennis on snowshoes if you could find a partner."

"Tennis or any other game," Jack added.

Mom nodded and winked at Jack. "The one game Mallory Huntington can't play is the game of Sit Still."

"Humph," Dad said. "I sit still for your dinners."

Jack thought about Kristi sitting up with her mom, waiting for her dad finally to arrive home for a cold dinner. He wished she had answered the phone.

CHAPTER 7

The next morning, when Kristi arrived at school, her sad eyes shocked him. He approached her locker after math class, whispering to her slumped back, "What's going on, Kris?"

She stiffened. "Not much," she said, then tossed her shiny black hair as she turned toward him. "I guess I got the flu from my mom."

That sent ice down Jack's back. He should have been there, helping her find a solution.

"I'm sorry," he said. "I wish I'd known."

She pushed away from her locker. Her face muscles tightened as she focused glittering eyes on him. "Yeah, well. You can't do anything about it, and it's gone now."

"Next time you're . . . when you're sick, call me. I can help."

She jutted her jaw. "You don't tell me you're going to the hospital for tests. Why should I tell you when I'm sick?"

That hit him in the chest. "I just didn't want you to worry."

She pushed past him. "Ditto." And she was gone.

Kristi didn't return his calls on Saturday. On Sunday, he went to her high-rise and knocked loudly. Inside, a radio blared, but no one answered. After he knocked a third time, the neighbor across the hall came out. The thin woman put on her glasses and peered as if she'd never seen him before.

"Hello, Mrs. Bartlett."

"Boy," she said. "It lookin' like that girl don't want to see you, so take yourself off and leave us *all* alone."

Back at home, Jack kept reminding himself Kristi was strong. She hated alcohol.

But then he remembered Friday. She'd looked defeated. He'd seen that kind of defeat in Mom once, right after baby Kaitlyn died. It had taken a long time, weeks of stifling silence to get his smiling Mother back. Something in his father had changed forever that year. Jack wished he knew how to reach inside his father and pull heart-deep joy to the outside once more.

. . .

While waiting for test reports, he tried not to care about his iffy leg or about being cold-shouldered by Kristi. At home, he labored over his metal boat frame – his Industrial Design project. He painted a picture of it in the river, with Sacagawea and her baby sitting on the plank across its beam.

Wednesday, he handed in his draft-drawings of Lewis' iron-frame boat. His design teacher gave the drawing a second look. "Who created this thing?" Mr. Williams asked.

"It was designed by Meriwether Lewis, of Lewis and Clark. The explorer."

Williams grinned and ran a finger over the pencil lines of the design. "Well, necessity breeds invention again. I'm going to want to see this boat."

After such a reaction, Jack believed he might make it through fall term in spite of his long absences. School might be fine, but everything else was lousy – his jumpy legs slowed him down on the track. And his girlfriend avoided him.

Girlfriend? He'd never allowed himself to think that thought. She was Kristi, his climbing buddy, his belligerent friend since the day she slid into him stealing second base during Pee-Wee Baseball.

"Girlfriend." He tested the sound of it. It didn't ring. Not yet. Not while she was so ticked off at him.

. . .

On Thursday after school, Kristi thawed enough to ask him if he had the results of the biopsy yet. He shook his head.

"Would you tell me?" she asked.

"Yes. Yes, I'll tell you."

"Good. Don't you be closing doors on me," she said.

He held up his hands to call a truce. "Cross my eyeballs."

She cracked a smile, then caught herself and turned into Tough Cookie again. "Don't you be assuming you know what makes me tick, either."

Shame flooded his face.

"I saw your expression last Friday," she said. "My friend, Gillian, gets that look once in a while when I've had a bad time at home. I know I don't look great, and she's got 'Oh blessed Jesus, she's drinking with her mom' written all over her face. I said I had the flu, and you were giving me that look."

He'd been imagining the worst, all right. "I'm sorry, Kris."

She stood with books on one hip and her fist on the other. "You know me better than what you've been thinking."

He could barely swallow.

"Right?" she asked.

"Right." His voice squeaked like some scrawny fourteen-year-old.

"No more." She thrust out her hand, "Deal?" she said.

A weight lifted. They shook. Kristi whipped around. Walking down the hall she called over her shoulder. "Now let's get something to eat. I'm starved."

CHAPTER 8

Kristi flashed her bus pass at the Tri-Met driver and strode toward the last seats. Jack fumbled out his bus ticket and dropped it into the slot. The bus took off. Forward motion, combined with his own long strides, threw him into the seat, next to Kristi.

As he righted himself, he said, "I've got track workout in fifteen minutes."

"Coach Cotton will live without you," Kristi answered, not looking at him. She pretended to be absorbed in houses and telephone poles she saw every day.

"I thought you wanted to eat," he said.

"There's a neat place, downtown." She still gazed outside. "Health food. Fresh air. No responsibilities."

He stared at her profile, straight, slim nose and dark eyes with thick lashes, like her father. Gone was the soft golden look she used to share with her mother. Hell, her mother didn't have that look anymore.

"Kris, what's this about?"

Kristi talked to the seats in front of them. "I found a place to go when I've had enough."

"Enough of what?"

"Of washing empty glasses and bottles, of cleaning up vomit, of making dinner for people who don't eat it, and of earning super grades so our Dads can brag on us."

"Hey, Kiddo," he said, hoping for a smile, "you can come over to my house for a vacation."

"Hah! Jack the great leader, the fearless athlete, the genius . . . You need to know about this escape as much as I do."

He ignored her nuttiness. "Where are we going to eat?"

"You rich?" she asked.

"Not last I looked, but I think I can swing one sandwich between us."

For some reason, that made her laugh. And then she was giggling, and hysterical. He didn't like that word – hysterical. She'd hit him if he used it on her, but she was acting way strange.

"Sorry. Sorry," she wheezed between bouts of laughter. "Swing a sandwich . . ."

"It wasn't all that funny," he said.

"Between us . . ." she gasped. That image set her off again. And he knew there was more sadness than humor in her reaction. "What's going on, Kris? What's got you so wound up?"

She still didn't look at him, but buried her face behind her fingers, her shoulders shaking. He reached a tentative hand to her shoulder. Any moment she would shrug him off. Instead, she leaned toward him and took a deep breath. He could feel the depth of her sadness in that breath, way down . . . and down.

And then it whooshed out, and she turned away, curling up on the seat with her back to him. He glanced down the aisle. No one watched them, so he put his arm around her waist and leaned over, close to her ear. "What happened?" he asked.

"He didn't come home. Three nights in a row," she whispered.

When Jack made out who she meant, he was stunned. Her father always came home. Of course, he waited until her mother had drunk herself into a stupor, but he came home to watch over Kristi. And he stayed until breakfast was finished and the dishes were in the washer. At least he did that much for her.

"Where was he?" Jack feared the answer. Ever since the drinking started, back when Kristi was nine years old, he'd been expecting her dad to find another woman and kiss the family good-bye.

"I don't know where he went," she said. "After the third night, I left. I won't be there alone when she dies."

"You can't be doing this anymore," Jack said. "He has to put her in that hospital again."

Kristi flipped around to face him. "I know that. Don't you think I know that? But I'm only sixteen. I can't force her to go."

"And your dad? Can't he sign papers and take her there?"

"What good did it do those other times? He gave up on rehab a long time ago."

"But you – why leave you to face it?"

"You never understand. Drunks scare him," she said.

"But he's the grown-up . . ." Jack said.

Kristi stood abruptly, yanked the bell pull, and grabbed her pack. "My stop," she said. He thought she meant this stop was hers alone. He was no longer invited to her new space.

Then, as the bus doors opened, she turned and motioned for him with a yank of her head. "You coming?"

He bounded off the bus behind her and discovered they were at Sixth and Yamhill, the business section of downtown Portland. He and Kristi and the fellow sleeping in a nearby doorway were the most ratty-dressed people on the block.

"We've got some crowd plowing ahead of us," she said, and took off up Yamhill Street.

. . .

Several blocks and a quick deli stop later, they settled onto a low wall at the upper end of Pioneer Courthouse Square. Jack pulled their sandwich out. Nearby, a group of high school kids clustered around the statue of a man carrying an umbrella – the symbol of rainy Portland. The statue reached out with his free hand as if hailing a cab. One of the kids had stuffed a joint between two bronze fingers. A wisp of smoke rose from it.

Jack handed Kristi half of their sandwich. Her dark shine of hair swung down and covered her face as she made a big ceremony of unwrapping the wax paper. He gazed at the cowry shell necklace that lay against her fragile collarbone. She set their smoothie on the wall between them and then looked up.

He was surprised to find a tentative, questioning look in the sharp rise of her jet-black eyebrows. "Nice place for lunch," he said, even though it was four o'clock in the afternoon. He wanted desperately to know if she'd been here on those nights when he tried to call her. If he didn't pry, maybe she'd want to talk. He knew independence was her prized possession.

The need for independence had been what sent her up the walls at Goat Rocks on those days when his father made her do it over and over again. They'd been twelve that summer. Her body had changed, making it harder for her to use brute force to hoist herself up the sheer cliff faces. Dad taught her how to finesse her climb rather than rely on shoulder strength.

And Jack had suddenly realized how much he liked the changes that time brought to her shape. His body's reaction to that new knowledge had embarrassed him.

Her voice jerked him back to the present. "Nobody pays any attention to you down here," she said. "No bother. No questions."

He stretched out his tight legs as he gazed around. "You know any of these kids?" he asked.

"No attention. No bother. Didn't you hear me?"

He tried to smile. "How can they not pay attention? You're the smartest mouth in the square." He'd almost said she was the most beautiful, but beautiful made her scared. Tough made her feel safe.

"Huh!" she bit into her sandwich and then glanced around the square while she chewed. "See that girl with the purple-spiked hair?"

He nodded. The girl wore a scummed-up sleeveless shirt that revealed a snake tattoo down the length of her arm.

"She's the mouth," Kristi said. "Never heard so much venom and shit. Berto could learn a thing or two, hanging down here."

"Maybe, but he'd have to go home evenings and Sundays." Jack hoped to steer the conversation toward her own evenings.

"The choir boy," Kristi chuckled. "Jesús El Salvador Baptist."

"Hasn't hurt him any. He got the lead in the play. Did you know?"

She glared at him. "Just because I hang down here doesn't mean I can't keep track of friends."

He saw she was going to turn this into a fight if she could. Jack gazed over the action in the plaza. Lots of kids rested their butts on this same wall, or leaned against the trunks of Sycamore street trees. On the downhill side of the wall, open spaces of brick were stair-stepped to create an amphitheater focused on the lower end of the block. People in business clothes crossed the open area in small groups, headed for stores or offices.

Most who stayed in the square were middle school or high school-aged kids, sprawled on the wall or on the wide steps. One guy's thick neck muscles and jaded smile gave him away as late twenties or early thirties. He sat on the steps in the shade. Younger people came to him, one or two at a time. They talked. They high-fived. The older man's hand always came away from that move with something in it. His acquaintances hurriedly stuck their hands in their pockets and ambled away without looking back.

Not too tough to figure out what went down over there.

At the upper end of the square, a younger fellow, tall and brown-skinned, seemed to hold court near the street vendors. Jack watched the guy's easy smile. He waited to see the merchandise exchange, but he never caught it. If the fellow sold something, his hand-off was smooth.

"Stop judging people," Kristi said.

That stung. "Why?"

She stood up as if to distance herself from him. "Because you think you know, but you have no clue." Her wish to fight was as clear as the flash of her shell necklace. She brought her anger down here with her and was looking for a way to hang it on him.

"I know that big guy is selling something," he said, nodding toward the man in the shade. "And I know that guy over there is doing something smooth, but I can't figure out what."

"And you won't know. You can't even guess."

At that moment, the young, dark-skinned man seemed to see them. He strode across the steps toward them as if he owned the whole plaza.

"What's he up to now?" Jack asked.

"Taking care of his own," she said.

As if ice had formed in his chest, Jack could hardly breathe. *His own. Kristi.*

"Hey, Girl," the guy said as he approached. Jack rose, aware that his left leg wouldn't stretch out easily. His bad muscles made him feel inadequate, but he stood as smoothly as possible, just to be on a level with this new man. He hid his reddened hands in his pockets.

The fellow glanced at him, then reached out to bump fists with Kristi. "You okay here, Kristina?" He asked.

"Doin' fine, Swede," she said.

A joke, Jack thought. *A guy as dark as my dress shoes chooses the street name Swede.*

"This is Jack," Kristi said. "He's uptown."

Swede looked him over. "Name's Swedish Pete," he said. "You that climber she's been telling me about?"

What had she told him? "I climb some," Jack said.

Swede grinned. "Kilimanjaro is no little climb."

"That was my dad."

"Oh, the dad," Swede said, nodding. "Dad's are hard to follow, yes?"

"We climb together some," Jack countered. "Closer to home."

Swede raised his eyebrows and pursed his lips. "I understand. Everyman's dad has gotta be lived up to. Or lived down."

What is he getting at?

The guy turned his blazing smile toward Kristi again. "You got that address I gave you?" he asked.

"Got it."

"All right, then. Carry on, Girl." He turned back to Jack. "Nice to meet you, Climber. Visit us here, anytime."

The way he said it was like a slap. He meant 'slum here all you want, rich boy'.

As Swedish Pete strode away. Jack picked up the empty container of the smoothie and dumped it in the nearby garbage can. "I gotta walk. Stay or come as you please."

"Was that your last bus ticket?"

He nodded.

"Here, take my pass. I'm staying."

He stared at her. "Don't do this, Kris."

"It's okay. I got a place."

"Kris."

She bit her lip. "I don't need the bus pass now. I'll pick it up from you tomorrow."

"No!" he blurted so loudly that she jumped. Across the square, he saw Swedish Pete's head jerk around. Aware that half the kids in the square were watching, Jack turned on his good heel and marched off down Yamhill toward the Steel Bridge. He hoped she would follow, but he didn't hear her boots. What he heard was the scrape of deli sandwich paper. When he turned around, she was sitting on the wall, facing away from him, eating the rest of his half sandwich.

CHAPTER 9

As Jack charged down the stairs to Friday's breakfast, Dad met him at the bottom landing. "You've got a few minutes. Let's do some stretches before breakfast."

"Dad, I do stretches."

Dad nodded. "Humor your old man. I want to make sure you're well before I leave for Denali." He gestured Jack into the living room. The chairs and coffee table already were moved aside. Jack gave in.

As they sat on the floor, stretching legs and arms, Dad asked, "Do you know where Kristi stayed last night?"

Jack's hair tightened on his scalp. Had he talked in his sleep? Or had Dad started reading minds? "Why do you ask?"

"Her father called me. He came home and couldn't find her." Dad stood and started a yoga stretch he always called 'the triangle'.

"Mr. Labbé should worry about being home more himself," Jack said. "He wasn't home for three nights in a row."

"I don't know about that," Dad said, not looking at Jack. "He was pretty worried and hoped she was at our house." Dad's ponytail obscured his expression.

Jack stopped stretching. "Dad, she's staying someplace downtown, at some address a guy in the square gave to her."

"Some guy? That's not like Kristi. What's happening?" Dad gestured Jack to stretch with him.

Jack stood still. "Kristi's finished with taking care of her mother by herself."

Dad stopped. "That woman . . ."

"It's her dad who needs to get some backbone," Jack said.

"Her dad?"

"Hell, he leaves them alone until Mrs. Labbé is passed out."

Dad glanced out the garden window where fall had begun to redden the Sumac, then bent over to stretch his back muscles. "You must have misunderstood Kris. Her dad came home last night."

"What time did he call you?"

"I don't know. Maybe an hour ago. Five this morning."

"That's what I mean." Jack heard his voice heat up. "Why not come home by six or seven o'clock at night when Kris really needs him?"

"Jack, there's got to be something you don't know about this situation. Maybe his work keeps him . . ."

"If I needed you, would work keep you away?"

Dad stopped moving. "What do you think?"

Jack pictured being in that bicycle wheel chair he'd dreamed about. He couldn't imagine Dad pushing it. After a moment, he realized Dad noticed his hesitation.

"Of course you'd be there for me." Jack smacked his hand on his thigh for emphasis. "So work is not an excuse for him, is it?"

"That woman ought to buck up, get herself dried out."

"She?" Jack's voice rose with anger. "She's sick. He's absent. So Kris pays. Where's fair in all of that?"

"Kris is a big girl. She can choose not to . . .."

Jack waited a moment to see if Dad would realize what he was saying. Dad blinked.

"Exactly," Jack said. "She's choosing not to."

"Mallory," Mom's voice broke in, "How about if you call Wolf Labbé and tell him what Jack knows. Jack, stick around and be ready to answer questions. Then let's eat."

Mom sure knew when to let Dad off the hook.

. . .

No one answered at Kristi's house or at Mr. Labbé's office.

Jack could hardly bolt down any food. Dad promised to stop by Mr. Labbé's office. Mom told Jack to bring Kristi home when he found her.

He ran all the way to school.

Kristi didn't show up, so Jack skipped out to find her. The bus trip downtown netted no sighting. Swedish Pete was not at Pioneer Courthouse Square, either. Jack asked around for both of them, but got shrugs and turned backs. He looked too square, he figured. They'd decided he didn't deserve any answers.

So, imagining the worst, but disgusted with himself for caring so much, Jack ran all the way home. As he crossed the Willamette River on the Steel Bridge, he had to stop several times to stretch his tightening legs. He spent the rest of the afternoon skipping school and calling her cell phone and her house while trying to do homework.

At four thirty, she called to say she'd dropped her cell phone in the river, but heard about a zillion messages from him on the home phone.

"Come here," Jack ordered, and knew he'd made a mistake.

"Can't. Got work to do here."

"Mom really wants you to come for dinner."

"Stop worrying about me. Tell her thanks. Gotta go now."

CHAPTER 10

By five forty-five, Jack sweated in his basement, determined not to think about Kristi or her limp excuse for not answering her cell. He told himself he didn't care about his test results. And he couldn't do magic on the fading cut on Berto's forehead, though he felt guilty every time he saw it. What he could do was get in shape for the next cross-country meet.

With his cramping feet pressed against the end of the weight bench, he reached the bar in the cradle above his chest and lifted weights. He didn't want his arms to wimp out like his legs. During this week, his legs only bothered him when he ran home from town. He figured he was improving.

About six o'clock, his father's key turned in the front door lock. Jack listened to the familiar sounds above him. Dad dropped his gym bag in the front hall even before he shut the door. Next, Jack heard the light clunk of his father's laptop. That meant tonight he would be working on a magazine article.

"Alison," Dad called to Mom.

"In the kitchen."

Then came a squeaky-shoe trek to the back of the house followed by silence during their hug, then Mom's laugh. "Watch my sugary hands, Big Guy."

Jack liked their ritual. They loved each other. They looked for each other at the end of the day. He knew lots of guys whose parents could hardly care, or some who had split. A few took their disappointment out on his friends. Kristi's mom took it out in alcohol, which was the same as taking it out on Kristi.

While he rested his muscles for another set of repetitions, Jack heard Dad say what he always said after greeting Mom.

"Where's Jack?"

"Working out in the basement."

"He find Kristi?"

"She called. All's well."

Not likely, Jack thought.

Upstairs, there was a silence, and then Mom's voice again. "Honey, I think we should let up on him. Maybe the cross-country team is too much for this year."

Never, thought Jack. *This week's been great. I'm getting it together at last.*

"Babe," his dad said, "I work with athletes all the time, motivating, telling them when they aren't ready for an expedition . . . trust me. It'll be all right."

Jack braced his back and pumped the weight up again, slowly. He wanted to prove he was not backing away from challenges. As his arms reached extension, his father opened the basement door and bounded down the steps.

From the low perspective of the weight bench, Jack watched him turn the corner at the bottom of the stairs. It struck him that, except for Dad's bigger shoulders, they must look a lot alike – tall, and all sharp angles. Their hair was the same dark black, and so tightly curled it looked like they'd trekked together through a lightning storm. Dad's hair grayed at the temples. He kept it long and pulled back in a thick tail. Jack controlled his hair by whacking it short.

Dad plopped down on the stool near the weight bench, subjecting Jack to the intensity of his cobalt-blue gaze.

Jack lowered the bar and its two fifty-pound weights, showing Dad he could do it slowly.

"Hey, son," Dad said as he leaned over to check the size of the barbell weights. "Guess what?"

When the bar rested in the rack, Jack said, "My guess is . . . you want to buy me a Pizzicato Pizza. Right?"

Dad chuckled. "What other kind is there?" As he pulled his blue shirtsleeve below the cuff of his woodsman's jacket, Jack recognized the opening gesture for a serious talk.

"Doc Edwards called," Dad said.

Jack swallowed hard. Here it came – the verdict about his legs.

"Edwards says you're strong as a bull and twice as healthy."

Jack breathed out.

"They did get your muscle biopsy back. That enzyme Edwards was looking for was only slightly elevated."

"Elevated?"

"Just a little." Dad shrugged. "Probably means something was wrong, but it's going away. You've been doing okay all this week, haven't you?"

Jack nodded, thinking it was mostly true. It had to be true.

His father clapped his sturdy palms together. "I've got an idea for a celebration."

At his excited tone, Jack glanced up. Dad leaned forward. His ponytail fell over his shoulder. "What say we make the last climb of the fall this weekend? Tomorrow we can tackle the north wall of Mount Tecumseh."

Jack was stunned. He knew the route – a mid-Oregon Cascade mountain, a tough climb first soloed by a guy who went on to be among the first up Mount Everest. The place required a crawl up a two-hundred-foot rock chimney. Above that, the route was exposed. Tecumseh was a place where you had to trust your partner.

And Dad wanted him there. Trusted him. His chest filled with the warmth of pride – until a sudden rush of concern made him back off.

"I thought you had a climb with Dave Evans on Denali," he said.

"I postponed it again," Dad said. "I think it's time for you and me to get back into it. This leg business has kept us from climbing together for too long."

"I . . . I want to do it. I like Mount Tecumseh. But I'm not sure you'd be safe when I belay. What if . . ."

His father shook his head and took a light jab at Jack's shoulder. "Buster, you've been running on that leg all week. Doesn't seem to give you much trouble."

Pretty true, Jack thought. *And I want to climb with him.*

"Well, what do you say, kid?"

He glanced at his father's flushed face and felt the pull to be part of his team, to forget the cramps and have a good time with his dad again. He'd been given all the tests and nothing came up. It would be fine. Great.

"I'll do it," he said.

"Great," Dad said, standing as abruptly as he'd sat. It struck Jack that his dad could hardly sit anywhere. Even when he wrote articles, he seemed constantly up and down: checking his resources; refilling his water bottle; taking a pit stop, or reading his work aloud as he paced.

His father's hip bumped into the woodworking bench, which made him notice the boat model. "Got ribs and sheathing, I see. But it's still a weird-looking thing."

Jack smiled. "That's what Captain Clark thought when he first saw it."

"Yeah? Well, who designed such a hippopotamus?"

"I don't think *hippopotamus* is what Meriwether Lewis was thinking," Jack chuckled, "but it's a good comparison. Hippos carry a lot of cargo."

He realized Dad had just handed him an idea he might use in his presentation for Industrial Design class – maybe make some point about designing by studying what works in nature.

"You doing this for social studies?" his father asked.

It struck Jack then that he'd also been staring at the solution to his American history problem – tools that helped the settlers. Why not talk about a tool that failed? Same speech, different emphasis – win points in both classes.

"Dad, you're a genius, and a life saver."

His father's smile flashed out, a little crooked, one side up, the other trying to remain unmoved. Dad's one-sided smile made him a lot more human, more like a guy who could be hurt by what you said. No wonder he didn't smile much in his documentary films.

"Well, better get to work on the *Sports Illustrated* article," Dad said, starting toward the stairs again. "Finish your reps," he added as he reached for the newel post, "Then talk your mom into ordering pizza, eh? She'll do anything for you, especially now that we've got this muscle problem behind us."

After his father took the steps three at a time, Jack glanced up at the weight bar. He lifted it once more, and let it down as slowly as he could. Then he stood up and leaned on his woodworking bench. He thought about Mount Tecumseh, and about how much he wanted his father to believe in him. It helped to have a father you could talk to.

In fact, thanks to Dad's idea about Lewis's boat, Jack figured he nearly had his part of the American history project written. There'd be time left over to work with Berto and Kristi on the oral presentations.

He fingered the ribs on the boat, working a piece of deerskin leather into place around the wide frame. From an old baby-food jar, he added a smear of pine-tar pitch to keep water out of the seam. He knew without the pine tar the whole thing would sink.

Still, the genius of Lewis's design was that it would carry a lot, and the iron frame could be taken apart and made into smaller boats when the rivers became shallow and narrow. The frame's clumsy look disguised its flexibility. It might have worked in spite of obstacles.

Too bad its journey hadn't turned out the way Lewis hoped.

CHAPTER 11

Mom slapped down the pizza pan and whacked into it with the rolling cutter. "Mallory, there is absolutely no reason you have to celebrate by climbing something. Give Jack a rest."

"Mom, I'm all right. This afternoon, I ended my workout by bench-pressing one hundred pounds for ten repetitions."

"With your legs?"

Dad dropped the utensils into the salad bowl. "Alison, don't be ridiculous. He's got a clean bill and we want to have some fun. And while we're gone, you can finish the last of the paintings for your show next week."

Plopping a large slice of pizza on his father's plate, she gave Dad her dagger-throwing look. "I want to celebrate Jack's health, too."

Trying to lighten the moment, Jack teased. "So, come climb with us, Mom."

His mother rolled her shoulders, as if to rid them of tightness. With deliberate motions, she slid a piece of pizza onto her spatula. Finally she said, "Do you climb because your father wants you to climb?"

Her question startled Jack. "How can you think that? I love climbing."

"What do you love about it?"

He stared at her, aware of the frozen motion of his father's fork. He remembered Mom loved hiking and camping, but she never climbed. Maybe she really didn't understand.

"I guess . . ." he hesitated, then plunged on with whatever came to mind. "I guess I climb because of the smell."

"What?" Mom and Dad both reacted.

Embarrassed, he tried to explain. "It sounds stupid, but I really like the hot-sun smell on shale and basalt, and the salt smell on my face when sweat starts up. I like the wind over algae in the snow, and the pitch smell in the pine trees."

His mother and father gazed at him, a question in the rise of Mom's eyebrows, as if she'd never met him before. He shrugged, thinking what a ridiculous start he'd made on it.

"That's not all of it," he said quickly. "That's just what I thought of first."

Mom laughed. "Thank you. You've answered my question. You like climbing – with or without the great Mallory."

"But he's the best." Jack blurted and was embarrassed to see his father's eyes widen like a startled deer.

Mom smiled down at him, pushing back her wavy red hair, looking happy. "That's the truth," she said. "He's the best. Let's eat."

Dad tried hard not to smile, but Jack saw a grin start at the edges of his mouth just before he leaned down to study the contents of his pizza.

Jack decided to press his advantage. "Hadn't you heard, Mom? Climbing's the best game in town. Man against nature. Man against himself."

She slid a slice of warm pizza on his plate and leaned toward him, saying, "As your Uncle Jackson has so ably pointed out, climbing mountains is not the only test of manhood."

Jack darted a quick glance at his father. A dark red washed up

Dad's neck. He tossed his fork on the plate and stood. "I have a lot of work to do," he said. "Thanks for the dinner, Alison."

He picked up his plate, strode from the room, mounted the stairs and shut the door to his office.

After a moment of silence, Jack looked up at his mother. She stared at the place where his father had been, her spatula poised. As she plopped into her chair, her shoulders slumped.

"I shouldn't have done that."

"I don't get it. You guys name me after Dad's favorite brother and all that crap, and then suddenly, I'm eight, and Uncle Jackson can only show up to visit me when Dad is not here."

She glanced up. "After all your visits with Jackson and Samara, and you really don't know?"

"I know it's got to do with Grandma's death," Jack said, "but I had to guess that much."

She let her head droop, stared at her lap and took a deep breath before saying, "Jackson was with your grandparents on Nanda Devi. He should have been on her rope team. Grandpa's version is that Jackson quit the climb."

"Is it true? Did he leave them short-handed that day?"

"Jack, I don't know what's true. Jackson tried to explain, but your dad told him there was no excuse for what he did. But I know this, I trusted your Uncle Jackson before that day, and I trust him now."

"But Dad . . .?"

"Wasn't there."

He knew that. Dad was here, helping Mom recover from losing that baby – the baby that wasn't well and died before it was born. Kaitlyn.

His mother picked up her uneaten pizza and walked to the sink – a perfectly good pizza.

"Mom, don't toss that. I'll eat it."

Finally! That got her to laugh. It was sort of a sob-laugh, but in a second, it turned into her sunshine smile. "You will not, Jackie.

I'm going to eat this one and at least two more. I just forgot to get my salad."

A lie, but an okay lie. Jack saw the tears standing on her lower lids. He knew she still cried about Kaitlyn sometimes. He thought about the baby, too. All through fourth grade he'd planned how it would be fun to have a baby sister, watch her learn things, maybe teach her how to climb on the furniture.

But Kaitlyn died, and then grandma died on the mountain. And his father had hidden in his office for days, weeks. Two months after her death, when Dad went alone to take grandma's ashes to Mount Rainier, Jack was certain he would not come back to their sad house.

A week later, however, Uncle Jackson had brought Dad home, dirty, tired and wheezing with pneumonia. No one ever said so, but Jack thought his uncle had followed Dad to Mount Rainier.

At first, his mother and Uncle Jackson took turns stuffing medicine and food down his father. Jackson stayed around, quiet and calm, even though Dad often called him Mr. Artsy-Fartsy, and later, when Mom was in another part of the house, Dad called him a bloody coward.

Then, one day while Mom was at her office, Dad shuffled down to the living room where Jack and Uncle Jackson were in the middle of a game of Crazy Eights.

"Jackson," Dad said, "I want you to leave my house."

Uncle Jackson didn't look up. He sighed, and laid down his cards. He caught Jack's attention with his somber gaze. "I guess you win this hand, Little Buddy, but, I'll be back."

Smelling his pizza again, Jack straightened, sitting up and away from his memories as Mom watched him across the table.

"Jack," she said, "you don't have to prove anything tomorrow on this mountain. Everyone, including your father, knows you are a great climber."

· · ·

That evening, Jack wrote an outline draft of his paper about Lewis's boat, and then he hauled his climbing boots out of the basement storage closet. One floor above him, he could hear his mother setting out the boxes Dad had built to carry her paintings to the gallery for her show next Tuesday. Two floors above, his father concentrated on finishing a magazine article – or maybe he chewed cold pizza and brooded about his brother. Jack hoped Dad wrote.

Jack sat down on a stool to work on his boots. Tomorrow, he wanted dry feet.

As he rubbed wax into the seams, he glanced over the gear he'd laid out on the rec-room floor: water bottles, first-aid kits, climbing helmets, and the safety devices they would use. Jack wanted it all in order. His father planned to check the stuff after he finished working on his article.

Next to the CB radio, stood his dad's boots, the seams already waxed, and the welt of the sole already shellacked to preserve the bond. Dad's boots were solid, stiff and capable of withstanding all kinds of strain.

His father was the man *National Geographic* sent to dangerous spots in the Andes and the Himalayas to film adventure features. Yet, Dad trusted him to be steady on a dangerous climb up Mount Tecumseh. He wanted to deserve that trust.

While rubbing the last welt on his boots, Jack's hand bumped into his cell phone in his jacket. He took it out of his pocket, clicked it on and saw that it had a pretty good battery reserve. Maybe it would work. Call Kristi from the top of Tecumseh. Maybe sing Climb every Mountain to Berto. Why not?

He chuckled at the idea and pushed the phone into the daypack next to his salt tablets. He set the last boot on the floor by Dad's. Leaning over the workbench, he stretched out his hamstring muscles, bounced a few times to stretch his Achilles' tendons before he went upstairs to do the second draft of his part of the history project.

. . .

Dad glanced up from his desk as Jack walked past his office. His eyes didn't focus until Jack said, "I'm done putting climbing gear out."

"Oh!" Dad seemed to be jerked out of the world he wrote about. "Oh . . ." he said again. "That's great. I'll check it when I'm done here."

"I'm gonna do homework," Jack said, but Dad was already back into his article.

Once at his desk, Jack revved up his computer. At first, he wrote without stopping. He knew this stuff. He'd been reading about it for weeks, ever since he discovered the story of the boat in a magazine article. He figured to look up his footnote references after he nailed his ideas down.

If President Thomas Jefferson's information had been correct, the iron-framed boat would have carried the explorers and their goods from the headwaters of the Missouri clear to the Pacific Ocean. Jefferson had read early explorers' diaries and reports. They wrote about a mountain range located between the Missouri and the Columbia River headwaters.

Both Jefferson and Captain Lewis imagined those mountains were like the mountains and pinewoods of Virginia and Kentucky. They believed the expedition members could carry the parts of the iron boat for a day or so across the mountains, then rebuild it and float down the headwaters to the Columbia and on to the Pacific Ocean well before the winter of 1805.

But this plan was based on misinformation.

President Jefferson and Captain Meriwether Lewis had no idea of the huge distances and the murderous altitudes of the mountain ranges called the Rockies. When the men entered these uncharted territories, this miscalculation almost cost their lives.

Jack's work on the assignment was going great until he tried to explain why the boat design could be both ingenious and the cause of near-disaster. Instead of writing, he caught himself imagining how he might have solved the transport problems if he'd been there. And then he started daydreaming about the crew that had to abandon the iron-framed boat in Montana.

One kid had been on the expedition – a guy named George Shannon who was close to Jack's age. Shannon was hired to go the whole way. Every day, he'd hunted and built shelters, paddled a pirogue or hiked over rough terrain. George Shannon had seen the unknown, the unimaginable, the majestic. He was the luckiest kind of guy.

However, the kid didn't seem to have a great sense of direction. At least twice, Shannon got lost for several days. But each time, Lewis or Clark sent men out to search for him. The captains cared when he didn't show up. They celebrated when they found him. Jack liked to reread those parts of Lewis' and Clark's diaries.

Thinking about being with Shannon on the expedition was a whole lot easier than writing about why the iron boat had failed, and why Jack believed it still deserved to be counted as a tool for opening up the West.

None of his explanations seemed to say what he wanted. He was about to trash what he'd done when he heard his mom bang on the clothes chute between the second floor and the basement. He shoved back and strode to the hall to open the little door to the metal-sided clothes drop.

"What's up?" he called.

"You're up. I'm down," Mom said.

"Very funny," he said. "And your point is . . .?"

"I could use your help framing my last painting."

"Now?"

"Yes."

"Sheese!"

He heard her laughter echo up the chute.

"You gotta write the rest of my paper, then," he called.

"How about if I help you with it on Sunday when you come back from the climb?"

"Deal."

He forced himself to shift gears from homework to woodwork. He was stumped on the paper anyway. Besides, Mom had to have all her stuff ready to deliver on Monday. This show made her nervous. It was the first time most of her friends would see her watercolors. Most people in Portland thought of her as an architect, not a painter.

He saved his history file to a disk, and then hopped down the steps to her basement office. Thirty paintings stood all around her desk and on her meeting table. Some, he'd helped matte and frame. Some, she'd done herself. She held out one painting. "I can't decide what matt to put with this one."

He took the nubbly paper and looked over the picture – a pair of heron, standing in long-legged dignity at the edge of a shallow river, eyes alert for dinner. The female had one foot raised, preparing a silent move toward her prey – a shadow fish in the blue-green water.

Jack recognized the moment right away. "These are the birds we saw last summer, camping on that creek near the Umpqua River."

"Their last silent moment."

He chuckled. "When your camera clicked, they must have thought it was a gun, and whoosh."

She smiled. "That fish owes me his life."

Jack looked over the whole picture, the way his mother had taught him. He sought the focus of the painting that could be enhanced by the matte colors.

"I'd use a thin matte of this light green" Jack said, pointing to the deciduous trees growing among dark fir on the low hills beyond the river bank. "And outside of that, a wider matte of the sunset gold from the sky. See here, how you've captured those colors in the glints on the heron feathers and in her eye."

Mom took the painting and studied it. "Right."

"That combination would draw attention to her and to the fish she's about to eat," Jack said.

"It sure would."

"Want me to do the wood?"

"That would be a big help. I'll cut the narrow matte first."

Jack walked deeper into her office and opened what looked like a coat closet. Inside, several widths of pre-stained wood lengths with different profiles stood in between the dowels. He and Dad had installed these dowels to hold the framing wood upright. He selected two lengths of cherry with a simple shape and carried them out past his mother, who was measuring the painting at her cutting table. At his workbench, he moved aside his boat model and then brought out the miter box and the saw.

"The total with two mattes is going to be eighteen by twenty-seven inches," Mom called from her office. Jack set the wood in the miter box and cut the pieces to fit.

His mother came out of her office holding the green matte up to the painting. "You are so right, Eagle-eye. Look how great that is going to be."

It was good. With the gold, it would be even better. He grinned and held up a piece of cherry wood for her to add to the test. Its profile would create a shadow-box effect around the herons.

"Perfect," she said. "And when are we going to start framing your paintings?"

Startled, he put her off. "Maybe this summer, sometime."

"I think your friends would be proud of your work." She raised her eyebrows at him. "Berto and Kristi won't make fun of you."

"It's not that," he said. "I'm just real busy."

"Busy never stopped you from doing great paintings," she said, tilting her head and staring at him in a way that made him uncomfortable.

"I gotta get this glued, Mom."

A half-hour later, leaving the wood frame nailed, glued and clamped to dry, he returned to his bedroom and tested five lousy explanations of the importance of a failed iron boat.

CHAPTER 12

At one o'clock in the morning, Jack flung off the covers and grabbed at his foot. He pulled back on his toes with one hand and switched on his bedside lamp with the other. The cramp in his foot grew tighter.

Swinging out of bed, he stood upright, clutching his tall chest-of-drawers.

He put all of his weight above his foot, to force his muscle open. Slowly, his toes loosened their grip. But each time he lifted his leg, the muscle contracted down the length of his sole. He had to slam the foot to the bedside rug again to get relief.

His feet warmed in the thick yarn of the rug his mother had made for him, but warmth didn't stop the cramp. Each time his arch muscle threatened to tighten, Jack thrust his other foot forward as if he were a fencer lunging toward his opponent. This stretched his back foot enough to convince the muscle to stop cramping – for a while.

He was in this stretched-out position when his father opened the door. "Glad to see you're getting ready early, son."

Tentatively, Jack turned, leaving his feet extended to prevent a recurrence of his cramp. "Dad, my foot woke me up. I've been trying to work out the muscle."

"That's the idea. Just let your muscles know who's in charge."

"The foot's in charge. It's taken me twenty minutes to get it flat on the floor."

"Perseverance, Buster. You've always been good at sticking with a job."

Jack tested. "When I lift it, the foot tightens again."

Finally his father stepped fully into the room. "Kid, it's normal to be up-tight before a climb. Back when I climbed with your grandpa and grandma, I can't tell you how many times I had to woops my cookies before I hauled out of the tent on the Eiger."

"Dad," Jack said, "I'm not tossing ginger snaps. I've got a by-God cramp in the bottom of my foot."

His father motioned him to the floor, the way he did when he wanted Jack to give him twenty push-ups. "Let's see this famous cramp."

Jack collapsed to the warm surface of the thick rya rug and lay on his back, raising his leg. Dad took the foot in his hand and tested the rotation of the ankle joint. Jack tensed, waiting for either the hamstring or the foot to pull up tight. But neither happened. Dad pushed backward on his toes and then ran a thumb along the muscles of his sole. It didn't even tickle.

"Yeah," Dad said. "I can feel that it's a bit tight. Wait here, I'll get you some Mineral Ice and some aspirin." He let go of the foot, expecting Jack to lower it to the floor.

Jack couldn't stop its fall. It crashed onto his heel bone with a bang. Dad jumped. "Lord, don't do that," he said. "You could break that bone."

Jack held his breath, waiting for the pain to register, but it came to him that the sudden impact didn't hurt as much as he thought it would. It hurt, but in the distant way he imagined it would feel to the stretchable comic-book character Plastic Man – a blow to the heel so far removed from the brain it seemed hardly connected.

"You okay?" his father asked.

"It's okay," Jack said.

Dad squinted at him and glanced at the foot on the floor. Then, he marched into the bathroom to find the Mineral Ice.

Jack rolled over on his side, opening his eyes into a forest of his mother's wool yarns. Before him stood all the colors Mom loved – red, purple, pink, blue, yellow – a chaos of cheer at the end of his nose. Wanting to wrap those colors around him, he wished for their brilliance and warmth to give him a clear signal.

He had a choice to make and he knew it was important to make the right one because it could never be unmade. He could call off the climb. Safer for him, and for Dad. If he did, however, he was sure this would be the last time his father ever asked him on a trip. Like Uncle Jackson – cut off for failing. Or for giving up at the wrong time.

Maybe Dad and Doc Bradley were right. Maybe the cramps were caused by his mind, by worry that he didn't have what it took to get to the top. The hospital tests showed nothing – just that trace of some enzyme. And the cramps hadn't happened much since Crown Point – one cramp as he ran home from town, and this one tonight, of course, but it was gone now.

He heard Dad rummaging around in the bathroom cupboards.

Imagine Dad throwing up in a tent.

Confessing to throwing up – that was even harder to imagine. Until three minutes ago, that idea had never entered Jack's head. If Dad could throw up, Jack's cramps might be his own reaction to not knowing. And if he didn't climb, he'd never know.

He had to do it. Had to find out if he had the courage. He knew he had the strength, the concentration, and experience. Maybe not as much experience as his father, but enough. Even got down from that very sticky place on Crown Point in spite of everything.

Then he remembered the feeling at Crown Point. He'd put his tortured foot on solid ground at last. Nothing. No triumph. No joy. Merely exhaustion that had forced him to sleep two hours in the hot car while Berto drove them to the Hamburger Hide-Out and then home.

He rolled to his stomach and tested himself in a set of push-ups. The feet, the shoulders, the arms, all working as if nothing unusual ever happened. In his last push-up, he shoved hard enough for his hands to leave the ground. He clapped twice, landed on his outspread hands and walked his feet up to his palms. He rose and stared at his big-shouldered silhouette in the dimly lit mirror.

No twinge in the leg or foot.

I can do this, he said to the obscure face in the glass. Just then, his father flipped on the overhead light. The silhouette in the glass became a boy with a face full of beard stubble, and hair sticking out in all directions. Jack glanced away.

"At least I could find the Bengay tube," Dad said. "That ought to do it. Put it on before we leave. Give it time to work itself in."

He took the Bengay from Dad's outstretched hand. "We going soon?" he asked.

Dad nodded, staring at the tube like it was the answer. "I'll make some oatmeal. You toss the gear in the Outback, and we're off."

Half an hour later, Jack walked through the dining room on his way to the car. He stopped to look at mom's paintings, ready to pack into the wooden boxes. The herons looked hungry in their green and gold matte. The show would be great. He and his friends would be there. And so would Dad. They planned to return from Mount Tecumseh by Sunday morning. The show would start Tuesday evening.

CHAPTER 13

In the dark of early morning, Dad handed Jack the keys to the Outback and let him drive down the Willamette River Valley to the Santiam Pass. They turned east across the Cascade Mountain Range. In the dark, listening to KOPB radio, Dad peered through the windshield, looking for the highway number sign. After they traded drivers and turned south, the radio station faded to a constant static. Dad flipped it off.

"So, what's with the metal boat?" Dad asked.

His question surprised Jack. He hadn't thought Dad paid it much mind. "People only know about it from descriptions in Captain Lewis's letters and the diaries. I don't think there are any drawings of it."

"What was it for?"

"Lewis hoped it would make the last part of the trip easier, so they stored the metal parts in the big keel boat during the first year of the trip. But when they got to the shallow headwaters of the Missouri and put it together, they discovered they couldn't get enough pine tar to caulk the seams of the covering skins."

"You mean they carried that heavy frame all that way and then couldn't use it?"

"Yeah. It floated great, but the caulk recipe they created from the local trees didn't hold up."

"I'd fire the man who did such piss-poor planning."

Jack laughed. "Well, that was the boss, Captain Lewis."

"Meriwether Lewis?" At Jack's nod, Dad shook his head in disbelief. "Why are you writing about something that didn't work?"

"It was a cool idea."

"It was a failure. Move on. Find another topic."

Jack rubbed his thigh. Maybe he *should* dump the boat idea – a boat that ought to have been a design winner, except for the lack of pine trees in upper Montana. But it was the boat that had attracted him to their story in the first place – the failed boat and the kid, George Shannon, who kept getting lost, but always figured a way to get back together with the explorers. Jack thought he would have liked Shannon. He was absolutely certain, from their journals, that Lewis and Clark both liked him.

"Look," Dad said, pointing off to the side of the car.

Through the gray of pre-dawn, they caught glimpses of broad-shouldered Mount Jefferson and the ragged silhouette of Three Fingered Jack. At sunrise, they traded drivers again. Dad directed Jack to take an old logging road toward the north side of Mount Tecumseh. Driving over the bumpy rocks, Jack studied the mountain. Near the top, a black, straight-sided tower of ancient rock soared to the summit.

He could tell that the tower once was the volcanic throat of a bigger, older mountain. The lava in the throat had cooled and hardened into a plug. Over thousands of years, freezing water expanded cracks in the outer rock. The rock broke off and tumbled down the mountain leaving boulder-strewn jumbles all around the upper flanks.

Whenever he could take his eyes off the road, Jack glanced from the plugged throat down the mountain toward the steep cliff on the north side. The path up that side was through one of several tall, three-sided chimney-like chutes where water and ice had eroded away soft-rock pillars leaving only the surrounding harder rock. Those chutes could act just like the clothes chute in their house. Anything dropped down them ended in the basement – in this case, in the jumble of boulders.

Soon, they had driven too close to see the whole mountain through the pine forest. A few miles of dusty, switch-back road brought them to a dead end. They locked up and carried the tent and other gear for three more miles to a remote meadow at Tecumseh Ponds. After pitching the tent to establish a base camp, Jack and his father lifted their daypacks and set off for the mountain. His father's rock-climbing shoes were tied to the back of his daypack. For the next eight miles, Jack followed the rhythm of swinging shoes. They finally arrived at an alpine meadow bordering the rocky north face of the mountain. Dad halted and held up one hand.

"Listen."

Jack stopped. Bells. In fact, what sounded like a whole chord of bells rang softly in the distance. He glanced about him. Four goats stood at the scrub-pine edge of the meadow.

"Somebody owns those goats," Dad said, "but they've wandered a long way from the nearest ranch."

The gray and black billy raised his head to glare at the human interlopers. Jack and his father stared back. For a moment, silence filled the cool air, and then one of the nanny goats took a step toward them. Her bell rang once. The brindled billy snorted at her and banged her rump with his head. She jumped and skittered into the scruffy trees, chased by the nipping male. The other nanny goats followed, swift and graceful. Bells clanged softly with each leap.

"The nannies out-number him," Jack said. "If they figure that out, he'll be in Deep Goat Dip."

"They know he's got their safety in mind," Dad said. "So they do what he says."

"Sure, Dad," Jack chuckled. "Can you imagine Mom or Kristi taking a butt like that?"

Dad grinned at him. "Never. Not the women we love."

Jack's face heated. He'd never told Dad he loved Kristi. Dad smiled and started across the meadow. Jack tried to regain some pretense of calm. On the far side of the alpine meadow, as they approached the first rise, a rock rolled out from under Jack's boot. He stumbled and turned his ankle. The quick pain scared him for a second, but a couple of steps later, it went away. Dad, in front of him, hadn't even noticed the incident. They began hiking up the steep slope toward the chimney-chutes.

Three hours later, they stood at the top of the chimney of columnar basalt, triumphant from having conquered a difficult part of the climb in record time. Jack took off his goggles by pulling them below his chin. He was glad to have them – they'd saved him from getting a handful of grit in his eyes as he followed Dad's trail up the chimney.

His ankle registered occasional twinges, but he thought it would be fine if he just kept using it. His father always said muscles didn't seize up until you stopped for a long time.

Atop the chimney they faced a climb up a slab of dark andesite. Hundreds of years before, the slab had broken off of the exposed throat of the volcano and tumbled to a stop on the slope above the chimney-like chutes. It lay at a sixty-degree angle, steep, but not vertical.

After studying their best path up the slab, they planned a clear route from the top of the slab to the plugged and eroded volcanic throat – the peak of Tecumseh. The throat would be a vertical climb.

A trail of thin clouds had hung over the peak when they started up the chimney. Now, when they were at the bottom of the andesite slab, those clouds had become a white fluff, billowing into the mountain from the northwest. Jack shivered. A cool breeze tugged his jacket strings.

"We'd best do this quickly," Dad said. "Get in and get out in case that becomes a storm."

"Okay," Jack said. "Your turn to belay."

Dad nodded. He and Jack had already created safety anchors on their ledge. While they set up the ropes, preparing for Jack to climb the slab, Jack put his goggles back on and then stood on his toes to find a good first handhold. His heels shimmied up and down like the chassis of a car with bad suspension. He put his heels down flat and the shimmy went away. He figured he ought to stretch those muscles before he tackled the slab. He bent slowly, pretending to tie and untie both boots.

"You about done with fiddling there?" Dad asked.

"Just stretching."

"That take care of the problem?"

Jack stood on his toes. No shimmy. "Good to go," he said.

"No time to quit on me, son."

Jack blurted, "I said I'm fine."

"Great." Dad went back to setting up the rope.

Jack regretted his quick anger. He figured being tired had made him too fast to judge. The ropes were safely coiled and his father settled in for the belay. Jack tested his legs again. The rattling in his heels had gone. He started up the wall.

Twenty-five feet up, mist darkened the rock and the color of his jacket as it soaked into the fabric. At forty feet, almost halfway up the slab, the mist was thicker. Occasional heavy drops splashed his face. Jack yanked his goggles around to the back of his head. In this rain, they were useless.

On hands and toes, he crawled up the wet slab wall. His father stood on the narrow ledge fifty feet below him. In spite of the rain, Jack gritted his way toward their next belay stance, placing safety devices in the rock as he climbed. Jack drove cams or chocks into cracks in the rock. He clipped an aluminum carabiner into each device's ring-shaped head, looped his rope into the carabiner and kept moving up. If he slipped, the duplication of protective cams and chocks would prevent him from falling all the way back to the ledge where Dad stood.

"Ten o'clock, up, left." Dad called. Through the wet air, Jack saw it – a great handhold, wide enough for three fingers. He grabbed and pulled himself up another foot of the wall, then moved his right foot to the next niche in the granite.

His thigh burned. The shimmy had returned to the foot on which he placed his weight. He knew he should not have begun climbing this wall. Now that he'd gotten so far up, however, the safest way to get down was to finish this next bit – get to the ledge formed by the upper end of this slab. The peak, with its exposed volcanic throat, loomed above him, a distant goal in the rain, another three hundred feet of near vertical climbing.

Jack no longer believed his leg would carry him to the summit. He wished he'd never started this. His own stupid optimism and boundless confidence had made him do it. He'd wanted to think Dad was right, that the cramps might be a creation of his imagination. He dreaded giving up, but he knew it was the smart thing to do, the only thing. Now, he'd have to admit defeat. For their lives, they both had to stop.

"Time to place more pro," Dad called.

And he was right. The safety devices would work, if they held – if he'd placed them at the right angles. He wasn't sure of anything anymore. The pain in his leg and a new, burning heat in his shoulder made concentration difficult. The growing fear of his own incompetence made him slow, tentative and shaky. The rain made him cold.

He must not fall. His father counted on him. His mother . . . Mother would . . . He wouldn't let his mind go there.

The rock on which he now inched upwards, allowed few handholds. Moss and lichen combined with rain to slick the surface. Water drooled from the brim of his climbing helmet onto his worn parka. His leg cramp grabbed again, twisting his right thigh.

"Damn!" he yelled out once, and then the pain went so deep he could not yell, but had to rest his forehead against his hand, grasping the webbing in the device he'd just put in the rock.

Hanging onto that nylon web and his rope, Jack closed his eyes and blew air out his mouth to force his muscles to relax – the trick his mother taught him, but the muscle refused to let go. He reminded himself to breathe, just breathe and put in the next piece of protection, to get a foot closer to a place to where he could sit.

Glancing behind him, Jack checked the rope leading from his harness through all the safety devices and back to the harness on his father. The great Mallory Huntington stood ready, feet apart and propped against a boulder, rope belayed through a stitch-plate anchored at their belay base.

It wouldn't matter how determined Dad might be. Jack feared if he fell from this slab, if the chocks and screws didn't hold, his weight would rip both Dad and the anchors from their narrow ledge.

And below that? Nothing, until the alpine pasture they had walked through six hours ago – the goats now so far away even their tuned bells could no longer be heard.

Scrabbling, Jack found a place to rest the toe of his left boot. He leaned away from the slab, putting his center of gravity over his feet, a counter-intuitive move that forced careful thought when thought seemed impossible. The constant and excruciating heat in his twitching shoulder took over his attention for long moments. Reaching into his belt and pulling out the next chock became the work of minutes. The effort to place the chock into a fissure in the rock caused lightning jolts from his hand to his head. White pain reduced his field of vision to the particular piece of pro and the carabiner he attempted to clip together. Attaching the rope and the loop for its knot demanded his entire mind.

"Jack," Dad called, "can you go any faster? We're getting soaked."

"My hands aren't doing things right."

"If you increase the tempo," Dad said, "they'll warm up and start working again."

Jack knew that was true, but if he moved faster, he was bound to make a mistake. Each knot and carabiner, each device of protection had to support his weight and then Dad's, up, then down again. Down – he could not begin to imagine the process for down.

An hour passed in this way, moving ever upward, following his father's suggestions sometimes, making his own opposite decisions at other times. The motion of each finger became a triumph of concentration until at last Jack pulled himself to the top end of the slab. He created two safety holds, one a screw in the rock on which the slab leaned, the other a tie-off around a huge boulder solidly resting at one end of the shelf on which he sat.

Next, he shrugged off his daypack and set it beside him while he took a salt tablet and then drank water from his bottle.

Sitting on the crack between the slab end and the wall behind it, he became more clearly aware that centuries before, this enormous piece of rock had broken off and fallen from the tower above. In that long ago moment, the andesite tumbled end over end until something, maybe a boulder or a pile of earlier rock-fall, halted its plunge toward the valley. Jack grew certain that at any moment whatever held the slab up would give way. Then, gravity would yank the rock, Dad and him down hundreds of feet to bury them in a pile of rubble.

He forced himself to stop thinking and check the anchors to which he'd tied himself. Then he wiped rain and sweat off his face, placed his feet against the edge of the slab and called down, "I'm set, Dad. Come on up."

Dad waved, then untied his rope from the lower belay anchor. Jack propped himself to belay as his father began to climb.

Within fifteen minutes, following the path Jack had made with his protection devices, Dad arrived at the ledge. "Good leading, son."

Jack, though tired, warmed at his father's praise.

Dad stood atop the ledge end of the slab. He anchored his ropes to Jack's belay. There, beside his approving father, Jack could have had the best moment. He hated to break the spell. He pushed himself to stand

and spoke before his courage failed him.

"I'm through."

His father glanced up at the peak. "It's gorgeous in the mist. Almost magical."

Jack steeled himself. "Dad, my leg is one huge knot. I am through."

His father chuckled, then dropped his big hand on Jack's shoulder – a heavy thump that reverberated down his spasming side. "Naw, son," he said. "We're close. Only a couple hundred feet. See?"

"Three hundred," Jack corrected. "Three hundred to the bottom of the volcanic throat. I am not going to make another move upward."

His father started gathering rope in his hands as if he were going to stand. "Suit yourself, son," he said, "but your old Dad has never been one to give up. It'll only take me. . ."

Jack took a grip on his father's Gore-Tex lapel, "I have a better idea. Drag me up there with you, Dad. Bench press me. Dead weight can't slow down Superman."

His father glared up at him. "What's the matter with you, Jack? Let go of my coat."

For the first time, Jack realized he'd grown taller than his father, and probably outweighed him. An image roared vividly into his mind – a picture of himself slamming his father against the rock wall behind them. His features must have telegraphed the idea to his father, because Dad's eyes widened in a swift moment of terror. As soon as the ugly thought came out, Jack's stomach rose into his throat

His hands shook as he released his father's jacket and rolled away from dad's eyes. After a moment, Jack said what had to be said to keep them both safe. "You're going to help me get down, Dad. If you want to finish this climb, do it another day."

He heard his father straighten the front of his jacket and take in a shaky breath before he answered. "What the hell do you think you're doing, giving orders?"

Jack turned to hold his father's gaze. "I'm telling you the cramps are not in my mind. I don't know what they are. I don't know why they are. I'm afraid."

His father scoffed. "Afraid?"

"Scared shitless. I need you to help me down." Jack stared at his father. A bleak, defeated sag took over the muscles of Dad's face. He slumped against the wall.

"You can't be sick," he said, staring into the chasm in front of them. "You're barely seventeen."

His father seemed lost, and suddenly small. Jack wanted to tell him there wasn't any big-deal wrong. But he couldn't. If he said it, his father might try again to jolly him into the climb. That way led to disaster. Even now, they'd probably gone too far.

"Dad, I won't get better by pretending nothing's the matter."

For a moment, he thought his father hadn't heard him. Slowly, Dad sank to his haunches. His head bowed onto his knees. He seemed to be planning. And if the past taught Jack anything, it was that his dad was probably planning how to talk him into toughing it out. Two minutes passed in strained silence. Then, Dad reached across the narrow void between their cooling bodies and placed his hand gently on Jack's burning shoulder muscle.

"I wanted the climb to show you how good you are. You were a heck of a climber, you know."

"You were?" Jack dragged in a deep breath. "I'm still good." He looked his Dad square in the face. "If I weren't great, I wouldn't have gotten this far on one leg."

Dad's head jerked back as if he'd been slapped. His gaze darted out over the mountain and up to the overhanging peak. Then he stared at the rope in his hands.

"Your runs last week," Dad said, "How were they, really?"

Maybe his father meant to listen this time. "Uneven. Good some days," Jack said. "Gimpy on others."

Dad turned to face him through the drizzle. "I wish we could have worked out together. We could have fixed those legs."

Jack swallowed his bitter retort. Dad would never understand that he had work hard to get over these cramps.

"I wanted to come," Jack said. "I wanted this to work."

"Yes." Dad's voice came out rough. "I wanted it, too." He cleared his throat. "Let's get you out of here."

Relief washed through Jack. He glanced at his father and found him gazing into Jack's eyes. Dad rarely looked directly at him, but this time, his look never shifted. Jack saw that the blue of Dad's irises was ringed with an off-white color. Dad's face was pale beneath his windburn, and fine crinkles of skin surrounded his eyes. He was not invincible.

Then his father took charge of their retreat. "You rappel first," Dad said. "Start now, before this rain makes you too cold to move."

As much as Jack longed to rest, he knew Dad was right. He crawled to an upright position, checked the rope where it ran through his stitch-plate and anchor. He watched Dad check the safety system Jack had created. His father nodded and then pressed his feet against the edge of the slab for support. At last Jack, center of gravity over his feet, was ready to back down the slab.

"Jack," Dad said.

Jack glanced at him.

"That little pine near the ledge down there is strong. Its roots dig deep into the crevices of the rock. You are as strong as it is. Breathe. Think, and tie yourself to the mountain before I come down."

Jack nodded. He took a last look at the clouds surrounding the high peak, then gazed down at the rain misting the valley. He shuttered his mind and focused on the work of descending, and of bringing both of them down safely.

Chapter 14

During the next minutes, Dad lowered Jack down the long basalt slab to the top of the chimney, the first leg of their descent. The rain soaked into Jack's supposedly rainproof coat and drooled down his neck into his sweater. Jack sent the rope back up to his father and slumped against the wall of the eighteen-inch-wide ledge. Then he remembered he had to tie himself into the safety anchors they'd left in this place.

First. I should have done that first.

At that moment, he became acutely aware of the long mist-filled drop below. In the rain, everything seemed different. The shelf was smaller than he thought. And when he looked for anchors, they were lower in the wall than he remembered placing them as they climbed up.

Still, he had to tie into the anchors. He grabbed a D-shaped carabiner from his harness and hung it through the round end of the bolt that had been stuck in the cliff wall. Opening the gate on the carabiner, he looped nylon webbing from the front of his harness into it. The webbing slipped off the open end. He tried again. He couldn't get the nylon to go into the wide-open jaws of the carabiner.

Must be my eyes. He wiped rain off his goggles.

Above, his father shouted "On rappel" and began coming down. Jack had to tie into the anchor soon, or Dad might accidentally bump him off this narrow space. He grabbed the anchor carabiner with his left hand, pulled his face up close to it so he could see what he was doing, and guided the nylon web into the open jaw. Without warning, his left arm muscle twitched. His hand shook and dropped the metal latch. The webbing fell out.

The unexpected jerk in his arm forced him to step back. His left boot scraped the edge of the rock platform. Then, the boot contacted air beyond the shelf. His center of gravity shifted.

Grabbing at the bolt, he yanked himself close to the rock wall. He laced one finger into the anchoring bolt and steadied himself. Sweat trickled down his sides – fear sweat. His foot searched for a solid place, but he couldn't be certain his mind had clear knowledge of where anything was. Up, down, back, forward, it all seemed the same in the mist. He couldn't read any messages from his foot.

His left boot bumped into rock again, but he didn't dare lean on it, unsure as he was about what kind of rock it had found. It might be on the loose shale to the left end of the ledge.

Slowly, he forced himself to open his eyes. Glancing down, he saw that both boots were on the solid ledge. He wondered why he couldn't feel where the left boot was.

Still gripping the bolt and the carabiner in freezing fingers, he inched his feet closer to the wall and took a deep breath. His mind messed things up, and he knew that meant he wasn't getting enough oxygen. At least that's what it usually meant.

His father was now only forty feet above him. He had to get his harness tied into the bolt, before he caused an accident as Dad arrived.

He guided his nylon webbing into the open gate of the carabiner as if he were threading a needle. This time, it went right in. Breathing easier, Jack threaded the webbing through his second anchor point on the left. He was fully hooked in by the time Dad approached the ledge.

Jack leaned his forehead against the cliff and took another deep breath. His legs were weak. He wanted to sit, but he had to look calm by the time Dad arrived, or Dad would guess how close he'd come to losing it. He moved his arms and legs trying to create a little heat and help him forget his near disaster.

In another minute, his father stood next to him, reeling in their long rope. Dad shivered and then blew out, probably trying to make his own muscles relax.

"Where's the little pine tree?" Dad asked.

"Somewhere in the fog, I guess," Jack said, realizing he'd forgotten to look for it.

Jack sank down, sitting on the ledge, wishing he felt ready for the next step. They had yet to descend through the two-hundred-foot chimney that ice and water had carved in the lower section. If they made it through that chute, they faced another long rappel down the steep shoulder of the mountain to the meadow.

So far down . . .

Jack steeled himself. Long ago, he'd taken the last of the Gatorade. He'd also finished his bottle of water. Pain still cramped his thigh and shoulder. He breathed out whenever cramps twisted him. His head reeled from too much air, or maybe it was not enough air. He'd lost track.

"I cleaned as much gear as I could," his father muttered, counting the chocks and carabiners he'd brought down with him. "We've got to get out of here the fast way this time."

"I'm sorry, Dad." Jack wasn't sure he'd said it out loud, but his father bent over him.

Jack tried to avoid his gaze, but Dad took hold of his head, "I have to see your eyes."

He guessed his father searched for signs of shock. Jack didn't think shock was his problem. He was cold from the rain, and driven to concentrate on his damned leg, but he wasn't going unconscious. He wouldn't leave Dad to solve this alone.

"You're okay, boy," Dad said.

"Stop studying me and hook in," Jack said.

His father snorted, but hooked into two other bolts farther along the wall. Then, he stared off into the mist again, and back at all the bolts and carabiners. "This isn't right," he said.

"What isn't?"

"These aren't the ones we left here. This isn't where we were on the way up."

"Where else could we be?"

Dad looked up into the rain. "As you climbed the slab, you followed the natural line of the fallen rock. The top of that slab is about ten degrees farther north than the bottom. I should have remembered that."

"So where are we?"

"Your rappel rope would go straight down like a plumb line. We're probably using somebody else's bolts." Dad began checking all the anchor points. The one on Jack's left came right out of its fissure in the rock wall. Dad stared at it a moment and then stared at Jack. "Notice the details, Jack," he said.

Stupid. He'd been so busy trying to make the nylon do what he wanted in the first anchor that he hadn't tested his second anchor at all. Dad moved the left one over and screwed it solidly back into the wall.

"Raise your arms," Dad ordered.

Puzzled, he raised his arms. Dad slipped the daypack off Jack's shoulders. "We're going to need your second rope after all," he said, yanking the clip that held the coils of nylon to the pack.

"Are we sitting above the longer chimney chute?"

"I think we are."

Jack remembered this chimney on the topographic map. Its lower end was farther down the steep northeast side of the mountain, making it about two hundred-forty feet – forty feet longer than the chimney they had come up, and longer than their longest rope. That meant they would have to tie two ropes together and later, pass the knot through their braking device – not an easy trick to pull off.

"Can you still use your feet to guide a rappel?" Dad asked.

Jack moved his feet. They seemed to be connected to his brain – too connected. The foot cramp started again.

"Looks good," Dad said. "At least you won't be swinging in the breeze."

Jack didn't tell him about the cramp. His father had enough worries. Dad removed an extra balaclava cap from his own pack and handed the cap to Jack. Staring at it, Jack wondered what he was supposed to do.

Dad frowned. "Shit. Why didn't I see this coming?" His father worked the clasp on Jack's climbing helmet.

Understanding dawned. Jack unbuckled his chinstrap and removed his climbing helmet. Dad pulled the balaclava on and covered Jack's ears. The cap was dry, and extra warm from being in the pack and near Dad's back.

Then Dad placed the helmet over the cap. "Can you buckle it?" he asked.

Jack nodded and reached up to work the strap through the buckle. His fingers didn't seem to know what to do, but he finally was able to grasp the buckle.

Dad watched Jack's struggle before he took over and buckled the helmet. He shook his head and rummaged in his own pack. His search became more and more intense.

"What the hell?" Dad said.

"What is it?"

His father sagged against the cliff wall. "This is unforgivable. I always bring the damned radio."

Jack stared at his father. He was certain he'd seen the radio with the other equipment. Then he remembered his phone. When he dropped it in his pack, he'd been thinking about trying to get Kristi, or Berto from the summit – do a little bragging, he'd thought. Some bragging!

"Dad, in my pack. My cell phone."

His father was already rifling Jack's daypack. He pulled out the phone as if it were a precious gem. "There are towers at Black Butte, Bend, and at Sisters," Dad said. "This better work."

Jack turned to look over his shoulder at the far distances. The rain was so thick he couldn't see the gray hulk of Mount Washington, less than ten miles north. To the northeast, where Black Butte would be visible on a clear day, he saw nothing. The town of Sisters was as remote as Pluto.

His father punched buttons and studied the read-out. "Top of the Cascades, a bee line to Sisters and the blasted phone's still got to go roaming."

He punched in ten digits.

Jack frowned. "What about 911?"

Dad shook his head and motioned for quiet. It seemed forever that they both waited, then his father spoke. "Bradley. Huntington here, on Mount Tecumseh. Yeah. Long story, but Jack's in bad shape."

His father had called the man who never took Jack's cramps seriously. He shrank into his jacket and shivered. Why not call emergency?

"You're breaking up," Dad yelled. "Bradley!"

Dad pulled the phone from his ear and stared at it. "Not now!" he muttered. "Not now."

"Try again," Jack whispered. "Try mom this time."

Whoever Dad called, they needed help. If they had to hike back to the car, Jack knew he'd be crawling the whole eight miles. His father opened the phone and tried again. He closed his eyes, as if to listen, or pray. Then shouted, "Bradley, call the sheriff of Deschutes County. We are on the North Face."

Silence. Jack hoped Bradley was taking notes.

"That's right," Dad said. "The sheriff should call in the Nine-thirty-ninth. Yes! The Air Force Reserve Rescue Wing."

I'm not that bad, Jack thought.

"So what if it costs?" Dad said. "It should cost. Tell them this is hypothermia."

Another silence. Then his father said, "He's worked like heck to get down this far."

Jack felt ridiculous, but grateful for Dad's praise.

"We'll meet the helicopter in Big Meadow – northeast side, eight miles west of Tecumseh Ponds, and nine miles southwest of Bluegrass Butte."

Jack couldn't have given such specific directions. He'd let his father be the one who knew the area. He should have studied the map himself.

"Bradley?"

Jack glanced up. His dad's face tensed in concentration. "Bradley?" He pulled the phone from his ear and stared at the read-out. "Lost signal," he muttered. "I think he was gone before I said Big Meadow."

His father blinked and glared at the phone. Rain dripped from the end of his nose onto his open palm. He shoved the cell phone back into the pack. "We gotta hope Bradley figures it out. You and I need to haul."

"Why call him?"

"911 doesn't know the mountain, and neither does your mom."

Jack admitted to himself that Dad had done the right thing, but he hated that Bradley knew he was sick. Dad set to work looping the rope through a tube-shaped braking device.

"Wish we had the Grigri," he muttered.

Jack swallowed hard. Dad never used the Grigri brake. Always said it was too danged heavy to be of any use. But the mere fact that he wanted it worried Jack. It meant his father wasn't sure he could lower his son down this long chimney.

"Dad," Jack said. "Maybe you should go down first and just help guide me. I can rappel myself down."

"Don't talk like that, Jack. You can't even buckle your helmet on."

True, Jack thought. *But if you went down first, at least I'd know you were safe.* "Dad, I'm fine. I can do this."

"Cut it Jack! Get ready to go."

He started to knot Jack's rope to the first rope to make it long enough to lower him down two sixty-meter lengths. Later, Dad would bring himself down to the same level and do it all over again until they reached the meadow.

It occurred to Jack that he didn't know how his father would pass the knot of the second rope through the brake device while hanging in mid-air. He figured Dad had something in mind, but Jack couldn't focus enough to figure out what.

He watched his father's hands slip and then grab the two ropes again, attempting to tie a knot joining them. Glancing at his father's face, he saw his right eyelid jerk several times. His cheeks had gone from ruddy to translucent gray. Jack had noticed those signs in guys who were tired and tense.

"Breathe, Dad," he whispered.

Dad glanced sharply at him. "Don't talk, Jack. Keep your mind on doing the rest of the rappel right."

But his father lengthened his intake breaths. That's okay, Jack thought. He doesn't have to admit taking advice. He watched his father breathe while setting up anchor points for a short side rope. Later, Dad would use that third rope to take the pressure off the main rope so he could pass the knot around the tube-shaped brake.

Jack remembered there was something he should ask his father about that knot, but he couldn't get the question to form itself in his head. Instead, he watched his father wrap the short rope. Dad tied a prusik knot attaching the shorter rope to the longer rope. That special knot would take Jack's weight while his father moved the bigger knot beyond the brake.

Dad seemed to be better now, so Jack reached into his pack and pulled out nylon webbing to create his own chest harness. He wanted to contribute to this rescue.

"I brought a chest harness," Dad said. He fished out a prefabricated harness. "Put this on."

Jack sighed, stuffed his web back in the pack, and then tried to get into the loops of pre-sewn nylon. For the last few minutes, his father hadn't looked at him, just barked at him. Silence and failure crowded in between them.

A few moments later, Dad glanced at the harness. He reached down and tested the carabiner where the harness would attach to the rope. Jack was certain he'd put it on with the gated-opening away from the pressure of the rope – the safest way, the way Dad had taught him and Berto and Kristi to do it when they were ten years old.

"Was it right?" Jack hated himself for having to ask.

"Fine." Dad said. He hooked the rope to Jack's sit harness and chest harness, then handed Jack a stick of beef jerky. "Best get some protein and fat into you before we start this. It'll be a while 'till we're down."

Jack had trouble biting into the salty jerky. Chewing was hard work. Swallowing, even harder.

Frowning, Dad studied the darkening sky. He checked his anchors again, then sat and braced his feet against rock, preparing to let Jack down. "We've got to move," he said.

Jack wanted to tell his father he was sorry about grabbing his jacket, but he knew Dad never trusted people who had to apologize, so he shoved the last of the jerky in his pocket and then swiveled his hips sideways to the edge of the shelf.

"I'm good to go."

"Okay." Dad said.

Staring at his father's boots, he let his body fall into space. The yank of the rope on his hip and chest harness jarred him. Elevator nausea brought beef jerky into his throat. In a fraction of a second, he felt Dad's control of the rope, firm and sure.

Jack bit his lip and kept the beef in his mouth, but his father must have sensed something, because the last close glimpse Jack had of him was the worried blue of his gaze raking Jack's face. Then, his father returned his attention to the rope.

Stomach acid burned at the back of his throat, but Jack swallowed, and leaned his face against the smooth threads of nylon. Moments later, he glanced up the narrow chute of weathered rock, through the pounding rain. In the cold and wet, Dad sat, harness tied to the protection in the rock wall, his feet apart, braced. His hands played out the rope, lowering Jack down the face of Mount Tecumseh. Dad looked only at the rope and the braking system, never at him.

Jack stepped down the chimney chute. On the way up, they had climbed a nearby chimney, pushing feet against one side of the vertical shaft and their backs against the other. Now his legs could not have moved three feet with that technique. At each step, his hand had to push on his left leg. If he didn't push, it didn't work for him.

Dad let the rope out smoothly. Within a few minutes, Jack arrived at the elevation where the chimney wall angled away, leaving him hanging in air. From here on, he would move down like a simple elevator, completely relying on his father's concentration and skill.

Jack kept his chest close to the rope. A breeze blew across the rock face and forced his body to twist to the right.

Careful, he told himself. *Don't bang against the chimney wall.*

Move the legs. Touch the cliff face. Keep your distance. Stay awake. Stay awake.

Thirty seconds later, he couldn't look up any more. His neck had stiffened. He leaned against the rope to rest his shoulders. *Just for a moment*, he told himself. *I need to close my eyes. Just for a moment.*

He pushed against the cliff with his boots. Right, then left. He could do this in his sleep. His left shoulder muscles tightened, so he stopped pushing his leg with his hand. He would need his left arm to get him out of the harness at the bottom, so Dad could retrieve the rope.

Jack thought two hundred forty feet would be a butt-busting long rappel for anybody to control – worse for a man with graying skin, a man who was wet and cold and probably not as strong as he was that last time he climbed into trouble – the time Dad got trapped in a crevasse in the Andes.

Balance, Jack said to himself. It was a good word, he thought – a balanced word – heavy letter B on one side of the L . . .

He jerked awake hanging upside down. Enormous pressure flooded his face. Blood had rushed to his head. His heart pounded in his ears. Instinctively, his right hand still gripped the rope. He rolled his head toward his chest, but the pull of his helmet strap across his neck choked him. He had to get upright before he fell out of his sit harness. He couldn't understand what had happened to the chest harness. It hung across him, dangling from the carabiner that still kept it attached to his rope. But it no longer surrounded or protected him.

When he tried to pull himself upright, his legs slipped in the sit harness, inching the webbing toward his knees. He had to get up and back into the harness. The fabric of his chest harness flapped into his face. At that moment, he saw the package for the beef jerky fall from his jacket pocket, whirling away toward the rocks below. His grip on the rope tightened.

If he yelled, his father would lean over the ledge to see him. That would put them both in danger. He grabbed at his thigh with his left hand so the leg wouldn't fly up and let him drop. Unable to loosen the helmet strap, he forced himself to use quick shallow gasps. Moving his hand on the rope like a crawling caterpillar, he inched upward. With the useless harness blowing across his face, he could hardly see what he was doing.

The wind blew his freezing body, banging him sideways into the cliff. As he swung out from the collision, the wind turned him, face away from the rock. He knew this was the most dangerous time. Most climbers get broken wrists or ankles from colliding with rock.

The eighty-foot pendulum of rope swung his hanging body again. Jack hunched his shoulders and tucked his chin toward the helmet strap. The blow against the cliff rammed his helmet upwards. His head snapped toward his knees, driving his body upright.

Jack shot his right hand far up the rope. He closed his eyes against the pain, but he gripped hard in the new higher rope position. As he swung away from the face of the cliff, his head was again above his hips, and safe. The chest harness fell away from his face. Far below, he could see the boulders on which he might have dropped. And there, staring up at him, were the goats they'd met in the meadow this morning.

They're thinking, "Hey stupid, got any more tricks?"

Thrusting out his right leg, he caught the cliff face on the next swing. His father might have felt a jerk on the rope when Jack banged into the wall, but Jack hoped he didn't know his son had been up-side down. He'd tell Dad someday, maybe – when they were both old men – if they got the chance to be old men.

He couldn't tell what had happened to the chest harness. He guessed it had to be his carabiner opening. He must have used it incorrectly.

To calm his fear, and avoid thinking about his mistakes, Jack studied his surroundings. His descent finally approached the lower belay stance. Through the rain, he could tell it was far to the north of the one they had used as they climbed up.

"Dad," he called. "bottom of chimney-chute coming up." His voice was stronger now.

"How far?" his father yelled.

"Sixty more feet."

Then he remembered the knot. "Dad," he called again, "the knot's coming to the brake."

Jack wished he had watched Dad tie that knot. His life now depended on the prusik knot. It might be no better than the chest harness that hung limply on the rope, doing him no good.

Jack shook the water out of his goggles, lowered his head against the rope and slowly moved his limbs to keep warm, always facing the dangerous rock. Renewed rain made a pounding drum of his helmet. The rope stopped. The knot had arrived at the braking system. He couldn't see Dad because of the angle, but he knew from hours of practice under his father's demanding eye, that Dad had his hands full at the moment. With one hand, Dad would tighten the prusik sling – the third short rope – to relieve tension on the primary rope. His father's other hand would move the big knot past the brake. Then he would reattach the long rope to the brake device and slowly unwind the load-releasing hitch, allowing the main rope to take the weight again. Careful work always seemed to take forever.

"Jack," his father called at last. "I'm ready to lower you."

"Ready, Dad."

Within minutes, Jack was all the way to the bottom of the chimney. His feet touched rock. He stood a moment and then limped to the bottom of the next chimney. His shaking hands hooked him into the protection they had left there. He sent the rope back up to his father and huddled, unable to stop shivering as his father brought himself down. Minutes only for Jack to get down the chimney, but it had seemed like hours.

Then he realized that Dad had a two-rope descent and no one to relieve the tension when the knot came to the brake. That was the question he'd forgotten to ask.

He glanced up and watched his father already lowering himself. One rope had been looped and attached to his pack. The other rope carried Dad's weight as he walked his legs and his back down opposite sides of the rain-slickened chimney chute.

Jack frowned and cleared his goggles again. His father's foot slipped against the wall. The other foot held. Dad got a new grip with both feet and started down again. Jack couldn't imagine how much leg strength this descent must demand. It was bad enough going up when it had been a dry rock face.

Beyond halfway down, Dad arrived at the end of the first rope. He halted, hammered a camming device and a bolt into the cliff face. Then he routed the second rope through a pear-shaped carabiner and tied a Munther hitch and attached the rope to his seat harness.

Jack knew the Munther hitch knot would give his father pretty good friction control, but it tended to twist the rope and slow the descent. It was a clever, but arm-wrenching way to come down.

Jack glanced below him at the gray and black billy goat. He could barely see under its beard where the big bell hung around its neck.

As soon as Dad arrived on the ledge next to Jack, he grabbed what was left of the chest harness and studied it. "The damned sewing failed," he said. "I've never seen that before." He rummaged in Jack's pack, pulled out some of Jack's purple nylon web and tied it around Jack. Jack shivered too much to help, but he was grateful to hear the harness failure hadn't been his fault.

Dad held Jack's shoulders, looking into his eyes. "I'm sorry, Jack," he said. "I should have checked that harness. I had it at Nanda Devi last winter and just assumed it was still in good shape."

Through his chattering teeth, Jack tried to whisper, "It's okay, Dad." He couldn't say much, but his nod seemed to get through to his Dad. He wondered if Dad knew he'd been dumb enough to fall asleep.

They began the process again on the new cliff face, but this time Jack had trouble making certain he faced the mountain so he could touch the slope with his feet as he backed down. At some points, he hung free. In other places, he could put his feet down and use the rope at his waist and chest to steady him as he moved down the near cliff-like grade.

His legs grew more and more rubbery. The taut rope hummed in the wind. At this point, Jack's descent was on a steep slope rather than a drop-off. Several times he had to stop merely to breathe. Down at the bottom of the slope lay a heap of boulders, the scree of debris that had fallen off the mountain and come to rest at the edges of Big Meadow. Beyond the boulders, grazed one very wet, unconcerned billy goat, and a nanny who watched Jack closely.

Above, Jack could imagine his father, the great Mallory Huntington, sitting stone still, playing out rope for his halting and slow-witted son.

"Jack. What the hell's going on down there?" Dad's voice was as strident and impatient as ever.

Jack realized he'd stopped walking his feet down the slope. He stared at the rope. His forearm rubbed against the Buck knife in his pants pocket.

He remembered Kristi's angry voice. *Mallory loves you because you make him look good.*

No longer, Jack thought. *I can't run. Can't climb. Can't even stay awake. I don't make anybody look good.*

With a rope under this much tension, one touch of the knife would cut through and he would fall to the boulders fifty feet below. He would never again have to prove himself worthy.

"Jack?" Dad's tense voice flooded the face of the mountain. "Jack, are you conscious?"

Jack's hand jerked away from his pocket and his knife. How could he think about that? If he cut it, the sudden release on the rope might pull his dad off the ledge. His father leaned over the cliff, staring down. A risky position. That moment – that show of concern embarrassed Jack, but it also flooded him with an unaccustomed hope.

"I'm awake, Dad," he called. "Just a Charlie-horse." He was disgusted with himself for thinking about quitting. He might have killed them both. As he concentrated again, he tried to remember what it had been like to run, to leap over high hurdles, to climb monoliths in the Columbia Gorge. He tried to remember trusting his legs.

Fifty-feet lower, he touched the first boulder at the edge of the meadow. He pushed with both hands and his right foot to shove away from the boulder. He worked his way down ten more feet to the sparse grass and late fall's blue Michaelmas daisies.

"My toes are on the ground," he yelled.

The rope inched its way, allowing Jack's feet to settle fully on the meadow. After three tries, he was able to open the carabiner and released the rope. His legs were soggy noodles, but he leaned on his stomach across a big boulder and yelled, "Off belay."

His father took up the rope. Jack made certain it didn't get hung up in the crack between two boulders. As soon as the rope was free, he collapsed into the wet sand and grass.

Dad would have to do the last pitch without him. And then, they would have to get to the car. He couldn't imagine how.

. . .

He woke when his father's big hands held his head. "Jackson," Dad said. "Look at me, boy."

Jack tried, but startling sunlight hurt his eyes until Dad's head created a shadow over his face. Dad had whipped off his own goggles. His stiff brows brushed his upper lid as his left eye squinted to study Jack's pupils.

"Damn," Dad said, his fingers resting on Jack's throat at his pulse. Jack breathed in the odor of fresh grass warmed by the sun. Nearby, a deep bell rang. They were in the meadow with the goats.

"When did the rain stop?" he asked.

"You went out on me after you got here," his father said.

"I'm cold."

"The helicopter has passed over once. They got our message."

Jack listened. Faraway, copter blades whopped the air. Jack thought about what his father had not said – nothing about getting on his feet and toughing it out.

"Dad?"

His father had looked away, toward the copter.

"Dad, do you sometimes wish you could let up?"

His father's head jerked back toward Jack. "What do you mean?"

"When you're worried, you sound . . . you know . . . more like Mom."

The air whooshed out of his father's lungs. Dad's head hung down between his shoulders.

Jack reached up and touched his father's arm. "I wanted to be here with you."

Dad's attention returned to Jack's face in an instant. "Don't get crazy on me, boy."

Jack warmed at the concern in his father's voice. Then, he noticed a change in the sound of the helicopter. "That copter is looking to land."

His father raised his head to see the incoming rescuers. He stood quickly and held out his arms to show the pilot which direction the wind blew.

CHAPTER 15

Jack saw that the meadow was too small for a safe landing. The helicopter hovered – a huge machine. The whack of its blades drummed inside Jack's head. Through thin grass, he watched the brindled billy-goat retreat to the cover of scrub pines. Peaking out, the billy's head swung from side to side. His gaze focused on a moving object.

A squinting glance upward showed Jack what the goat saw – a dark knot of feet and jackets wrapped around a cable, men descending from an opening in the side of the hovering helicopter. The copter blades blew dust in his face.

"They're bringing a litter down with them," Dad said.

Jack blinked to clear his eyes. One of the nanny goats inched her way into the clearing. Her bell rang a low note. Jack was amazed at her courage. The billy must have worried about her, too. He nipped at her haunch, but she reared her hind leg with a swift kick. The billy backed into the pines again.

But she moved closer to Jack. Her bell clapped out a soothing ring below the whapping copter. Jack thought he must be dreaming her. He closed his eyes, exhausted from shivering.

"Sergeant Scott Light here, sir," shouted a young man. "The copter is going to leave while we get you ready to hoist."

With a revving of its engine, the helicopter circled away toward the east.

"What's the patient's name?" Light asked.

Jack tried to answer for himself, but he couldn't stop shaking.

"Jack Huntington," his father yelled. "My son."

Scott Light put a warm hand on Jack's forehead. "Did he fall?" His fingers moved along Jack's neck and then his arms.

"No fall." Dad said. "No breaks, but an unbelievable cramp in his left leg."

Unbelievable. That's why he'd ended up this way. Dad couldn't believe. Bradley wouldn't believe. Worst of all, he'd allowed this craziness to happen because he pretended the cramps were nothing.

"What's your name?" Light asked Jack as a second fellow took Dad away to talk to him.

"Jack." That was all he could get out. While Light checked Jack's body for breaks, he asked other questions: What's today? Who's the president of the United States? – questions designed to tell Light if Jack still had any brains. He thought he answered, but he wasn't certain.

"Barnes," Light said to his partner, "we've got to package this kid. Bring the immobilization board."

"But there's no break," Dad said.

Light glanced at his buddy and pursed his lips before he answered. "We have to take all the precautions, sir, just in case."

From that one glance, Jack believed they were treating his father as if he knew nothing – in fact, might be part of the problem. Jack tried to sit up, to set them straight. Light stopped Jack's feeble rise with a hand to the chest.

"It'll be all right, Jack. I'll ride up with you."

Jack wanted to see his father, but Light and Barnes surrounded Jack, their orange parkas and rain gear cutting him off from any view but their faces. Light spoke to Barnes. "Careful with the neck. Leave the wool caps on him."

Light reached for the zipper on Jack's soggy rain parka. "Gotta get you out of wet stuff." In Light's hand rested a pair of small scissors.

Breathing grew hard. Jack's mind went dark for a few moments – a fleeting space. In what seemed like a short time, they had him wrapped in wool blankets, a rain-proof cover, and strapped on the immobilization board. Jack remembered photos of servicemen coming home in body bags. He tried to push the blankets away.

"Into the Stokes," Light said. "One, two, . . . "

On three they lifted him – Houdini levitating, he thought, but no Houdini escape. His breath grew quick and loud with fear. They laid him like a baby inside a metal frame, a bed surrounded by a cage. In moments, they pulled wide nylon web across his chest and legs. The finality of thunks at his side told him they had closed the straps into strong buckles. There was no crawling out. He heard nothing from Dad.

If this Stokes litter weren't safe, his father would protest.

The whole move took no time, but then Jack couldn't be sure he'd seen it all. Every muscle in his body had tightened, the way his foot always clawed up. The pain of the cramps was gone, but this time Jack figured lack of pain was not good. It meant he no longer felt what normal people would feel.

The Stokes, his bed-cage, tilted slightly to one side. Sergeant Light leaned over him. The guy's jet-black eyebrows nearly met above his nose. His brown and gold eyes concentrated on Jack's face. When he saw Jack's eyes were open, his worried frown became a bright smile.

"What hey, buddy. It's not every day you get to fly while wrapped in a cocoon."

Jack pushed hard to shout out a few words. "Wrap Dad."

Light leaned closer. "Wrap him up?"

Completely worn out, Jack couldn't nod. He had to let blinking his eyes mean "Yes".

Light picked up on the blinks. "My friend Barnes got your Dad in a down parka. He'll warm up pretty quick, here."

Light seemed to be only a little older than Jack – maybe in his twenties. Jack liked him – his serious attention to detail, and the contrast with his offhand talk.

The other para-jumper, Barnes, signaled the helicopter. It returned to hover over the meadow. Light and Barnes lifted a rope of steel that had been lying next to Jack. They hooked the cables from the bed to a cable on the helicopter. Jack saw Barnes lock down the hook opening.

"We're about to take off, Jack," Light said. "I'm covering your eyes. Don't want dust in them. We're going up, and then Barnes here will ride the Penetrator with your dad."

Jack had a vague wish to see what a penetrator looked like, but Light pulled the blanket over his eyes.

A grave is like this, Jack thought. Darkness. Panic. No muscles to get you out. The space inside the blanket smelled like his bad breath and the stale sweat of fear.

In a moment the litter tilted up at the head end. The sides of the cage bent inward under tension. As they rose, Jack's mind flashed on the iron-frame boat of Lewis and Clark. The Stokes was that boat in another century – a good idea that failed.

God, don't let this cable break. He was aware of every jerk and waver, the wind blowing him from side to side, and the long, tugging whine of a motor under stress – the hoist motor, he believed.

Then Light shouted, "Don't bump my patient."

A voice answered. "We've got him, Scott. Move your butt."

Within seconds, his litter glided in and settled on something solid. The rumble of the copter motor beat right through the metal bed. Light removed the blanket from Jack's face and tightened the blanket about his shoulders. Jack watched the guy's calm concentration as he adjusted another blanket around Jack's head.

"Dad?" Jack managed only a whisper.

Light watched his lips and then answered. "Your dad's on his way up. We'll get you both to Trinity Hospital in twenty minutes."

Cool air brushed Jack's forehead, a breeze from the open side of the copter. He heard the crank of the hoist engine bringing up its second load. Someone in the distance gave orders – "step here" and "move back to the Stokes." Then, his father, wrapped in a parka and wool blanket, loomed behind Sergeant Light.

"How is he?" Dad asked.

"Warmed and steady. Responding to questions."

"Aren't you going to IV him? You said his temperature was down to ninety."

"Sir, we've found that warm IV fluids often push cold blood back toward the heart. In hypothermia patients, we've learned to be extra careful not to stress the heart."

"We used IVs in the Andes." Dad sounded frustrated.

"Believe me, IV warming has been studied. We're using the accepted protocol for situations when we're close to the hospital and to better equipment."

"Not even warmed oxygen?"

"No, sir."

"Damn it, I . . ."

"We'll be at the hospital in fifteen minutes," Light said. "This is safer."

"I've used it. It works."

"Yes, sir," Light said. "Jack's worried about you, Mr. Huntington."

"Jack?" His father still stood behind Light. Jack wished Dad would bend down and touch him, maybe shove some of his hair back from his eyes. When he tried to get Dad's attention, he coughed.

"I'm here, Jack. Mom's meeting us at the hospital."

Jack remembered the cell phone. Maybe Dad called Mom while Jack was out of it, down in the meadow with the goats. What a show for the goats – something to tell the kids about.

He wanted to share that joke with Light, but he couldn't dredge up the stuff to talk. His chest felt heavy. His eyes wouldn't stay open. The drone of the helicopter engine made talking too much work.

. . .

Jack remembered the helicopter setting down, the rush of people in blue-green cotton suits who lifted him from the Stokes to a litter on wheels. His legs were constant knots. The crew wheeled him from the heliport into the hospital. A huge gray and white cross hovered over the doorway.

All about him, he heard terse orders and the swift click of his wheels. At the speed they were hauling him around corners, he feared for the life of anybody on crutches.

"Slow down," a woman shouted. "You don't want to start cardiac fibrillation!" His ride became sedate as her voice continued to give orders. "Don't stop in Emergency, take him to Cardiac Care. His mom's already signing papers."

Cardiac Care? That meant heart trouble. He didn't have heart trouble – he was only seventeen.

As his moving bed turned a corner, the smell of disinfectant bit the insides of his nose. Overhead, lights flashed past. Voices came at him from all directions. From behind him, a familiar voice sounded louder than the rest.

"For God's sake, Mallory, why didn't you follow my advice?" That was Dr. Edward's voice, but the angry tone was nothing like Edwards. And no one yelled at Dad.

"I told you we needed more tests. What didn't you understand about the word 'elevated'?" Jack heard him nearly shout. "We could have avoided this."

As the voice receded, Jack noticed his body wasn't shaking any more. Wrapped up the way Light had mummified him, his arms and legs had grown stiff. His muscles had locked.

In despair, he stared at a passing wall where a polished wooden statue hung, a mother, a father and a baby. *Where's Mom?*

They rolled into a brightly lit room. A woman leaned over him. She had dark hair tied back in a ponytail. "Hello," she called as if he were deaf, "we'll get you warmed up soon. You hang in there, guy."

He blinked 'yes'. She didn't seem to see the signal. Jack wanted Sergeant Light in the hospital. In moments, Jack was transferred to another kind of boat, another bed with metal sides. Cool air washed over his body as two orderlies opened the blankets.

"Get a temperature," a voice called from the hall. "I can examine him in a minute."

"Getting it, Dr. Crescent."

In moments, someone rewrapped him in warmed cotton. The nurse leaned over him, pulling the new blankets over his chest and throat. He felt a tug on his head as she slipped a mask over his face.

"Take those blankets to Scott Light, the fellow from the rescue helicopter," she told someone off at the side.

Watching his only link with Light disappear out the door, Jack began to shake again. He couldn't control it, although this time, the shivers were about more than the cold. He was damned scared.

And embarrassed. Until they unwrapped the blankets, he hadn't been aware that someone had taken off all his rain-soaked clothes. Maybe Light did that when they wrapped him up on the mountain.

He just wished his nurse were a man.

"Core temperature is now ninety-three," the pony-tailed nurse called to the person in the next room.

A second person, behind Jack's head, said, "Doctor Edwards has called in Ambrose, too."

The nurse hung a bottle from a metal stand. She glanced beyond Jack at the second voice. "You're the electrician. How would you know this?"

"Edwards was making calls as I came past the nurse's station. He says this includes an immune system breakdown."

Immune system breakdown! What does that mean?

"Hey," she glanced angrily at the speaker. "The kid's sick, not stupid."

She studied Jack, and must have seen the panic in his face, because she took his hand, right through the blanket. "It's okay, kid." She glanced at some papers near the bed. "Jack," she said in a tentative voice. "You like to be called 'Jack'?"

He blinked.

She smiled. "When you did that before, I thought you were just blinking. So, you heard the blabbermouth behind you. That's Chuck, our tech in charge of electrical equipment. He'll try not to scare you again. And when Dr. Edwards and Dr. Crescent arrive, they can explain what's going on."

She raised her eyebrows. "You got that?"

He blinked again.

"Good. Now our big job for the moment is to raise your core temperature. That's what the warmed blankets are for. And the air in the breathing gizmo is heated to forty-two degrees centigrade. That's like one hundred seven degrees Fahrenheit. Understand?"

She watched for his blinks and then continued. "With this needle and this bag up here, we're sending warm liquids into your system, too. Have to get your major organs re-warmed. Then, we can get you back on your feet."

Yes! Back on his feet. Out of here. He breathed as deeply as he could. The mist felt good against his nose and all the way into his throat. But breathing too deeply hurt his chest.

Shoe soles scuffed as another person turned the corner at the end of Jack's bed. "Jack, Dr. Edwards here. You remember me?"

Jack blinked.

"Blinking means 'yes'." The nurse explained.

Edwards smiled at her. "Ah. You've got a system worked out already. What means 'no'?"

She glanced at Jack and winked. "You ever say 'no', Jack?"

Inside the respirator mask, Jack wrinkled his nose.

She tilted her head toward Edwards, but kept her eye on Jack's face. "Making pig noses is the 'reply negativo'," she said.

Edwards moved closer and put his hand to Jack's throat, but spoke to the nurse. "I see you started the D-S."

"Dextrose and saline dripping now," she said, as if telling Jack as well as Dr. Edwards.

Edwards whipped out the end of his stethoscope, rubbed it warm, then applied it to Jack's chest. Jack heard someone in a room off to the side of this one turn on a water faucet, maybe washing hands.

"Dr. Crescent," Edwards said. It looked like he was speaking to the person in the side room. "When Jack is stable, let's get a blood draw," he said. "I'll need a metabolic panel. Include a CPK level."

"We'll do that, and copy to Dr. Ambrose," a woman's voice said from the side room. The water in there turned off. A tall woman entered the room. "Where's the heart monitor?"

"Working on it, Doc," said the electrician, Chuck, from somewhere out of sight.

"Be quick," she ordered in a stern voice as she strode to Jack's side opposite Dr. Edwards.

Jack's eyes drooped. He tried to open them again, but he had no strength, only a surprising heaviness in his chest.

"Let's start the lavage," Dr. Crescent said to the nurse.

A sharp jab told him someone had punched him in the stomach with a needle. Jack moaned.

After moments of fiddling with tubes, Jack heard Edwards say, "I asked Ambrose to come down. Only a floor away."

"Good idea," Dr. Crescent said, "But we have to deal with hypothermia first."

High heels clicked in the hall, and then swiveled, swishing the door open.

"How's our young man?" The voice was another woman's, but not his mother. Less worried than his mother would sound. He should open his eyes.

"Dr. Ambrose, Dr. Crescent, this is Jack Huntington. Jack . . ."

Edwards' hand was at his neck pulse again. "Get that monitor hooked up now," he shouted at Chuck.

The electrician answered from somewhere beneath the bed. "I have to tape the cord in place."

"The pulse? Jack!"

Without opening his eyes, Jack tried to wrinkle his nose. Nobody seemed to see the gesture. Maybe it didn't happen.

A blip of sound invaded the room.

"Ah, there it is," Edwards said. "Good. Much better."

"Yep," Chuck said, climbing from beneath, and jarring the bed in the process. "There's the sound of Jack's heart."

The nurse's voice was cold and sharp. "Duct tape!" she said, "I've seen that broken plug twice today, and that's twice too many."

"Yes, sir." Chuck must have saluted her. Jack could hear the motion of his rising starched sleeve and the click of his heels.

"Young man," Dr. Crescent said, "a better machine. Right now."

Jack couldn't care less about jerks like Chuck. His head seemed to be floating in a heavy liquid. Through the liquid, he heard people's voices distort, wowing in and out like a radio that is not on the station.

"Core temperature?" Dr. Crescent asked.

"Ninety-three." That was the nurse again.

" Mountain climbing?" Dr. Ambrose asked.

"And poly-myositis," Edwards said.

The gasp Jack heard next was his mother's. He tried to wake up for her. Nothing worked.

"What's happening?" his mother asked, her voice moving closer very quickly.

"Don't jolt him, "Edwards said. "Might set off his heart."

"How?" Mom's voice was tight.

"Fibrillation," said Dr. Crescent. "Hypothermia. Until stabilized, .
. . heart . . . risk."

"Is he unconscious?" Her voice rose. Jack had never heard her sound
hysterical.

"Asleep," Edwards said. "Exhausted."

Dr. Ambrose said, "Talk to him."

"Jack, I'm here, honey." Mom's voice receded, as if she were heading
out the door. Jack realized it was his mind that was leaving the room.
He heard only pieces of what was said next.

"Warm . . . fluids . . .respirator," Ambrose said.

"That other word. *Poly-myo...*" Mom said.

Now Jack's mind went on alert. He needed the answer to her question.

"Muscles burning," Ambrose explained. "His immune system
thinks his muscle is foreign matter."

Jack's mind wowed in and out, hearing snatches of words.

"Clue was . . . rash," Edwards said. "told . . . husband . . . Friday.
CPK . . . five hundred."

"CPK?"

" . . . an enzyme . . . leaks. . . as muscles break down," Ambrose
said.

At this, Jack's mind returned fully to the room.

"Did you tell my husband the CPK was slightly elevated?"

Edwards was silent.

"Did you say 'slightly?" Mom asked.

"I've seen . . .numbers in the thousands."

"'Slightly' handed him the excuse he wanted to ignore it."

"That's not what I meant."

"That's what 'slightly' means . . . parent who grasps for chance . . .
pretend nothing wrong." Mom sounded very angry.

At that moment, Jack heard himself gasping. He heard the blips on the monitor go wild.

"Fibrillation," the nurse called. "Code blue."

A loud alarm sounded out in the hall.

"Move back to the wall," the nurse yelled, probably at Mom.

Behind the roar of liquid in his head, Jack heard machinery being wheeled into his room. His monitor bleeped and whizzed. A vice seemed to grip his chest.

"What are you doing?" Mom shouted.

"No electric shock," Crescent called. "He's hypothermic."

His monitor danced a syncopation. His head cleared. For a moment, his mind rose above pain.

"Epinephrine!" Dr. Crescent's harsher voice shouted. "He's about to flat-line."

Flat-line was the only thing Jack understood. Even as she said it, his monitor hiccupped and then came back on, humming one low note, broken by two blips.

Dr. Crescent called out, "Give me the syringe!"

A swift jab smashed into his IV tube. Heat spread through his arm and chest, but his mind dragged him from the hospital, back to the body bag, in the helicopter. And somehow, Sergeant Light was smiling at him. "Crazy ride, huh, Jack?"

CHAPTER 16

Much later, Jack returned to his body. An ache in his chest grew closer and closer until agony forced all else to recede. People fussed over him, putting a needle into his IV shunt, fiddling chest bandages onto him until he wanted to hit them. The center of his being grew into a crescendo of pain.

And then, he realized that for minutes at a time the pain receded. During those moments of relief, he was able to hear people, but not to respond to them.

Several times each morning he heard Dr. Ambrose clip into the room. He remembered her high heels from the first night. She took Jack's hand, whispered "Good morning, Mrs. Huntington. Hello, Jack. It looks like you are making progress. Dr. Crescent, your heart doctor will be in later this morning. Keep up the good work, young man."

He liked the sound of her voice, her belief that he might actually have something to do with getting better. But even as she clipped out the door, all he could do was return to sleep.

• • •

"Hello, Mrs. Huntington," Kristi said, and deep in his mind, Jack felt morning sun gliding into the room. This was a different room, he could tell by the softness of Kristi's voice. The room before, where his heart had stopped, that room had given off sounds of metal and hard surfaces and the echoes of loud voices. That room had been filled with monitors, machines and whispering people.

But this room had fabric.

"Mrs. Huntington?"

As Kristi spoke again, his mother moved her hand within his. He felt the mattress dent as Mom turned toward the door.

Berto spoke next. "Mr. Huntington said we should sign in as your other kids."

"Oh," his mother let out a surprised chuckle. "I suppose that was the only way."

"Well, hey," Kristi said, "at least we all have black hair."

"It's been days," Berto sighed. "They wouldn't let us in Intensive Care even if we *were* your kids."

"He'll be glad to see you when he wakes up," Mom said.

"How is he this morning?" Berto asked.

"His temperature is still high."

Jack waited to hear Dad, but there was no sound of his boots, nor the pine-pitch smell of him.

"Here's a chair," his mother said.

A whomp of air left a seat cushion. Only Berto's whole weight could have made that noise.

Jack felt Kristi's hand take his hand opposite Mom. "Why are his lips so blue?" she asked.

"It's . . ." His mother's breath caught before she could answer. "It's the pneumonia. He's not getting enough oxygen."

"I thought his heart stopped," Berto said.

"It did. They had to open his chest and massage his heart to start it again."

"Not a defibrillator?"

"They can't use that on hypothermic patients. They had to find another way . . . a way to coax it instead of jolt it back to life."

Kristi's fingers tightened on his fingers. "Did the operation infect his lungs?"

"No," Mom said, "his heart doctor says he had this lung problem even before the heart stopped."

Kristi's hand covered his fingers, as if she were trying to warm him from the fingertips to his chest. Jack wanted her to stay like that, but there was no way he could tell her. Even if he could get his eyes open, or his mouth, he couldn't say that to her in front of his mom. So he absorbed as much of the feel of her as he could.

Kristi blurted the question he wanted answered. "Could his heart stop again?"

His mother's hand stroked his arm, making him aware of the tube her fingers had to avoid. "Honey," she said to Kristi, "I think he can hear us."

"Oh! I'm sorry."

"Some questions are okay. He probably wants to know how he is, too," Mom said.

Yes, Jack thought. *Tell me the truth.*

"So," Kristi began slowly, as if carefully picking her words. "What's with all the wires and tubes?"

"The oxygen is helping him breathe. These wires monitor his heartbeat. It's been regular. We're still worried because all of his systems have been fighting to function."

"Is that why he doesn't wake up?"

"The head nurse, Mrs. Sawyer, says he needs his strength to get well, not for talking."

A long silence followed. He expected Dad to say something. It would be something positive, about how Jack would conquer all this and be back to track workouts in a month. But Dad said nothing. So where was he?

Then he felt the mattress move as if his mother sat up straighter.

She took in a deep breath, maybe to make herself more alert.

"How did you two get to the hospital?" Mom asked, her voice attempting brightness.

"I've got my dad's old car, now," Berto said. "I picked Kristi up from downtown."

Downtown? Jack thought. *Is she still hanging out downtown?*

"Kristi," Mom said, "Why *are* you down there?"

"I'm all right," Kristi said. "I just can't be at home right now."

"You know you can sleep in our guest room."

"I know. But there are people who . . . well, they'd miss out if I weren't working downtown."

"Honey . . ." Mom began.

"Please trust me, Mrs. Huntington."

Another silence followed. Jack imagined his mother and all the questions she wanted to ask, and then decided not to ask. Berto moved, making the chair whoosh. He was probably really uncomfortable with this conversation. Jack wanted to shake the story out of Kristi, but not one muscle obeyed his command.

Kristi squeezed Jack's hand. She seemed to sink into a chair, but she never let go of him. "Mr. Huntington said he was better. How is this better?"

"Saturday night was bad, Kristi," his mother said, "Very bad."

Berto shifted in his noisy chair. "Why is Mr. Huntington staying out in the hall?"

Jack tensed for her answer.

"Mallory has a chest cold. He could make Jack worse," Mom said.

He relaxed. Dad wasn't mad at him. He was taking care of him.

"Jack was sick way before this weekend," Kristi said. "Why did they even go on this climb?"

"I don't know, Kris," Mom whispered. "I should have argued harder. I should have . . ."

"Nothing would have stopped them," Berto said. "You could have stolen their climbing shoes and only slowed them down going out the door."

Jack knew Berto was correct. They went because Jack never admitted it was too much for him. He should have said it – just a bold and solid "No, Dad. I can't."

He felt Kristi's forehead touch his hand. Her hair brushed his arm as she lay her head next to his fingertips on the bed. He wished she would do that sometime when he was awake and no one else was in the room. Helplessly, he recognized somnolence invading his mind, dulling the throb in his chest, making his limbs heavy. The last thing he felt, before he slipped into torpor, was a small drop of water plopping onto his open palm.

And then he dreamed about Kristi, huddled in a doorway in downtown Portland.

CHAPTER 17

Jack couldn't swallow his own saliva. He thrashed in the bed, pulling at the oxygen tube, trying to roll over on his side so he could breathe. Desperate, he clawed at his face.

He smelled the cut-grass aroma of his Uncle Jackson. Jackson's hands opened his mouth. A nurse thrust a suction device beside his tongue. Jackson's low voice talked him through terror.

"Thank you, Mrs. Sawyer," Jackson said quietly to the nurse. Then he began a slow chant that helped Jack concentrate. "In through the nose," Jackson said in his compelling rhythm. "Out through the mouth. All the way down to your solar plexus. That's it, Jack. In through the nose, let your back relax. Out through . . ."

Uncle Jackson's calm took him down into rough breathing and deep into release.

Over the next hours, when he couldn't swallow, others talked him down from fear – sometimes Mom, sometimes Kristi, or Berto, or the nurse, Mrs. Edna Sawyer. But it was Uncle Jackson's calm that brought the longest relief.

He dreamed he worked with Uncle Jackson on a landscaping job. They pruned a Japanese maple so carefully that the main branches seemed ancient. When they finished, every branch and leaf contributed to a feeling of airy permanence.

"No need to conquer the tree," Jackson often had told him. "When you're done, the tree should recognize itself."

With Uncle Jackson and trees, Jack recognized himself. With Mom and their paintings, with Kristi and Berto at the cliffs, Jack recognized himself. And as he drew slow, smooth breaths, he recalled himself in the woodworking shop. In his memory, he remodeled the basement to create his mother's office.

But in that creation, he worked alone. He no longer saw himself as building with Dad. His father was never in the hospital room.

Jack knew he'd been right to insist they come down from the mountain. And he shouldn't have had to convince anybody. Dad needed the rattling Jack had given him, but Jack couldn't forget that moment when he grabbed Dad's jacket and thought of taking them both off the cliff.

. . .

Through closed eyes, Jack felt the gray and shadowed lack of sunshine on this new day. He'd stopped gagging the evening before, yet he still had a tube in his nose and was stuck flat on his back. He wanted desperately to curl up and cover his aching chest, but he couldn't.

He heard the squeak he knew belonged to Mrs. Edna Sawyer's shoes. He opened his eyes long enough to watch her hand him something. She explained that when he felt pain, he should punch that button and deliver painkiller to his body.

Jack didn't want to become addicted. Although he never talked about that fear, by noon, Mrs. Sawyer figured him out.

"That button is calibrated," she explained. "It won't deliver medicine every time you punch it. It gives you a little bit, and no sooner than every fifteen minutes."

When he used the relief it offered, the taste of ashes and copper washed through his mouth. A buzz of orange and white heat raced through his whole body and he knew oblivion was not far behind.

Today, his incision hurt clear to his backbone. He tried to breathe in without raising his chest.

A noise startled him, but he didn't have the energy to open his eyes.

"Don't wake him up," Kristi whispered.

Jack recognized the thump and shuffle of Berto's boots, but half his mind still concentrated on the pain in his chest. A sharp ache threatened to split open his stitches. It was time to punch the button again, but he wanted to stay awake. So he moved his fingers away from the tube.

"Mrs. Huntington said we should talk to him," Berto whispered. "She's pretty sure he can hear in spite of the pain medicine."

Beyond his pain, Jack heard a whoosh exhale from the noisy chair next to his bed. That put Berto beside him near the window. And Kristi, maybe she was at the foot of his bed.

"Yo, Jack. Berto here. Over and out."

"Yo, Berto," Kristi said, "We're not on the Enterprise"

"Yeah? Then how do you account for all this weird equipment here?"

A chuckle came from Kristi. Berto spoke to Jack. "Xindi Colonel Kristi Labbé has beamed up from somewhere in the Andromeda Galaxy. She has important things to tell you," Berto said. "And it looks a lot like luvvvv, big guy."

Jack imagined Kristi making faces at Berto. He wished he could join in their teasing – but any motion at all was a knife stab.

The chair whooshed again. Berto must have stood up and moved around the bed where he could face Jack.

"Jack." This time it was Kristi's low voice. "I want to apologize for this dork here interrupting your nap."

"Just tell him how you've been out in the hall crying."

Jack waited, hoping.

"So," she said. From the closeness of her voice he knew she was now talking directly to him. "You got stupid and climbed when you should have laid off."

That wasn't what he wanted to hear.

"I am pissed," she said. "You promised to talk me into doing the Home-coming thing. 'Get dressed like a lady and go dancing,' you said. This is a lousy a way to back out."

Jack felt a laugh bubble up, but instead of laughter, a streak of lightning crossed his chest.

Oblivious to Jack's pain, Berto snorted. "Dance with you? Jack's found a charming nurse who doesn't give him such a hard-ass time."

Jack tried to smile, but he wasn't even sure his mouth moved.

"You see that?" Berto said. "His nose wiggled."

"You brush your teeth this morning?" she asked Berto.

"I think he was trying to say something."

"With his nose, it was probably 'Breathe elsewhere, big fella.'"

"Jacko, you gonna let her dish out that stuff to your best friend? She's killing me here. All you do is blush and let her at me."

In that instant, Jack felt exposed and stupid – a turtle on its back with no way to protect himself. He wanted to brush his hand through the mess of his hair, jerk the tube out of his nose, wipe the drool off his downhill cheek.

He forced his eyes to open. It took a moment to focus on her.

"Oh, Jack!" Kristi stood so close he could almost reach out and touch her long green shirt. Her eyes were shadowed with darkness – the look she had after days taking care of her mother.

"Kristi," he whispered, "You're exhausted."

"That's what I've been saying," Berto chimed in. "Can't be any good for Jack, if you make yourself sick."

"I'm . . . I'll be fine," she said. "But Jack, you been sleeping for days."

"Pain medicine," he said. "Crazy dreams."

"We made your mom go get something to eat," Berto said. "She'll be ticked she wasn't here."

"Dad?" he had to ask.

Kristi and Berto glanced at each other. Berto put a hand on her arm and spoke fast. "Your dad . . . he can't come in here."

"I think he'll be okay soon," Kristi said quickly. "He's just, you know . . . he's got a whopping cold."

During the next minutes, Kristi and Berto told him all about track practice, about their friends at school, about funny things that happened in the halls and the lunchroom. They said nothing more about Dad.

Jack felt his lids growing heavy. The pain in his chest yelled for morphine.

Berto noticed Jack's tired look. "Kris, Let's go find his mom."

She glanced at her watch. "Geez, I've got to get downtown, too."

"Look," Berto said, "Jack's mom said you could sleep in their guest room."

"But . . ." she said.

Jack worked to be heard. "Please, go to my house," he said.

Kristi frowned as if not certain what to do. Her hand brushed Jack's arm. And then her fingers stayed on his wrist. It was the softest thing she'd ever done.

"I guess I'll take the bus to your home then," she said.

Relief spread through him. She didn't have to go downtown. "Get mom to take you," Jack whispered. "She needs rest, too."

Kristi smiled and nodded. "I'll talk her into driving me, right after she sees you."

"Great," he said. His eyelids drooped. "That would be great."

"Well, old Buddy," Berto said. "Looks like you need to sleep. We'll wait for your mom in the hall."

Jack nodded, but the motion was so slight he didn't think they saw it. He heard them tiptoe out – if tiptoe is what you could call the thud of Berto's boots. The door closed, and then popped open again. He figured it didn't fit the jamb very well. He imagined working on that jamb with his father, re-setting the hinges, planing the door, cutting a new hole for the knob and the latch. Then he heard Berto talking to Kristi.

"I'll tell that Swede you can't work anymore."

Work? Jack thought. *What work can she be doing for Swede?*

Kristi said, "No, don't make Swede worry. That would be hard on the girls."

Jack wanted to holler at her. *You don't have to do this, Kris.*

Berto said, "Dang it, Kris. What girls? What are you doing down there?"

At that moment, the quick, squeaky-shoes of Mrs. Sawyer approached them. "Jack's heart monitor says you are acting too much like brother and sister. He needs quiet. So you'd best scoot."

"Oh, Lord!" Kristi said. "Jack, I'm sorry."

"Scoot. Scoot." The nurse waved them away from the door.

"Come on, Kris," Berto said. "We need to find his mom."

"Okay," she said, "but no more butting into my business."

After they left, the nurse came into the room. She rested her cool hand on his forehead, but Jack could only think about Kristi and the big guy he remembered in Pioneer Courthouse Square – Swede.

CHAPTER 18

The next morning, Jack woke hungry, but warmed by the sun through the window. He hoped Mom had taken Kristi home last night. He wanted to talk sense into that girl. Maybe Mom could do it.

He glanced at the button for pain medicine and decided he didn't need any right now. Maybe he'd see how long he could hold off on that stuff.

The scent of baking made his mouth long for warm texture and melted butter. Biscuits. Maybe he was near a bread factory, or the hospital kitchen. He glanced at the tower of hanging bottles on his left and hoped those blue-tinted liquids didn't represent his only food. For the first time since the disastrous climb, he craved a good hamburger.

Then, he gazed about the room. He'd never been in a hospital before. None of his family ever got sick. Well, hardly . . . Kaitlyn.

Jack studied the curtains that hung from the ceiling on a track, the empty bed next to him, the door standing ajar to reveal a bathroom. The toilet seemed miles away.

On the wall opposite the foot of Jack's bed hung a whiteboard covered with green words and numbers. A second blank whiteboard hung across from the empty bed. Above the whiteboards, a crucifix leaned out from the wall toward him.

The crucified Jesus looked to be in worse shape than Jack – at least Jack hoped he didn't appear agonized. Such a gaunt look would scare Kristi and Mom.

Jack focused on his whiteboard. *CPK 18,000. Prednisone 50 mg/day, Immuren 200 mg/day*

He stared at that CPK number. Wasn't that the enzyme Dr. Edwards tested for? Could it really be eighteen thousand? Edwards had told Mom it was only at five hundred before the climb.

As he read, the green ink blurred. No matter how he squinted, Jack couldn't force his eyes to refocus on that number. He held his breath, trying not to be afraid.

And that, of course, was the moment his father first walked into his hospital room. Even through the confusing extra lines and colors in his watery vision, he knew that long stride and that hair.

"Dad!"

"Hello, Jack."

"I can't see you good," Jack said.

Dad came closer and made funny faces at him. "I don't look all that good, actually. How's this for ugly?"

His father distorted his face in the clownish way he used to do when Jack was little. Then Dad gave him the same eye-crinkling smile he always used – a 'glad to be home with you' sort of smile.

Jack relaxed. His vision cleared up and he saw that his father's hair was in wild curls, almost dred-locks.

"You give up washing your hair, Dad?"

"Yup."

"I've thought of it myself," Jack said, "but it always was easier just to cut it."

His father chuckled. "Yeah, well I spent the day on the Ramona Falls trail – an article for *Field and Stream*. No time to wash the whole mess."

"I'm glad you came."

Dad tilted his head to one side – his usual way of shrugging something off. Jack waited, hoping to hear that Dad was glad to be here.

"You're kind of thin," Dad said.

Jack stuffed his hope. "I can't see myself," he said.

"Your mother says you've had a rough time."

"I . . . I don't even know what day it is."

Dad looked at his watch. "Wednesday."

"Dang! That was Saturday when we . . ."

"Yeah," Dad interrupted. "Well, that's all water over the dam."

Jack gaped at his father. What happened wasn't mere water over the dam.

Dad said, "I came to see if you're having as lousy a time as Mom described. You know how women exaggerate . . ."

Jack waited to see if Dad thought he lived up to Mom's description. But his father wandered around the room, shoving an ugly green chair out of his way.

Jack's hurt rose up in him like magma. His father hadn't been sick. He'd just been gone – gone hiking while Mom sat overnight at his bed.

"Dad, why did you stay away from the hospital?"

His father looked surprised. "I was out in the hall. You were asleep."

Kristi said that once, but it didn't seem to be a complete answer. Besides, Kristi also had said Dad had a cold and there was no sign of that.

His father kept moving, checking out the bathroom that Jack had never visited, looking into a closet between the head of the bed and the window. Mom must have hung a robe and a set of school clothes in there; Jack recognized the green and red plaid of his favorite shirt.

Dad's wandering stopped in front of the white board. He studied the green print. "That's got to be wrong," he said. "Who wrote this stuff?"

"No idea."

"Too many zeroes in this CPK number. And this says you're taking Prednisone."

The sound of clicking heels warned Jack they were about to be interrupted. The door, which had been ajar, swung open.

"Mr. Huntington, I assume."

That was the voice of Dr. Ambrose. He'd never seen her, but she looked exactly the way her high heels promised she would look – sleek, dressed in a nice suit. She faced his father who was at the white board. From behind her, Jack saw the cuffs of a light blue blouse and the tail of a colorful scarf. Fact was, she didn't look so much like a hard-working doctor as a short fashion model – really short. No wonder she wore the tall shoes.

Her black hair was slicked into a fancy braid at the back of her head. Jack guessed she'd wear bright red lipstick.

"Mallory Huntington," his father said, shaking her hand.

"I'm Anita Ambrose, Jack's rheumatologist." She turned toward Jack, revealing that he was right about the lipstick – magazine glossy and fire engine red.

"Hello, Jack. I think you've heard my voice before."

He nodded. "And your shoes."

She lifted one foot, studying the heel height. "My seven-league boots," she said, grinning at him. "I thought you could hear a lot in spite of the pain medicine."

"What's this Prednisone note here?" Dad asked.

She raised her eyebrows and turned toward Dad. "Let's sit down so Jack can ask questions, too."

Dad didn't even glance at the puke-green leathery chair she indicated. "Prednisone is a steroid, isn't it?" he asked.

"Yes, it is."

"My son is an athlete. He can't be taking steroids."

"Mrs. Huntington said she had explained these decisions to you."

"She said medicine, not steroids."

"Ah. In that case, let's sit down and talk with Jack."

Jack saw the flex of his father's shoulders and neck that signaled fight stance. Until today, he'd only seen him use that stance with Uncle Jackson, or some joker Dad thought was dangerous.

Dr. Ambrose gestured again at the chair. Dad's face reddened. He grabbed the back of the ugly thing and hauled it around to the side of the bed. He plopped into it, making the same whoosh of air that Jack recognized from Berto's visits.

Uh-oh, Jack thought. *I hope Ambrose can hold her own.*

Dr. Ambrose perched on the edge of a wooden stool, next to the tower of bottles. Neither of them spoke.

Jack wanted to break their standoff. "Can I have some real food?" He pointed at the tower.

"They're delivering breakfast as we speak," Dr. Ambrose said. "You happen to be the last room in this hall."

"About the stuff on the white board . . . ." Dad began.

She turned smoothly toward his father and waited a whole three seconds before she spoke. Then she moved slightly to include Jack in their conversation.

"CPK is an enzyme that leaks out into your blood when the muscles are injured. Normal CPK level is between fifty and two hundred. Yours was well above that at five hundred, a week ago. Now it's eighteen thousand."

Jack's skin went cold. The number wasn't a mistake. "I don't think I've had any injury," he said, "just muscle cramps."

"Right," she said. "And that's what tipped Dr. Edwards off. The high level without injury signaled something unusual. Another clue was this rash on your hands. That's a symptom of a disease called polymyositis, with the rash it's often called dermatomyositis."

Disease. The word alone was scary. *Does this disease take you downhill without a stop?*

Dr. Ambrose turned fully toward him, but he could see Dad was getting impatient. Jack knew the focused look on the doctor's face meant she intended to make Dad wait while she explained things her way. He tried to pay attention, but her close regard of him, and her back to Dad, made him very itchy. So did all the questions he suddenly was afraid to ask.

"Your immune system fights off invasions of foreign substances," she said. "It fights off cold viruses, flu viruses and bacteria of all sorts. It helps keep you healthy."

He knew that. As little attention as he'd paid in Health Class, he still got that info.

"But sometimes," she said, "for reasons we don't yet understand, a person's immune system gets the message to eliminate things you really want to keep. Your immune system believes your muscles are the enemy. It's attacking them."

She included his father at last. "Prednisone and Immuren are the least invasive way to turn down Jack's immune system. They allow his muscles to rebuild faster than they are being damaged." Refocusing on Jack, she added, "Your mother agreed we should try these medicines first and keep our fingers crossed."

"Turn off his immune system?" Dad said. "That leaves him open to lots of ugly stuff."

"Turned down, not completely off. And yes, it leaves him vulnerable. While he's taking the medicine, we check him frequently for signs of other problems."

"How?" Jack asked. He'd had about as many tests as he ever wanted.

"Regular blood tests. These two meds are less extreme than the others we may need to use. And they counteract the worst side effects in each other."

"What side effects?" Jack hoped they didn't include some of the things he knew happened to people on heavy meds – losing his hair might make it easier to control, but he didn't think Kristi would like the look.

His father sat in silence, jittering his leg up and down. Dr. Ambrose talked about things like loss of calcium causing brittle bones. The other side effects seemed to be long-haul – like maybe shooting up his blood pressure, damaging his liver. He didn't intend to be on this stuff that long. And his father would make sure they got rid of the medicine as soon as they could.

His father asked, "When can Jack start physical therapy – you know – get up, walk around, get off all these wires?" He waved at the heart monitor.

"Jack had a serious heart episode."

"That didn't do permanent damage," his father said.

"We hope not. He's young. He can rebuild his chest muscles and his heart. Your son must have a lot of will power to climb most of Mount Tecumseh in spite of his muscle disease."

He wished Dr. Ambrose hadn't mentioned their climb. It would only remind his father of Jack's worst moments. He saw Dad's jaw tighten.

Dr. Ambrose didn't seem to notice. "We hope he'll heal quickly," she said. "But we had to open his chest to start his heart again. Healing that incision takes weeks of rehabilitation. Also, polymyositis can attack internal muscles like the heart, so we have to monitor it carefully."

Dad's face looked almost as gray as he had on Mount Tecumseh, but he straightened his back and spoke with force. "Jack needs to get out of this place. He needs to start physical therapy."

"Yes, he does. He'll have therapy all along the way, at levels that benefit him."

"What do you mean?" Dad asked.

"This afternoon, a therapist will come in here and move his legs and arms through a series of motions that will help keep some tone in those muscles as they rebuild. And then the therapist will come back and do the same set of exercises this evening so Jack can sleep better."

"The muscle thing," Dad said, "how long will it take to clear that up?"

"We won't know for a little while. Many patients regain their full strength, but it takes time."

She turned from Dad to Jack again. "Any questions, Jack?"

After a moment he said, "Not now." His questions were too many, and too scary.

She nodded. "Well, let's take this a day at a time and hope the least medicine is all you need."

His father stood up, feet apart, hands on his hips. "You've got to do all this therapy and get well, son. Then we can chuck the steroids and get on with life."

Here we go again, Jack thought.

Dr. Ambrose looked at Jack. "Pushing yourself too soon can make it worse," she said.

Dad glared at Dr. Ambrose, who just sat there and waited for whatever his father had to say about it. Jack no longer worried about Dr. Ambrose. At that moment, he worried about how old his father looked.

A knock on the room door made all three of them jump. "Come in," Dr. Ambrose said.

"Breh-fast." The small voice was accented and timid.

His father pulled the door wide open. "Hi," he said. "My son is hungry. He'll be mighty glad to see you."

A young lady in her twenties carried the breakfast tray into the room. She looked bewildered by the trio she found staring at her. Jack thought she probably didn't know how welcome she was – an interruption to a tense moment.

Dr. Ambrose cleared a space on the table next to Jack's bed. "Here's a good spot, Yolanda."

"I hope you have a pile of biscuits and butter under that lid," Jack said to her. She nodded.

The news about his disease had taken away his hunger, but he tried to pull himself up. Dr. Ambrose put her hand on his shoulder.

"There's a safer way," she said. "Here's a button you can use to raise the head part of your bed. This raises your knees. I recommend you do the *knee* button first. It keeps you from sliding toward your feet as your head rises."

She handed the thing to him. He did a tentative pressure and his bed began folding up in the middle. Yanking his thumb off, he looked at her, startled.

"Fun, isn't it?" Ambrose said.

Jack's father slumped near the whiteboard on the wall, looking uncomfortable. "You eat up, Jack," he said. "I'll be back this evening." He sidestepped toward the door.

Jack wanted Dad to stay and talk, but he could see his father had motion on the mind. Even if they'd been alone, his father wouldn't have stayed long.

"See you soon, Dad."

Dad waved and walked out. Jack watched his wide-shoulders disappear into the hall. He knew he'd better get cracking on those exercises. If he didn't get well soon, his father would disapprove . . . Maybe disapprove wasn't the right word.

And that was when Kristi's words came again, unwelcome. "*Of course he loves you. You make him look good.*"

Jack's chest throbbed. His throat tightened around a hard rock of thought and he wished the doctor would leave. He had to think – get his mind around everything – this muscle disease, Kristi's life, and especially his dad's jaw-grinding anger about this hospital stuff.

Dr. Ambrose whipped out a small notepad and pencil. "How about if you keep this? Write down your questions. Ask me when I come here each day."

She pulled the table with the food tray close to him. "Smells great. Eat hearty."

To encourage her to leave, he lifted the lid on his breakfast. To his relief, she ushered the nursing student toward the door. "Yolanda, I want to hear about your anatomy class."

"Si, Dohtor Ambrose."

As they disappeared out the door, Jack dropped the lid onto the tray and let his head fall back onto his pillow. He stared at the guy on the cross above his white board. Then he let go and sobbed.

CHAPTER 19

The therapist, Bill Martin, came after lunch. His pager beeped while he worked at moving Jack's legs and arms.

"Aren't you going to answer that?" Jack asked.

"Naw. This is your time. That's a pretty tight foot muscle you've got there."

Jack forced a laugh. "You're telling me?"

Nurse Edna Sawyer sailed in. "Bill, can you spare a minute while we unhook Jack from this heart monitor?"

Jack panicked. Without the monitor who would know what his heart was doing?

"Sure," Bill said. "We want you more mobile."

"But," Jack started.

"Don't worry," Nurse Sawyer said. "We've still got you on our radar."

He sank back onto his pillow, putting on a devil-may-care face while inside his heart flipped out. In moments, the big monitor was silent. In its place, Nurse Sawyer gave him a small monitor attached to his forefinger. "This is a pulse-oximeter," she said. "It measures your blood oxygen. You can take it off when you want to move around the room."

As she explained, Bill hauled in an aluminum walker like

the ones old people use. Jack glared at the thing, hating what it meant.

"No more bed pans," Bill said. "Now you can take these colorful bottles and your IV tower and go to the bathroom on your own."

That would be a relief, Jack admitted. He hated the bedpan and the help he needed to use it. Yolanda, the nursing student, and Nurse Edna Sawyer were efficient and business-like about helping him use the bedpan, but it was damned embarrassing.

Later that day, the first time he walked to the bathroom he had trouble navigating his tower of hanging meds around the other bed and through the door. Yolanda finally pushed the IV tower in there with him and shut the door between them. Then he had to sit.

All done, he tried to get up, but he had no leg power. That was when he discovered that Yolanda had waited outside the bathroom to help him off the toilet. Jack wished he'd just sat on the can the rest of his life.

. . .

After school that day, Berto came. "Kris has to be downtown for something," he said. "She said she'd be by later."

Jack frowned, but took his cue from Berto. They didn't talk about what Kristi was doing down there everyday. They talked about every-thing else – even homework.

Kristi came to the door an hour later. Darkness under her eyes gave away her worn state. "Hey," she said, leaning on the doorjamb. "You're more awake today big fella."

He pretended he didn't notice how tired she looked. "Come on in." He gestured Berto out of the chair. When she had fallen into it, Jack said, "Berto says the girls' cross-country track team is leading the city."

"Don't know about that," Kristi said. "I'm not running this year."

"Why not?"

"They don't need me," she said and pretended to be interested in the view out his window, toward the lone tree and the power plant chimney.

"So who does need you," Jack asked.

"Nobody," she said, barely glancing at him. "Just taking care of number one."

"Coming to the hospital all the time is not exactly relaxing," Jack said.

"This is a piece of cake. Then, I go home and sleep until time for school."

Jack decided to leap head first into the problem. "We're not going to watch you get more and more exhausted and pretend we don't notice."

"Give us a break, Kris," Berto said. "All the years Jack and I have been your friends, and you pretend we can't know about your mother's drinking."

"You guys think because she drinks, I'll drink."

"Berto never said anything like that," Jack said.

"Is it because I'm part Indian?"

She isn't listening, Jack thought, *just pulling out old anger and hurling it.*

She put her hands on her hips. "That Kristi Labbé, she can't help it," she mimicked one of the girls at school. "You know how those people are. It's in their genes."

"Kris," Jack tried to soothe her, but she interrupted.

"That what makes you assume I'll turn to booze?"

"Now you're making the assumptions," Jack said, but he ran out of breath.

Berto jumped in to help him. "Your mom's Norwegian, and she's the one doing the drinking. Your dad just lets you deal with all the problems."

"My mother is a very smart woman. She loves my dad and he's scared of her sickness."

Berto shook his head. "Hell, at your house, it's like you're the parent."

"They hurt – they both hurt," she said.

"And you hurt," Jack whispered. "And you hide it, like your dad."

Kristi turned on him. "At least my dad doesn't up and totally bug out, like yours."

Shock hit him. *Bug out? What does she mean?*

Berto stood up. "Kris, it's time for us to leave."

Kristi glared at him. "You guys started this conversation about my mom."

"That's true," Berto said. "And now it's time to end it. Let's go to my house and work on the paper."

Kristi turned toward Jack, taking his hand briefly. Then she glanced down, saw what she'd done and moved her hand away from his onto the sheet at the edge of his bed. "I'm sorry," she said. "I don't mean half the things I say when I'm angry. Let's not talk about my mom again."

"We gotta talk about what's happening, Kris," Jack said.

"Yeah," she said glancing at his pulse-oximeter. "When you're better, we can talk about a lot of stuff."

Berto seemed nervous, nearly jumping from foot to foot as she talked. "Not now, Kris," he said. "Here's your book bag."

Kris took the bag. "Goodbye, Jack."

"You get some sleep, Old Man," Berto said. He waved at Jack as he followed Kris out the door.

Berto sure was in a hurry to get her out of here, Jack thought. *Didn't like her talk about Dad at all. What does she mean about Dad bugging out?*

The whole retreat from Mount Tecumseh re-played out in Jack's mind – the cold, the wet, his helplessness. Jack remembered that moment when he grabbed his father's jacket. He remembered his father's fear. The heavy ache in Jack's chest jolted into sudden pain. Of course his father avoided him.

...

Uncle Jackson came to the hospital in the late afternoon. "I was nearby, pruning Mrs. Vernaya's beech tree," he explained. "Thought I might as well visit my favorite nephew."

When Jack was twelve, he'd helped Uncle Jackson create Mrs.Vernaya's garden, a place of secret benches and ponds, all in the shade of an ancient beech.

"Does her old bull frog still live near those jazzy red lilies?" he asked.

"Him and his whole family." Uncle Jackson pulled his traveler's game board and magnetic chessmen out of his parka pocket "How about a challenge?"

"You like being cornered?" Jack jibed.

"In your dreams."

. . .

Uncle Jackson left as dinner came in. After dinner, Dad brought Mom. Dad had begun coughing a lot. Nurse Sawyer insisted he wear a mask.

"Picked up this cold on Ramona Falls, I guess," Dad said. "It was raining that day."

"Not on Mount Tecumseh?" Jack asked.

Dad looked surprised. "Heck no. You're the one that got sick up there."

Jack glanced at Mom. She didn't seem to see the problem. So Jack decided not to ask why his father had stayed away from his room so much. It didn't make sense, but Jack didn't want to rock the boat.

Dad paced, fiddled with flower vases and listened as Mom told Jack about Berto coming by for help with the group history paper.

Jack wanted to know how Kristi was, too, but he didn't want Mom to worry about Kristi's time on the streets. Mom already looked as worn out as Kristi.

Dad pulled down his mask and said, "Get this therapist, this Bill guy, to let you do pull-ups."

"You want to stay and see what he does tonight?" Jack asked.

"That'd be great," Dad said. "But I have a deadline. Maybe Thursday." He popped the mask back in place.

. . .

On the next night, Thursday, Dad left early for a meeting. Mom sat in silence for a few seconds. Then in a thin voice, she told Jack about what was happening on one of her building sites – trying to make laughter fill the empty space.

"Mom," Jack said, shattering a lull between her stories. "Why does Dad take off so soon?"

She tried on a fake smile, then frowned. "Oh honey, he's just got a lot of writing to catch up on."

Jack stared at her. "Don't give me that baloney, Mom."

Her eyes rimmed in red before she glanced away. "He doesn't know what to do with himself. The hospital, you being sick . . ."

"I won't be worthless forever."

She flicked a startled glance at him. "You are not worthless. Give him time. He'll get more comfortable here."

Jack could hardly breathe, but he had to ask. "What if I'm this way forever?"

She stood up, as if propelled by fear. "No," she said. "You've always been a conqueror, always."

Inside, he cringed. "So I conquer," he said. "Where will Dad be until then?"

Pacing away, she appeared not to hear him. "I should have told you not to go on that climb."

He sank into the pillow. "I wouldn't have listened," he whispered.

She turned back to him. "That's the damned truth."

After Mom left, Jack stared at the pallid green wall near his bed. He hated this building, this Clorox and lemon-freshener room. At home, he and Dad could talk and joke around.

Under the covers, his feet twitched like the dead frog in biology lab when he touched its muscles with electrodes.

. . .

The next day, Berto came alone. Jack wanted to ask about Kristi. Instead, they talked about the cross-country meets and the football team. As Berto shouldered his pack to leave, Jack said, "Bert, I need to know some stuff about this polymyositis."

Berto snorted. "The stuff nobody will tell you? I searched the internet."

"Yeah," Jack said, "I figured you'd do that."

"You know what?" Berto said. "Your doctor, Anita Ambrose, has written a lot about polymyositis. The others who write about it quote her research. She's 'the man', Jacko. Do what she says."

Suddenly, Jack sensed safety and a future. "Could you bring me copies of her articles?"

Berto swaggered back toward Jack. "It'll cost you big bucks," he said.

"How about I pay now, and bust your butt when I'm well again."

Berto shrugged, "As if . . ."

"Oh, by the way . . ." Jack began, uncertain how to ask the next question.

"I know," Berto said, "where's Kristi?"

Jack felt heat rise in his face. "I suppose she's studying for something, eh?"

"No. She's working in a place somewhere between the Pioneer Square and the Interstate Freeway – won't tell me what she does, or where. I pick her up at the Fourteenth Avenue freeway overpass. She claims secrecy is for the safety of the other girls."

"Other girls? Doing what?"

Berto shook his head. "Dunno. But tonight they had a crisis. She said I should give you hell by myself."

"Give *me* hell? What's *she* up to?"

"Wish I knew. She's at school most days. But she refuses to go home. Hops a bus and is gone."

"Follow her."

"Tried that. She ditched me both times."

Jack dropped his head back to the pillow. "I've got to get out of here. That Swede guy talked her into something." Berto nodded and then he left for home.

. . .

Jack wanted Kristi to come through that door and find a guy who could take care of himself – a guy who could take care of anything. He wanted Dad to see that he could get better. He had to get more exercise.

But he didn't want to walk around the hospital in a sloppy thing like an apron that opened at the back. In Dad's wanderings, he'd left the closet door open. So Jack snagged pajama pants from the shelf. It took him a little while to get the pajamas over his legs. He had to rest for a few moments afterward. Then he tied the waist string tight around his shrunken waist. The sight of his rib bones and his incision made him stop and close his eyes. He wished he hadn't looked at himself.

When he had his breath back, he pulled off his pillow case and wrapped it around his arm to protect the IV needle and the tube. He slowly slipped that arm through the sleeve of his robe, letting the IV tube rise from the neck of his robe to the tower. That accomplished, he hitched himself out of bed, leaned onto the walker and forced his legs to move. It took a lot of mental effort to get the left leg to pull itself forward. Jack remembered when he was seven, the first time he used ice skates, hanging onto the sidewall of the rink. His legs had splayed out in every direction except forward. Today, he had even less control, but he struggled forward, through the door and out into the hall.

Nurse Sawyer glanced up as he passed the nurses' station. "You go, Guy," she said, then went back to her computer screen. After that, each time he passed her, she didn't even glance up – seemed to have forgotten he was working out. The third time around, sweat rolled off his face. His arm muscles shivered. His left leg had to be dragged forward by the momentum of the walker.

He pushed through the door to his room. Nurse Edna Sawyer stood beside him, grinning. "You've done great! Three lengths of the hall on your first try."

He smiled, totally exhausted. "You a cheer leader back in high school?"

She snorted, "Nope. Line-backer, Powder-Puff Team at Pleistocene High."

Laughing, Jack took a nosedive. Nurse Sawyer caught him under the arms and helped him land butt first on his own bed. He'd long ago realized she was one strong lady.

Of course he weighed next to nothing these days. Embarrassed, he hitched his pajama pants off his hips and back up to his waist.

"I'll get you a better string for those things," she said while she opened his bed covers. "Got to keep you decent while you gain weight."

Ten minutes later, Jack hunkered on the side of his bed, wishing he could get up and walk again. He wanted out of here soon. His door opened. There stood Mom carrying a bright yellow package. His father stood behind her, holding a brown sack.

"I hope one of those packages is new pajamas," Jack said. "These fall down when I exercise."

"You're up," Dad crowed in his sideline cheering voice.

"Barely," Jack's voice came out with the assertiveness of floor fuzz.

"How about a walk down the hall and back?" Dad asked.

Hot anger flooded Jack's face. Couldn't Dad see how wiped he was?

"I just finished a long walk," he said. "Seems like three days worth of trekking just to hit the bathroom. And it's hard to pee around the walker – pardon me, Mom."

Mom bit her lip. Jack couldn't tell if she was trying not to laugh or cry.

At its mention, Dad's gaze flicked to the walker. He said nothing for a moment, then glanced at Jack. "How's it going, son?" he asked.

Startled, Jack felt his eyes fill. He glanced away, saying, "I don't know, Dad. I have a long way to go."

Dad plopped onto the wooden stool. "I wish we hadn't gone on that damned climb."

"Me, too," Jack said.

"But," his father said, straightening to his full height. "Here we are. We've got to work at getting out of this fix."

Jack imagined Dad giving himself that pep talk at the bottom of some ice crevasse.

"I am working to get out," he said. "Today, I walked the hall – three laps."

"Good. That's good." His father rubbed his hands together, the way he did right before he grabbed a rope and started up a cliff. "Now let's try for four."

"Mallory!" Mom's voice cut in.

"Okay. Okay." Dad waved her off. "Later, maybe."

Relieved, Jack started to ask his father to cover his cold feet, but Dad pulled a red Nerf ball from the sack he'd been hugging to his chest. "The salesman at Athlete's World said you could toss this to yourself in bed – keep your hand-eye coordination in shape."

"Mallory, I'd like you to give it a rest," Mom said.

"Ali, the kid's muscles are going to atrophy."

She walked past his father as if he'd said nothing. "I brought Kristi's pictures of the pep assembly. She can't come until tomorrow, and she wanted you to have them right away."

Jack squinted at Mom. Why would Kristi send him pep assembly photos? Mom handed them over with the expectant look of an artist waiting for audience reaction. So Jack flipped through. First was a snapshot of the football team lined up across the stage, each guy with big arms folded across his chest – awkward as a crowd of padded camels.

Next photo: the rally squad holding dinky Sally Johnson in the air.

Finally, the football team, the rally squad, the climbing club and the cross-country team crowded onto the front apron. They carried a big roll of butcher paper. It had been unrolled. Vastly different heights of guys and girls held the paper at funny angles. He leaned in close to decipher the message printed in red and blue letters.

"Jack! Lazy Bozo! Get out of bed!"

Tears pooled, obscuring the picture. He laughed, wiping his nose and glancing up at Mom. She grinned. "Hey," she said. "They're homely, but they love you."

He looked back at the banner. "Tell Kristi, I recognize the lettering."

"I will. Now, do you need help with those legs?"

"Alison." Dad said, sharply.

She paid no attention. She never ignored Dad like that, but Jack saw her face muscles tighten. She put an arm under Jack's knees and rolled him back into bed.

"Mallory, how about helping me pull up these covers?"

From his rolled up position, Jack saw a flash of anger in his father's eyes before he got up and strode to the bed. His mom and dad must have been arguing about him before they came.

Dad pulled the covers over Jack's legs and halfway up his back. "Don't let your mother baby you, kid. You need to get right back on the horse."

Jack's frustration burst out. "For Pete's sake, Dad! I walk myself to the bathroom every hour, and down the hall and back a lot today. I'm not giving up."

"That's the way. Here's the Nerf ball." His father tucked the crimson toy into the covers. His hand brushed Jack's cheek as Dad pushed the ball into the crook of his arm.

Jack remembered being three or four years old. Dad used to tuck stuffed animals into his bed in just that awkward way – never quite gentle, always reluctant to admit he was really doing it.

"Thanks, Dad."

"We'll have you out of here in no time, Big Guy."

Dad, he thought, *Get real!*

CHAPTER 20

Next evening, after his hall-walking workout, Jack summoned the energy for one more trip to pee. He stared at the empty second bed, a major obstacle between him and the bathroom. With luck, Berto would show up before Kristi, and help him get to the can. He sure hoped someone would come tonight. It was getting hard to sit here and not think about Dad. Sometimes in the afternoons, he believed he heard Dad's voice in the hall, but it would turn out to be a doctor or a male nurse. Dad came, but never for long, and mostly with Mom who could do the talking for both of them. Jack wanted to find a time alone – a time to talk with Dad about the climb. But he also didn't want to talk about it. Some things were better left alone.

Mrs. Edna Sawyer, bustled in carrying sheets and a blanket, which she plopped on a visitor's chair. "Need help getting to the bathroom?" she asked.

Embarrassed by all the times she'd already helped, he mumbled, "No thanks," and flopped back onto his bed. "You make beds, too?" he asked.

"Yolanda is in class and the housekeeping crew is cleaning another room. So you get me."

Jack reached into his bed-stand drawer and pulled out the drawing pad and pencil Mom had left for him. Nurse Edna Sawyer whipped out one of the sheets. Unfurling it over the other bed with a sharp snap, she sent the odor of freshly laundered cotton though the room. Jack remembered the smell of cotton shirts, hot from his mother's iron. A twinge of sadness plucked at him. His favorite shirts would no longer fit. He'd lost a lot of what Dr. Crescent and Dr. Ambrose both called muscle mass.

"A new patient is checking in," Mrs. Sawyer said. She tucked an odd-looking metal rail into the foot of the other bed. The upper sheet seemed extra-long. Mrs. Sawyer fitted it over the height of the metal crosspieces.

"What's that?" he asked, sketching the flange at the top of the rail.

"It keeps the weight of blankets off a person's feet. People with bad circulation, that weight is no good for them."

So that was what he needed all those nights at home when the heavy covers started his foot cramps.

Kristi peeked around the doorjamb. "You decent?"

At the sound of her voice, his heart thudded, then he looked at her and his breath caught.

She looked weird, and wonderful – her hair spiked around her tanned face as if she warded off diving bugs with mousse-sharpened spears. He relaxed again. Most of her beautiful hair had been tied in a knot at the back of her head. Only the front was short and spiked. Then he remembered Pioneer Square and wondered if she changed her hair to fit into Swede's street crowd. That thought made his skin go cold.

Mrs. Sawyer glanced around at her. "Come in, Girl. Come in. This boy doesn't bite."

"You want to bet?" Kristi asked. She lifted her backpack and danced a step to avoid Mrs. Sawyer's efficient bed making. "He can be laid out flat and still be giving me a hard time."

He remembered yesterday's hard time, and determined not to talk about her mom or her street life. He tried to sit up to greet her, but his head felt too heavy. Maybe he'd over-done his workout. "Hold on there, Superman," Kristi chided. "There's a lever for sitting up."

She reached down at the bottom of his bed, then with a puzzled frown on her face, she bent over, searching for something.

Nurse Sawyer glanced at her. "You been in some ancient hospitals if you are looking for levers and cranks to adjust the bed."

"My mom's bed . . ." Kristi started, but her face turned dark.

Mrs. Sawyer raised her eyebrows at Jack, but Jack stared at her as hard as he could. He didn't want Kristi having to explain that her mother was at a lock-in detox hospital for a month when Kristi was eight. Mrs. Sawyer heeded his warning. As she went back to blanketing the bed, she said, "There's an electric button attached to Jack's pillow."

Kristi slipped along-side the bed and reached out. Jack's knees lurched upward.

"Hey!" He grabbed at his blanket, afraid it might be yanked off. "Let me drive my own bed."

"I don't know," she said, unclipping the button from the pillowcase. "This is kind of fun . . . Three on the Richter Scale," she announced. "Just enough to bring down the crockery and make you buy more insurance."

"You're fired."

"I will stop, if you promise to dictate your part of the team's research paper for American History. Due in three days."

"I'll do it. Now give me that button."

She clipped the clothespin gripper onto the front of his ridiculous pajama shirt. "Your badge of power."

She came so close he let his glance stray to her throat, her lips. He inhaled the odor of rocks and sunshine. Her attention moved to his eyes. A sudden, solemn darkness played across her features, and he stopped breathing. She studied his face. He hadn't shaved, or combed his wild hair. He knew he looked ugly. Still, he held her gaze, wanting the moment to last. In the silence, he heard her swallow.

"Well," she said, straightening away from him. "We'd best get to work on that paper. I brought Berto's lap top, so you can talk and I can write."

He tried to gather his thoughts. Nurse Sawyer had slipped out, maybe to leave them alone at the critical moment. Too bad it hadn't gotten any more critical.

"What's with the spiky hair," he asked.

"The paper?" She hauled out Berto's laptop and opened it to write.

"The hair?" he insisted.

"I get enough grief from Dad. You can leave it alone."

He laughed. It was a relief to know she'd seen her father. "Maybe I'll do mine the same way," he threatened.

"Don't," she blurted, as if she couldn't stop herself. Maybe she didn't want him to change. But she recovered quickly. "Hair like yours standing on end would create havoc on the cardiac floor. People dropping left and right."

"Well, here's a heart-stopper piece of news," he said. "I wrote my part of the paper before I went on the climb."

She stared at him. "So where is it?"

"On a computer disc on my desk. Berto could bring it."

"He can't come. Rehearsals for The Sound of Music."

Jack had forgotten all about Berto's big role. Great friend he was.

"I think Mom could bring the disc to the hospital when she comes."

"I'll call her." She started searching on his nightstand.

"Call on what?" he asked.

"How come you don't have a phone?"

"They don't let you do cell phones in here."

"Land lines," she said. "I'd be surprised if they don't offer Internet hook-ups. Everybody down the hall has a phone."

Jack shrugged. "Not me."

"I'll find a pay phone."

"Tell mom it's in my disc drive. Labeled 'Homework, September'."

"Back in a few, then," she said. She hopped up and ran out to the hall. Outside his room, he heard her say, "Oops. Didn't see you coming."

As soon as she was gone, Nurse Sawyer turned into his room. "In here," she said, waving someone in from the hall.

Two fellows rolled a gurney through the door. After they parked it, they lifted a slender African-American man from the gurney to the newly-made bed. Fluffing pillows, tucking blankets, arranging the tray and plugging in various implements, the team that Sawyer commanded made the new patient at home. Jack pretended to be drawing so as not to stare. Kristi's new spiked hair appeared on his page.

Among the people working at the next bed, Jack recognized the voice of Chuck, the tech guy from his first night – the guy who used duct tape on bad plugs.

Between stifled moans, the new patient seemed to be asleep during these activities. As quickly as they came, the team left. Only Nurse Sawyer remained to check that the monitor worked smoothly and the patient was warm. Then she took out a green pen and wrote on the white board across from the foot of the man's bed.

She scratched the words, "Bed one, Myocardial infarction, diet diabetes."

Finally, she looked at Jack. "Your friend leave already?"

"She's calling my mom." Jack added Kristi's earrings to his drawing.

"Gloriosky! Did we never get you a phone?"

He shook his head.

"That darned Chuck," she muttered. Then she said, "With all the friends you have, you've got to have a phone. I'll see you get one." She tucked the pen in her pocket. "Probably be here by tomorrow." She glanced once more at the new patient's white board.

"What's myocardial infarction?" Jack asked.

"Heart attack," answered a low voice. Jack turned toward the man who lay on his back, one eye open and an arm over his dark forehead. "Name's Peterson," the man said. "Who are you?"

"Jack Huntington." He said. Jack liked the way Peterson's white mustache twitched as he spoke. The contrast between the mustache and Peterson's dark skin was startling and very dignified.

"Glad to meet you, young man." Mr. Peterson did not sound sick. His voice resonated in the small room, but he didn't reach out a hand.

"Your wife is on her way up from the in-take desk," Nurse Sawyer said.

"My wife and that minister who followed her," Peterson added. "You capable of shoveling the preacher man out of here pretty soon?"

"I can shovel out anything," Nurse Sawyer said.

"Fifteen minutes tops. Preacher man goes. Wife stays."

"Done," Nurse Sawyer said. And then she left.

Peterson let his eyes close. "Pardon my inattention, young Jack. Got to preserve my strength."

Jack was tired, too, and in a few minutes, it sounded like they were going to have a room full of people. Jack closed his eyes. Soon, he heard a bustling in the hallway and the ominous crinkling of cellophane. That could only mean visitors with flowers.

"The Lord be praised," a voice whispered. "We have found him, Sister. Just a few more steps."

Jack opened his eyes and discovered Kristi already sitting in his usually noisy green Naugahyde chair. Filling the doorway beyond Kristi, a sturdy man in a meticulously pressed blue suit entered the room. He carried the cellophane around flowers. In front of him, halting in the room, a tall, dark woman stood gazing at Mr. Peterson.

"Reverend Wilson," she said, "it's time for my husband to sleep. And you have a long trip to get ready for. Let me take the flowers. You say a prayer and then steal away home."

The reverend glanced at her, at his bouquet, at his patient. His shoulders slumped.

"I will do that, Sister Ada." He glanced at Kristi, then Jack. His eyes jerked back to Kristi's spiked hair. A frown creased his forehead.

"Let us all bow our heads," he said.

To Jack's amazement, Kristi bowed her head. The man's prayer was not brief. Several times he mentioned that August Peterson was a great sinner and yet should be forgiven and be honored with the Lord's healing power. At last, Reverend Wilson moved into the 'Our Father' and ended by glancing at the woman.

Mrs. Ada Peterson did not look up, but seemed to be doing her own praying for her husband. Her dark hair lay in orderly waves from her brow to a knot at the back of her elegant head. Her long-fingered hands calmly clasped the flowers. Jack noticed that Kristi watched her intently. So did the reverend.

From his low vantage point, Jack could see that, beneath the arm Peterson kept across his forehead, he too watched his wife. When she glanced up, Peterson closed his eyes.

After several more attempts by Reverend Wilson to offer Mrs. Peterson his support and the Lord's care, Nurse Sawyer poked her head into the doorway. "Time for all but family to leave," she said cheerily.

Kristi hopped up, way too happy to go away.

"Kris." Jack searched desperately for a topic, "We've got to plan our paper."

She glanced at him, "You heard the nurse. We've got to be going now."

He frowned. She never minded anybody this fast. She must be tired of visiting him.

"Reverend Wilson," Kristi said, "I understand you have a trip to get ready for."

Wilson studied her spikes of hair, and then her hiking boots. "Have we met, young lady?"

"My name is Kristi Labbé. Are you attending the National Convention of Baptist Ministers?"

"Why yes, I am. How did you know?"

"My grandfather, the Reverend Chief Jesus Wolf Labbé used to attend that convention every fall. He thought it was the most inspiring event in his liturgical year."

They headed toward the door, Mr. Wilson bowing Kristi out first.

"So your grandfather was a minister?"

Jack stared after them. He'd never heard of this grandfather. And he couldn't believe the girl just up and walked out on him for no reason. He fidgeted in his bed, pulling at his sheets and fretting his chest bandages, imagining Kristi hurrying off to Pioneer Square as the sun set.

While he twisted his sheets, Mrs. Peterson arranged the minister's flowers in a pink plastic water pitcher she found in the bathroom. Then she took her place in the chair next to the sleeping Mr. Peterson. She watched him breathe.

Jack swallowed hurt from Kristi's breezy departure. He closed his eyes.

Minutes later, Kristi returned, huffing out of breath. Jack couldn't stop the grin that spread over his face. She sat down next to him and whispered, "I forgot they lock the stair doors. Ran all the way up six floors and all the way back down. He'd got a cab and gone home. So then I could use the elevator."

Then Jack realized that Kristi was the shovel Nurse Edna used to pitch out the praying reverend.

"I never heard of your minister grandfather," he whispered.

She folded her arms and said, "You don't know everything about me."

That's the truth, he thought.

He reached out and touched her face. She didn't pull back as he expected. Instead, she turned her mouth into his palm and kissed him. His heart leapt into his throat. More than anything, he wanted to be well – well enough to pull her closer and seal this moment by touching her lips with his. He could have tried, but with others in the room, he knew she wouldn't like it.

Instead, he said, "I want to see you tomorrow."

"Silly. I come every day." She said this as if her return were a known, but her eyes looked vulnerable, wet and careful.

He sniffed. So did Kristi as she pulled back and asked, "Anything on that disc you don't want me to see?"

"Yeah," he whispered. "Love letters to a girl who won't listen to me."

"Must be a bitch."

"Always got her fists up, ready to fight," he said. "But her true self is a really swell person."

She leaned toward him again, and kissed his forehead. Jack closed his eyes and concentrated on the feel of her, the smell of her and the touch of her fingers where they held his head still. His whole being grew warm and seemed to float above the bed.

"I'll read those letters," she said, "and give you some pointers on how to win her over."

He opened his eyes and saw that she was still close. The softness of her breasts barely showed at the vee opening of her tee shirt. He couldn't breathe. And then she stood up.

"But, right now," she said, "I need to know the name of the American History file on your 'Homework' disc."

He dragged in air. "It's called 'The Iron-Framed Boat.'"

She smiled. "I knew you'd figure a way to get that boat model into this."

"Dad's idea."

She frowned. "See you tomorrow," she said. And then she just walked out. Never looked back.

He wished he hadn't mentioned his father.

CHAPTER 21

The next morning, Nurse Sawyer removed his IV. "The therapist will be in soon, and you can be off these for your exercise times."

Later, Bill Martin introduced himself to Mr. Peterson, then lifted Jack into a wheelchair. "I'll have your room mate back to you in an hour," Bill said.

Peterson nodded. "Take care."

Jack waved goodbye, then asked, "Where we going?"

"To the halls of Montezuma," Bill said, and then wiggled his Groucho Marx eyebrows.

Jack wiggled his eyebrows back. "Better have me back here for lunch, or you're in deep dog doo-doo."

Bill laughed and wheeled Jack into the back elevator, down to level B Two, and the length of a long hall where they turned right and squealed into a tiled room.

"You can get these on yourself," Bill said, handing him a pair of navy blue swim trunks.

"This a shower room?" Jack asked. He stared at the trunks he'd used for last year's swim team. Mom must have brought them.

"Pool room. Therapy pool. Can you get the pajamas off?"

"Easy," Jack said. "I just stand up and they fall off."

"That's no good. We've gotta get you some string to tie them up with."

Jack remembered Nurse Sawyer saying the same thing. "Promises, promises," he said and pushed himself up from the wheel chair.

"Those arms are still working pretty well," Bill said.

Jack sat back down, fast. The pajama pants had obliged him by falling before his arms gave out. He pulled them off his feet and reached for the trunks.

After handing the trunks to Jack, Bill went to a nearby cupboard and began folding freshly laundered towels. Jack sighed. He leaned over, trying to lift his left foot into the correct hole in the trunks. He was pleasantly surprised that he could control that leg. With one foot inserted, he had to stretch out the waistband. He picked up his right leg with his free hand, aiming it at the other hole. It stuck in the stupid waistband strings. From seeming unawareness, Bill surprised him by reaching down and untangling Jack's big toe from the strings. The foot slipped into place.

Still seated, Jack pulled the trunks up his legs and began to hitch them under his rear end. One side up an inch, roll over, hitch the other side an inch. Halfway through this tiring process, he glanced at Bill and found him reading a *Sports Illustrated* magazine.

"They pay you to stand around and let me fall out of this damned chair?"

"Nope." Bill flipped a page in the magazine. "They pay me to put you someplace you don't like, and make sure you have to work hard to get out of it."

Jack glared at him. He took a last hitch on his trunks. Bill lifted a foot and touched the lock on the wheels, checking that it held. Then he went back to the magazine. Jack noted the burly image of a boxer on the cover. It wasn't the swimsuit issue. There were some mercies in this life.

"Good work," Bill said, dropping the magazine on the shelf. "Let's get that robe off." He hoisted the terry robe and the pajama top over Jack's head. Jack stared down at his chest. The redness was way down from the last time he'd looked. Jack pulled one arm over his chest to hide most of the scar.

Bill wheeled him up a short ramp. "Punch the door button," he said.

Jack stared at the blue metal button. He'd punched buttons like this at Eisenhower High, and then he'd sashayed out and down the wheelchair ramps without ever thinking about what they really were for. For the first time in his life, he had to stretch up to hit one of these things. His throat tightened with sudden anger. He jabbed at it with his clenched fist.

The door swung out. His fist hurt. Bill pushed him down the ramp, turned right and stopped near a metal pole surrounded by rubber mats. A young lady in a chartreuse one-piece swimsuit appeared from behind the pole. Her sandy-colored hair was pulled into a wavy ponytail. Jack glanced away from her pretty face and down at his thin legs.

"You Jack Huntington?"

Jack nodded.

"I'm Carly Daniels, your pool therapist."

He stared where she pointed. What she called a pool was barely wide enough for two people. Blue and green tiles surrounded it, but he couldn't see the bottom through the churning water.

Jack remembered the baby-sitting part of health class. The teacher had said, "It only takes inches of water to drown a grown up. You can't leave a baby even for a second." He believed it now.

"Resistance exercises help bring back your muscle tone." Carly said.

"I just scoot out of the chair and roll in?"

She chuckled. "Maybe when you graduate to the walrus class. This time, we use the hoist."

She put her hand on the mats wrapping the metal pole. Jack looked up. There was a huge diaper made of sailcloth suspended from the pole. She lowered it with a crank. When it arrived at his chair level, Bill offered Jack a hand.

"Can you stand?"

Jack pushed down on the wheel chair arm and lifted himself. Bill held Jack by the waist, aimed his back at the diaper and lowered him into its seat. Carly punched a button and the water in the pool began moving faster, bubbling like a hot tub with the jets turned on.

"Ready?" Carly asked.

"What am I supposed to do when I get down there?"

"You can rest in the water for a little while, and then I'll give you some exercises to do."

"Move or drown, that it?"

Carly shook her head. "No drowning allowed. More like 'move and get well'."

"Huh!" he said.

"I know you're scared, Jack. Everyone is at first. But I'll be right here to make sure you're safe."

He didn't tell her he was no way scared. *Why bother?*

Bill folded up the wheelchair and walked up the ramp. "I'll be back in half an hour." Bill hit the blue button and swung through the door.

Abandoned to the swift current and a girl who is as small as Mom, and probably not as strong.

"Here we go," Carly said. The hoist lifted him away from the pole, rotated him slowly over the water and began to lower him in. He swallowed hard and then blew air out of his lungs, emptying them so he could take in a good deep breath just before he submerged. He calculated he might be under quite a while before he could pull himself up the rope and do a Tarzan swing over to the side.

Carly leaned toward him. "Don't look so worried. I haven't drowned a passenger yet."

Jack kept breathing, getting ready. His feet touched the water. The current dragged on them. The lower he went the more the warm water seemed to pull. Churning water buffeted his body. He saw Carly reach up to let the hoist relax into the water.

Don't, please. He knew he would thrash until his arms gave out. And then he would drown.

"It's okay, Jack," she said. "I'm here to catch you."

The sling sank beneath him, leaving him at the mercy of the current, his arms swinging back and forth to grab water and hold him in place.

"Relax." Her voice was firm. "This is just The Hellespont."

He kept swimming, but stared up at her. "The what?"

"The strait of water between the Sea of Marmara and the Aegean Sea."

Jack tried kicking, but only his right foot moved. He went back to using his arms to stay afloat. They were wearing out fast. "The Aegean Sea?" he gasped. "That supposed to make me feel good?"

"The great hero, Leander, drowned trying to swim The Hellespont."

"Get me out of here, Carly."

She reached her arm down, her hand ready to grip his, but he couldn't stop swimming to grab at her. She kept talking. "If Leander had stopped swimming and put his feet down, he would have discovered that on the out-going tide the Hellespont is only two feet deep."

Jack swallowed hard. He kept wagging his arms, but little by little, he let his feet drop. With an abrupt thud, his right heel hit bottom. He glared at her.

"Good work," she cheered and raised her fist in salute to him. "Now, let your head lie back into the cushion of water, and rest a while."

He let his butt rest on the tile floor of the pool. "Why was Leander swimming?"

"Had to. Hero, his girlfriend, was forbidden to him, so he couldn't come in the front door. Had to swim across to the garden entrance. But one night, she neglected to keep the light burning to show him the way."

"Women!" Jack let his head down into the water. His ears filled with the warmth and the rush of the tide. He closed his eyes and breathed in the smell of clean water and his own sweat. He hadn't sweated this much since the climb up from the goat meadow. He recalled the nanny goat kicking the nipping billy out of her way as she inched forward to make sure the boy in the meadow was all right.

Jack found he was smiling for the first time in a week.

CHAPTER 22

For the first morning after Mr. Peterson moved in, the man slept, except at breakfast. Even then, he didn't eat much before he went back to sleep. During Peterson's naps, Jack pulled out the drawing pad Mom had brought him. He sketched everything he could see from the bed: Peterson's face; his mustache; his thick eyebrows; the flowers people had sent them; the folds of their bed covers; the crucifix on the wall of their room; the television hanging in the corner, the fall colors on the single tree.

By noon, he was reduced to drawing the power-plant chimney that stood about fifty feet from their window. He became aware of a lack of snoring from his roommate and turned to find Peterson watching his pencil.

"You do good work, Jack," Peterson said. "I saw my mustache. Very swash-buckling."

"Do you mind me drawing you?"

"Not as long as you emphasize how dashing I am."

"No promises," Jack said. "Got to draw what I see."

Peterson smiled and closed his eyes again. At twelve-thirty, while they waded through soup and crackers, Chuck, the electrical technician, brought in a phone for each of them. He crawled around under their beds, plugging things in, checking other hook-ups. Jack remembered how mouthy Chuck had been to that first nurse in Cardiac Care. He wondered if the guy was as much a jerk as he'd seemed.

Chuck grunted once in a while, but said nothing. After a while, he picked up Mr. Peterson's phone, dialing some number. "Just checking," he said and then dropped the phone in its cradle. After fiddling some more with the cords, he picked up Jack's phone, dialed and said, "Hi Babe. You on the front desk today?"

Jack let his gaze drift out the window. The guy made a date for lunch, dropped the phone, gathered his tools and never said a word to either of them.

As he went out the door, Mr. Peterson chuckled, and then spoke in a girlish voice. "I'd love to have lunch with Mr. Electrical Tool Belt."

Startled, Jack watched Mr. Peterson do an eyelash-batting imitation of a girl going wacko over some guy.

Jack laughed, then patted his heart. "He's so dreamy," he crooned.

"I just love a man with good social skills," Mr. Peterson said.

They both cracked up. Jack decided he was going to like rooming with this guy. After the last bite of soup, Jack called his Mom and gave her the phone number in case she or Dad needed it. Within minutes, Kristi called. He figured she must have been at his house.

"Hi," she said. "I'm putting our American History Paper together, so I can't come over tonight."

"Oh." He didn't want her to hear his disappointment. "You working on my computer?"

"I'm not reading your secret files, if that's what worries you."

He smiled. "Those are password protected. I'm not worried."

"Yeah, sure."

Jack thought he heard her mental wheels grinding, figuring what he might use for a password. He was mighty glad he didn't keep a diary.

"Could I ask you a question?" she said.

"Sure."

"Why is this iron boat so important to you? I mean, the thing didn't work."

He stared at the wall. That very question had been bothering him as he wrote the paper. He couldn't figure it either. "It's just neat," he said. Even he knew that was lame.

"And . . .?" she asked.

"It's a great design. It would have worked just fine, except they didn't have the stuff they needed. They thought there would be pine forests straight across the continent, but when they needed the boat – no pine. No pine tar equals leaky seams. Boat sinks."

"It sure didn't help open the west," she said.

That was a problem. It hadn't opened the west. Thirty-three people counted on that boat, even wasted eight days trying to make it work. Its failure made them late into the vast, cold mountains where they all nearly died of starvation. What made him like the danged thing so much?

"Jacko, you there?"

"I don't know why it's so important, Kris. It just is."

There was a silence at her end, and then she said, "Don't worry. I'll figure something. You sure this Captain Lewis guy designed it?"

"Sure. Why?"

"Your mom loaned me one of your books about him. It looks like he was kind of a leaky boat himself."

"Not while he was on that expedition."

"A history of big depression? Killed himself three years after the trip. That's not exactly a guy I'd take orders from."

"William Clark liked him," Jack protested. "The other men liked him. He brought back more information about plants and animals than anybody else on the trip. He doctored everybody who got sick or injured. Saved Sacagawea's life from some kind of infection. It didn't matter if he had problems. During that expedition he was a leader."

"Okay, okay. Don't blow a gasket."

He hadn't meant to get so hot about it. Neither of them spoke for a long time. Finally, he said, "Kristi?"

"Yeah?"

"What do you do at Pioneer Square?"

After a moment of silence, she said. "If I stay away from home, my folks can't stay the way they are. I have to let my folks get desperate because I'm not there to fix things."

"This Swede a guy we should trust?"

"Yeah, I do."

Anything Jack said now would sound like an accusation. Finally he asked, "How about just talking to your dad?"

"Practice what you preach, Jack."

"Kristi . . ."

She interrupted him. "And when you succeed, let me know."

. . .

That evening, dinner rolled in, smelling of rosemary and pepper. The orderly left the meals on their bedside trays. It looked great, but Jack doubted whether he could swallow anything tougher than the mashed potatoes.

Peterson pulled his tray toward himself, gazed at it and groaned, "So much food, so few teeth!"

They both snorted at that one.

"Looks like we're stuck with the salad," Jack said, pointing to the red mound wobbling in a small bowl.

Peterson said, "The Jell-O sharks. We just gap and swallow."

As they spooned up elusive, translucent nothing, Edna Sawyer zoomed into the room.

"Never yet saw an improving patient skip the Jell-O," Mrs. Sawyer said, her voice as cheerful and solid as always. "You boys are on the mend."

Jack leaned back on his pillow, smiling a satisfied smile, but Mr. Peterson waved his fork at Mrs. Sawyer.

"I am nobody's boy." He held his fork in the air, waiting for her to respond.

A jolt of embarrassment hit Jack. He'd accepted the 'boy' title just as easily as she had dished it out. And he'd accepted it for both of them without thinking.

Mrs. Sawyer glanced up from reading Mr. Peterson's chart, calm, but alert. "I do apologize, Mr. Peterson," she said. "And I ought to know better. I hate it when a certain doctor refers to grown nurses as 'girls'."

Peterson said, "You got that right, Sister."

She smiled, said "I'll be back later," and left.

The two of them finished the jello and Jack ate some of his steak. But he quit and pushed the tray away.

A few minutes later, Nurse Sawyer came back. "You done eating?"

"Yes, we are," Mr. Peterson said, and he pushed his tray off to the side.

Nurse Sawyer pushed her tray of hypodermics toward him. "Need a blood sample, and the phlebotomist is out today, so I'm way behind," she said.

"Phlebotomist?" Jack asked.

"Blood-sucking vampire with a medical license," she explained.

Moments later, Mrs. Sawyer wrapped a bandage around Mr. Peterson's arm and pushed her cart toward Jack.

"This is a fine way to ruin a meal," Jack observed as he held out his arm for her needle.

"Doesn't ruin mine," she said.

"You might notice," Jack said, "that Mr. August Peterson is not eating any longer."

Mrs. Sawyer raised her eyebrows and bared imaginary fangs. "Vampires have that effect on people."

Mr. Peterson raised his hands as if to check for teeth marks in his throat. Jack laughed. So did Mrs. Sawyer. "You fellows are definitely better, tonight."

After she left, Mr. Peterson said, "Mr. August Peterson, eh? How come you to know my whole name?"

Jack hoped using Mr. Peterson's whole name wasn't an insult from a kid to a grownup. He held his drawing pencil in the air as he answered. "Last night, when the preacher came to pray over you, he said 'August Peterson' so many times I thought it was all one name. I guess he wanted the Lord to know for certain who he hoped would make it into heaven."

Peterson nodded. "Heaven can wait. I got other plans."

Jack's chuckle sent the pencil onto his drawing paper. "Your wife objected, too," he said.

Peterson sighed, "Mrs. Peterson has very fine taste." He winked at Jack. "What you in here for?"

"Mountain climbing accident," he said. "Well, not accident – nobody fell, but I nearly finished off both me and my dad."

"Your dad okay?" As he asked it, he looked at Jack directly. Real concern for him and his father shone in the man's dark eyes. So Jack told him most of it, the muscles, the climb, the rain, the goats, and even about his father nearly crying before the helicopter landed. He didn't mention grabbing Dad's jacket as they sat on the high ledge. Yet, when he stopped talking, Mr. Peterson leaned toward him and said, "You got a load of guilt inside you."

Jack's scalp tightened. The back of his throat stung. His nose suddenly itched and started to run, but he grabbed up one of his dinner napkins and wiped at his nose while Peterson went on talking.

"Our old preacher man, that Reverend Wilson, he's a funny soul, but he's got some things right," Peterson said.

Jack glanced up. Peterson gazed at him, seeing deep into Jack's heaviness and regret. "Reverend Wilson says you got to lay down your load so you can get up and move on toward life."

Jack fell into the softness of the man's eyes and the certainty with which he offered solace. "How do I do that?" he asked.

"Talk to your father."

He believed. For a minute there, he believed he could do it, and then he remembered that moment at the top of the granite slab. He had been a dangerous lunatic – crazy with fear. How could he ask Dad to forgive that?

The creaking of their door broke the awkward silence between him and Mr. Peterson.

"The Lord be praised." Reverend Wilson beamed as he entered the room. He balanced a Styrofoam cup in one hand. "Hallelujah, Brother. You lookin' mighty good."

August Peterson took a moment before he looked up from his fork, but when he did, he smiled at the preacher. "I thought we got rid of your sad self last night," he said. Jack saw from Peterson's smile that he was teasing the reverend.

Wilson raised his steaming Styrofoam cup. "My sad self been waiting at the airport too many hours," he said. "Mechanical problems, they said. Booked myself into a different flight. Nine tonight."

"Good decision," Peterson said, reaching a hand to greet the reverend.

Wilson carried his cup of microwave-able soup in his right hand, so he took Peterson's hand in his left. He must have squeezed with both hands, because the lid of the soup popped off. Salty chicken broth and noodles ran down the armature of Peterson's bed.

"Oh my goodness, Brother. Forgive my clumsiness. Where's a towel?" Wilson glanced over at Jack, as if he had a cache of towels on his side of the room. Jack held up his only clean dinner napkin.

"Now you never mind, Reverend," Peterson said, pushing his own napkin at the wet mess that covered the buttons on the arm of his bed. Jack dropped his napkin on his tray and pushed the tray table toward Peterson who grabbed the offered napkin and swabbed at the chicken pieces.

Reverend Wilson, obviously embarrassed, dabbed at the liquid with his handkerchief. "Goodness, Brother Peterson, I never . . ."

Peterson dropped the two wet napkins on his tray and waved Wilson's worries away. "Robert," he said, "you got to be all tired out, trying to get out to the airport and back. Rest your weary bones."

Bits of carrot and peas still dribbled down the armature, but Peterson paid no attention to them. He ordered Reverend Wilson to worry no more and to sit. The reverend sat. Peterson pointed out how nice yesterday's flowers still looked in their water-pitcher vase. The reverend calmed. Peterson asked about mutual friends. The reverend gathered his 'sad self' together and settled in to visit.

Jack watched the flurry and the settling and decided he liked August Peterson a whole lot. He pulled out his deck of cards and played solitaire while he listened to their friendly talk. Ten minutes later, Peterson lay back and closed his eyes.

"Afraid I got to sleep now, Robert," he said.

"The Lord loves you, brother."

"Well, then," Peterson sighed, "the Lord has a big heart."

"Amen," Reverend Wilson intoned. He smiled down at the resting Mr. Peterson, tipped an imaginary hat in his direction and then left the room.

Jack wondered if Wilson's Lord had a big enough heart to love a guy who acted crazy when he was scared – a guy who put the fear into his own father.

"Amen." Peterson whispered as he settled.

CHAPTER 23

"Hey, Jack." His father's booming voice took Jack by surprise. He started to jump from the bed, yanking back the covers, but his stupid, scrawny legs wouldn't move. Ashamed, he jerked the sheet up. He'd been about to act like a four-year-old – run and jump in Daddy's arms.

His father didn't notice Jack's childish moment. He stepped across the room, tanned and hearty as his old self. But as he came closer, Jack saw that something had changed in him – maybe he was skinnier, maybe – he couldn't put his finger on it.

His father glanced at the other bed. "Oh, I didn't realize you had company."

"Dad, this is Mr. Peterson."

His father stretched out his hand. "Mallory Huntington," he said.

As they shook, Mr. Peterson glanced at Jack, then back at his father. "You took those photos inside the crevasse in the Andes."

Those pictures had been in the *National Geographic Magazine* a good year ago. It amazed Jack that Peterson remembered the photographer's name.

His father smiled, and ducked his head. Jack had never seen him act embarrassed. "Yes, I took them," Dad answered.

"Got to do something good when you're trapped in a bad spot," Peterson said. "Got to make some beauty of it."

His father's attention sharpened. "How did you know I was trapped? The article didn't say that."

Jack looked more carefully at Mr. Peterson. The only reason Jack knew about that disastrous climb was that he heard his mother begging his father never again to work with the reckless climber she believed had caused the accident.

Mr. Peterson raised one hand, painting a swath in the air. "Man, that was one humongous scrape in the ice wall across the crevasse from your camera stance – over there where you tried to climb out."

Dad stared at Peterson, his eyes wide, as if seeing an apparition. Peterson continued to draw the photo in the air with his dark hands. "Those marks got you within twenty feet of the opening. Then something you counted on gave way."

Petersons' hands whipped sideways across the imagined ice wall. "You swung against the ice wall, and you fell."

Yes, thought Jack. He'd seen that row of furrows in the ice, but never questioned what they meant. They explained the deep scrape on his father's face and neck, and his broken nose. They explained the rips in his left pant leg and in the chest of his jacket. All the evidence was there when his father returned from that trip.

Dad's face paled under his tan. "Are you a climber?" he asked Peterson.

Mr. Peterson chuckled. "No way. Detective. Portland Police. Homicide Division. We look for evidence like that everywhere we go."

"I'll be . . ." his father said, his laugh shaky. "You saw it all."

Peterson is smart, Jack thought. Real sick, maybe, but real smart. All those months ago, his father had denied that anybody caused his fall. Mom had never brought it up again – at least not when Jack was nearby.

Dad nodded. "You sure know your job." He said. Then he turned back to Jack. "You need a hoist out of that bed?"

"I've had therapy twice today," Jack said. "'bout wore me out."

"Hard work, eh? You'll build up muscle again real soon. Just keep at it."

His father glanced once more at Mr. Peterson before lifting the lid on what was left of Jack's dinner. "It's not your mother's cooking, but it smells good." He handed Jack the unused plastic fork.

"You look great, Dad," Jack lied as he took the fork.

"I'm fine," Dad said, "Can't believe hypothermia had such a major effect on you."

Jack remembered what Peterson said about laying down his guilt. He wanted to, but if they talked about those awful moments on the mountain, they could never bury them again. So Jack held himself silent, and stabbed at the cold potatoes with his fork, pretending to eat. When he glanced again at Dad, he watched him fiddling with Jack's collection of flowers on the windowsill. Dad opened his mouth once, then twice, then shrugged and seemed to decide not to say what he was thinking.

Jack hoped Mom might walk in soon. "Mom parking the car?" he finally asked.

"No. The gallery rescheduled her opening for tonight."

At the mention of the gallery, Jack remembered – the opening was supposed to be last Tuesday night. She was at the hospital Tuesday.

"Shit! I wanted to be there. I sure didn't want to mess it up for her."

"The word is 'shucks'," Dad said. "The show is going fine."

"People came tonight?" he asked.

"Of course, they did. Your mom's got fans. Besides, Kristi and Berto rounded up a few of your friends to make a good showing."

Jack groaned. "Our friends will eat the food, but they won't buy the paintings."

Dad chuckled. "Kristi told that kid, Rambo Collins, his attendance would be great, but he was not to comment on the paintings. She said, 'Rambo, the only adjective you know is the 'F' word.' "

At last, Jack laughed. He didn't feel rotten any more. They could still joke around and have a good time. He didn't have to bring up uncomfortable stuff. "So how do the paintings look?" he asked. "Are they all hung and lighted and everything?"

Dad sat for a moment, gazing into the air as if recalling the ambience of the art gallery. Then he said, "Your mom's work is stunning. Several of her pieces sold by the time I left for the hospital."

"That's great," Jack said. Sadness gripped him as he imagined Mom's paintings in bright surroundings, gaily dressed people telling her how beautiful each piece was – her colleagues from Landis and Huntington Architecture, her friends from the neighborhood, all those past customers, people who liked her architectural work and who put down money to say how much they liked it.

"I wanted to be there," he said. And then there was nothing more he could think of to say.

Dad broke the awkward moment. "Eat up. You need the protein."

Jack stared at his meal, repulsed by the thought of more food. "I did half the steak and most of the Jell-O."

"Well, how about a walk? Then you'll be hungry again."

Jack braced for his father's go-get-em attitude. "My legs . . ."

His father glanced over his shoulder toward Peterson, then back at Jack. "Of course they won't work. Except for that little bit of therapy, you've been in bed for days."

Jack gaped at him. His father had not been here for any of his workouts. "Dad, I just got through jogging the hall about a half hour before you came. I'm wiped out."

"Look, I've been reading about recovery from heart attacks. Walking is the best thing. A little today. More tomorrow. All the websites emphasize that."

Jack felt a warp in reality. Dad had no idea how much his chest bone hurt him. He had no idea what his legs wouldn't do. "It's the disease, too," he said.

His father flinched. "Your muscles are inflamed," he said. "The Johns Hopkins med website says it's often started by an injury. Probably that fall in the hurdle race at the All-State Games, last spring."

"I don't think so . . ." Jack began.

"Sure," Dad said. "They say stress can make it worse, too. So stop worrying about it."

Jack snorted.

Dad clapped his hands together as if he'd solved that problem and was looking around for his next job. "No stress, plenty of exercise. You'll be back on the mountains in no time."

"In fact," Jack said, "that crash over the high hurdles happened *because* of leg cramps not the other way around. The *polymyositis* came first, then the injury."

"So, what other injury have you had?"

Jack shrugged, "Dr. Ambrose said the cause can't always be traced to an injury."

"Well, it's got to be the hurdles," Dad said.

Jack opened his mouth to point out Dad's lack of logic, but his father glanced at Mr. Peterson who busily read the newspaper. Mr. Peterson's good opinion mattered to his father, so Jack didn't tackle Dad's fuzzy reasoning.

Without noticing Jack's sudden silence, Dad talked on about what he'd learned via the internet. "This one site said that sometimes people with muscle cramps have to take medicine, but not usually this much medicine, and never steroids." He waved at the med chart on Jack's white board.

"Where did you find this information?" Jack asked, reaching for his water glass.

"Just type in 'muscle cramps' or 'inflammation of the muscles' and you get over a thousand choices."

Jack held the water glass poised. He had an idea about how Dad did his research. "Polymyositis. Did you type in polymyositis?"

"One thing I know about muscle cramps," Dad said, "you don't get over them by just lying here."

Jack slammed his glass on the tray table. Water sloshed. He wanted to wave a flag and call his father's brain to attention. Jack took a deep breath, trying to unscramble his tongue and his thoughts. In the best of times, you couldn't win a discussion with Dad. This wasn't the best of times.

"There's a reason you don't see the work I'm doing, Dad," he said.

"If you don't use muscles, they get out of the habit."

You're not here when I do it," Jack finished.

"So, I'm here now."

Closing his eyes, Jack tried to sink deep into his bed. His father didn't want to understand. And Jack couldn't step on his chest and force him to listen. Only someone really tough could get him to hear.

Jack reached out and fumbled with the drawer in the bedside table. When he finally got it open, his arm and chest ached from the effort. He dropped his hand at the side of the bed.

"What are you looking for?"

"There's a card for Doctor Ambrose in there. And copies of her articles. Call her. She'll explain."

His father fished in the drawer, pulled out the card and stuck it carelessly in his pants pocket. Nobody was going to see that card until Mom cleaned out the pockets to wash them.

"Her articles can be found online. Berto will show you where."

"Sure," Dad said. "Say, I see you've got a couple of history books in there. Want me to bring you something worth reading?"

Jack decided not to convince Dad he liked history books. "A good book will not be wasted," he said.

Dad rewarded him with a broad smile. "Great. I found an old copy of *A Climber's Guide to Oregon*. It's a hoot – describes some routes by telling the climber things like 'turn left at the grove of three scrub pines'. If those scrub pines die, everybody gets lost."

Jack tried to smile, but the possible death of three scrub pines made him ache for things he would not see again.

Dad fidgeted. After a moment, he clapped his big hands together again, and said, "Well, you need a good sleep, kid. So I'll head out and leave you to it."

Jack didn't want him to leave. "Dad, could you call me? Let me know how Mom's show went?"

"Uh, sure. It'll be late, though. Maybe Mom can call you in the morning." He was already at the door.

"You can call tonight," Jack said. "They get me up to take blood samples anyway."

"I hear you," Dad said, walking toward the hall.

A few minutes later, Mr. Peterson had pushed away his tray, folded his newspaper, and closed his eyes. However, as if he knew Jack was staring, he opened one eye and winked.

"Seem like you too tired to lay down your load, eh?"

Jack shrugged. "Can't talk to his back." Uneasily, he realized he hadn't tried very hard to talk to his father's front.

Peterson picked up his book and started leafing through it. "You want him to understand you," he said, "you got to be willing to explain who you are."

"He's my father," Jack said. "He understands me." This guy Peterson totally didn't get it and he was pushing Jack's 'Annoyed' button.

"Boy, you best go to sleep." He settled the book against his leg, ready to read.

In a burst of anger, Jack hissed, "Peterson, How come nobody gets to call you 'boy', but you feel free to call me that?"

Peterson raised one eyebrow. "So far, you haven't asked to be taken for a man."

"Like I should explain everything to my dad? He's the grown up here, not me."

Peterson closed his book around his forefinger and gazed at Jack. "What do you think your father is afraid of?"

Jack blinked, then rushed to answer. "The whole question is ridiculous. My father fears nothing."

Peterson shook his head once. "Boy, you got to take a closer look next time he comes."

Jack narrowed his eyes. He said it soft and slow. "I am nobody's boy."

"That's it, Jack Huntington," Peterson smiled broadly. "That's the first step."

Jack glared at him, and then turned his attention to the ceiling. Dad had no fear. That was the source of the only arguments between Dad and Mom. It was the reason his father didn't understand his own brother – the brother whose name Jack had been given. Uncle Jackson was a successful landscape designer, a hard-hitting tennis player, a great golfer. He was once a great climber, too, but since Grandma's death, he wanted nothing to do with the mountains.

Jack grabbed up a book, but he couldn't read. He lay there, wondering why he wanted so badly to see his uncle who refused to climb.

. . .

Peterson put down his book and lowered the head of his bed. It squawked on the way down. "Sounds like a hen-pecked rooster," Peterson said.

Close to ten o'clock, Jack gave up pretending to read. He closed his eyes for brief moments while he waited for Dad's call. The phone did not ring at ten minutes after ten. Or at ten-fifteen, or ten-thirty.

"That thing works both ways," Peterson said.

Jack's skin tightened. How did the man know what he waited for? "Mom's probably not home, yet," he said. "These gallery openings go on and on."

"Your mother's quite an artist, eh?"

"Sure is."

"Like you."

Peterson couldn't know the vast difference between dabbler art, like his, and real art, like Mom's. Before he could figure a way to explain, Yolanda, the nurse's aide, came in with a tray.

Peterson turned toward her. "My. My. What has Nurse Sawyer sent to us?" He raised the head and knee parts of his mattress. The motor made odd groaning noises.

Yolanda frowned and glanced under the bed, then she smiled as she wheeled the tray between their beds.

"You will like." She plopped bowls of ice cream and cookies on the tray and whisked herself out of the room.

When she had disappeared into the hall, Peterson said, "This would be a swell hotel if it didn't cost so much."

Jack glanced at Peterson. He seemed to hold no grudge for Jack's outburst about not being a boy. So, Jack took a chance and asked the question that had been on his mind.

"What did you mean, asking what my dad is afraid of?"

Peterson put his spoon into the dish and looked at Jack from under his gray eyebrows. "Everyone of us is afraid of something. And that fear, it drives our choices in life."

"Like what?"

Peterson pursed his lips and looked at the white boards on the opposite wall. "Well," he drawled, "take someone afraid of spiders. Maybe they clean house all the time. Or maybe they won't ever go down in their own basement."

His father did nothing like that. Mom did. She was afraid of cats, especially wild ones. Cougars were why she banged the pots and pans a lot when they were camping.

He pushed Peterson's idea. "What about someone who isn't afraid."

"We all afraid," he said softly. "Some of us just afraid other folks will see our fear."

"If we're all afraid," Jack asked, "what are you afraid of?"

As soon as he said it, he wished he hadn't. Peterson's sudden quiet warned him of the dangerous place he'd stepped into. The older man picked up his spoon again, stirring the ice cream. At last he spoke without looking up.

"I'm afraid I will die without finding my youngest son."

Jack swallowed hard. "I'm sorry," he said. His throat felt like someone had crammed straw down it.

Peterson took a deep breath and then sighed. "The way I set up this conversation, you'd have to be weak in the head not to ask about my fears."

Relief swept over Jack. "Okay" he said, "I'm not sorry I asked. But I am sorry he's gone."

Peterson nodded. "It's been six months since Malcolm left. I just hope I find him and that when I find him he'll want to talk. He was being a wild kid. I said things – hollered at him. Acted like a policeman. Two minutes after he left I wanted to take those things back and hug him. I don't want to leave it like this."

They sat in silence, and then Peterson said, "Best eat that ice cream before it sogs up both the cookies."

As he ate, Jack realized Peterson had never asked what Jack feared.

Chapter 24

In the morning, Mr. Peterson slept through breakfast. The man looked fragile when he slept. At ten in the morning, Bill Martin rolled a wheelchair into the room. Jack signaled him to be quiet for Peterson's sake. Bill glanced at the snoring man and nodded.

Minutes later, Bill wheeled Jack down to the therapy pool. By this time, Jack knew what to do, so Carly lowered him into the water and gave him a few exercise ideas. After her pep talk, he settled against the blue-green tile at the head of the pool, letting his arms float in the current. The heat and the low rumble of the water pumps made him drowsy. With his eyes closed, he imagined the rush and tumble of rapids, just out of sight around the bend of a river.

He braced his feet against the sides of the pool and reached forward. Pulling against the water with both arms, he imagined himself in a canoe, slipping through the river with the grace of a trout. He was in the Missouri River, above Fort Mandan, in what someday would be called North Dakota. It was May, 1805 and he saw with the eyes of Patrick Gass, the carpenter of the Lewis and Clark Expedition. Gass noted the lack of timber on the land rolling past their big canoes.

As Patrick-Jack rowed, plowing his cupped hands through the water, he imagined the call of birds from the prairie grass. In the canoe, or pirogue, in front of him, rode Sacagawea, her hair a long, wind-rippled version of Kristi's. Her curious baby boy trailed his fingers in the water. The other kid on this expedition, George Shannon, was only eighteen, but he worked among the men who rowed the lead canoe past mid-stream sandbar islands.

Pulling against the current and toward the sunset, Jack rowed in rhythm with Shannon and York and Drouillard, the hunter. He reached and pulled with his back and his stomach muscles, his legs.

Watching a sharp-eyed heron, Jack and his friends navigated the Missouri toward the west. A brown bear, fishing from the bank, raised his head. Jack willed Drouillard not to touch his rifle. The bear glanced at Jack, harrumphed and returned to its work, holding one paw in the stream, patient and careful, waiting for his prey.

The sound of a boot clomping on tile woke Jack from his dream. He glanced up into the light of the bright room. There stood his uncle. "Jackson. What brings you here?"

"Had to see what was making you stronger. Looks like you've been having a great trip down there."

His uncle hit close to the truth there, but Jack didn't want to tell anybody about working his way up the Missouri. He planned to be ready to use his legs by the time the expedition had to abandon boats. Then, he would trudge with the men and the one woman across the Bitter Root Mountains to the headwaters of the Columbia – his secret mental game for recovery.

Uncle Jackson bent down and winked "I'm amazed you close your eyes when there's a nice young lady over there waiting to be helpful. Seems to me you'd be asking for more ideas, a few pointers on how to work your arms better."

"I'm booked," Jack said.

Uncle Jackson's eyebrows rose in surprise, then he tilted his head back and thought. After a moment, he said, "Ah. Does Kristi know that?"

"I don't think so."

"You going to get the nerve to tell her how you feel?"

Jack chuckled. "Can't do that until I'm well enough to dodge for cover."

Uncle Jackson laughed. "Seems to me your best bet is to tell her while you're flat on your back, looking helpless."

"Yeah, sure!" Jack reached his hand up. "Get me out of here."

Uncle Jackson shook his head. "I believe I'll wait for the hoist. Much better for my back."

Jack snorted. "That's a crock." Uncle Jackson was as strong as any guy he knew – hefted heavy sacks of garden sand like they were nothing.

. . .

Half an hour later, Uncle Jackson wheeled Jack to lunch in the little café on the hospital's main floor. Jack sat at the table watching his uncle go through the cafeteria line. He noticed the electric current that always ran through his feet after exercise and rejoiced at what Dr. Ambrose had told him. His nerves and his muscles were working and the little zaps were a good sign.

Once his uncle set the tray of food down and they faced each other across the table, Jack tackled the question he'd avoided for so long.

"How come you never climb any more?"

His uncle put down his sandwich, studying his plate as if the words he needed were hidden in the salad. After a few moments, he looked up. "Your mom says you remember that last climb I went on."

"What I heard when you and Dad were arguing – that's all I remember."

His uncle moved his shoulders like an athlete loosening tension. "You loved your grandparents, didn't you, Jack."

"Sure I did. I mean, grandpa was kind of a grump sometimes, but grandma was fun, and she always got him to laugh."

"Your grandma was fun, as long as I fit into her image of our superior family. Conquering the world together – the photogenic, athlete family – strong father, daring mother, accomplished older brother. You know what role that left me? I got to be the adoring little brother, always a step behind the rest, but coming on strong. Your Dad couldn't go to Nanda Devi because he was needed here. So that climb was going to be my debut as competent son."

Jack leaned forward. What his uncle said set off alarms in his gut.

Uncle Jackson's gaze held his as he talked. "On Nanda Devi, however, I had altitude sickness. So did the other guy – Nick Thorne."

"Is he the guy that fell?"

Jackson nodded. "Fell isn't the right description. But that's what Grandpa told your father. Nick wanted your grandfather to admire him. Nick should have stayed in camp, or even gone down to a lower altitude, but he was afraid the great Thomas Huntington would write him off his list."

Jack knew that feeling.

"By fifteen thousand feet," Uncle Jackson said, "I was so sick I told my Dad to take his pep talk to hell."

Jack put his sandwich on the side of the plate. "I bet he blew a gasket."

"Yup. That was the most disgusted I'd ever seen him."

Jack stared at his uncle's long-fingered hand, as big and strong as his father's. He'd always known his uncle didn't stop climbing because of weakness or fear. He glanced at his own hands – big hands at the end of stick arms.

"How did grandma end up on Nick's rope?" he asked.

Uncle Jackson looked at the ceiling. The ends of his nostrils turned red. As soon as Jack saw wetness pooling at the edges of his uncle's eyes, he looked away.

Jackson's voice was tight. "Like your granddad, your grandmother believed grit could overcome anything. She convinced herself she could jolly Nick and me into each next step to success."

There was a sudden silence. Uncle Jackson's throat worked to swallow. He wiped his nose with one swipe of the napkin and said, "I told her to stop treating grown men like little boys and get on with climbing, if that's all she planned to do with the rest of her life."

Jack felt blood leave his face. The clamor of the café rang in his head. He could barely hear the next things his uncle said.

"So they roped up and started through the ice-fall. Three hours later, I crawled out of my tent to puke, and to see what progress they were making. In the snow, in front of the tent, I found that lily I've told you about – the one that blooms when the Himalayas are turning to spring and the snows are melting."

Jack remembered. He'd half expected to find the same lily among Meriwether Lewis' drawings.

"The first avalanche started then," Uncle Jackson said. "In the distance, I could see it – a puff of smoke rolling down hill toward the first rope of climbers. In seconds, they were gone, all except the leader, your grandmother. I saw her frantically stabbing at the snow with the handle of her ice axe – searching for the others. And then I saw the second puff above her. I yelled. But, of course, she couldn't hear me."

Jack didn't look at his uncle. He could only stare at the curved white space on the table between their plates, and listen to the growing roar in his head. Dazed and disoriented, he looked up to find Uncle Jackson gazing at him.

"I . . ." Jack could barely speak. "I'm sorry." It was all he could get out.

Uncle Jackson nodded, his red-rimmed eyes blinked twice and he swiped the napkin across his nose once more. "You look beat, Jack," he said.

"Yeah. I am."

"Sorry I dropped this on you."

"I asked the question."

His uncle exhaled slowly before he looked up again. "You asked. And you're the only one who did."

Uncle Jackson stood and dropped a bill on the table. He tucked Jack's sandwich back into the café plastic wrap and set it on Jack's lap before he wheeled him out to the elevator hall. When they got to the room, Mr. Peterson was gone – for tests, Nurse Sawyer said.

Jack slept most of the rest of the day, but it wasn't restful sleep. He spent it digging in heavy snow, trying to get Grandma out before she suffocated.

CHAPTER 25

That evening, the moment Mom walked in the door, Jack could tell she was tired. He introduced her to Mr. Peterson, who looked up from *The Oregonian* to shake hands.

"Your son's company makes staying in the hospital almost bearable."

"Let's hope you two don't have to be here much longer," she said.

Jack relaxed back into his pillow. Mom was tired, but this evening, Peterson looked a lot better than he had this morning.

A nurse bustled in. "Mr. Peterson?" she called.

Peterson glanced up. "Nurse Sawyer on vacation?" he asked.

The nurse fiddled with his heart monitor. "This is sending alarms to the front desk," she said.

"I'm fine," Peterson said, but she bent over, looking under his bed.

Peterson glanced toward the floor. "You find my heart down there?"

She popped up again. "No," she said. "Found that your monitor needs replacing. I'm going to call engineering." She hurried out.

Peterson smiled and leaned toward Jack. "I think we'll soon have another visit from Mr. Electrical Tool Belt."

Jack laughed.

At that moment, Mrs. Peterson arrived. As soon as introductions were made, and Peterson began talking to his wife, Jack concentrated on figuring out why Mom looked so wrung out.

"Is Dad sick?"

His mother hugged him without answering, then plopped her purse in the visitor's chair and put her hand to his forehead. "Your father is not doing too well, but he'll get over it. His brother is visiting. They're having a tough time."

"Uncle Jackson? What the hell . . . sorry Mom . . . but what's he doing at our house?" His dad and uncle couldn't discuss the weather without a fight. Jack remembered one of the few times Uncle Jackson had come to the house since Grandma's death. Jack was nine years old. After trudging home from fourth grade, he'd arrived in time to hear his father call Uncle Jackson a 'lily-livered cur'.

His uncle had stomped out the front door, nearly collided with Jack on the front steps and then pretended he'd been looking forward to greeting his nephew. He leaned down from his great height and whooshed Jack into the air. Dad had gone inside and slammed the screen door.

"Oh, Jackie, boy" Jackson crooned, using a tune Jack had heard each time he visited. "My heart, my heart is calling, from glen to glen and out across the sea," Jack had laughed at the silliness while his uncle carried him out to his gray BMW. It was planted slaunch-wise across the driveway as if Uncle Jackson had zipped in at an angle, slammed on the brakes and hopped out.

He set Jack on top of the warm car hood and said, "Jackie, my buddy, I want you to know I love you deeper than the ocean."

Jack watched his uncle's thick eyebrows rise at the end of the statement. They seemed to be asking if Jack understood him, so Jack repeated the part he liked. "Yup. Deeper than the ocean."

"Exactly. And here's the best deal," Uncle Jackson put his sturdy fingers up in the sign of the cub scout pledge and said, "You don't have to earn an uncle's love. You've got it forever."

This declaration made no sense. A kid didn't get love for nothing.

"I'm good, mostly," he said, hastily.

Uncle Jackson threw his head back with a laugh that Jack could feel clear to the bottom of his shoes. "Lord love you, boy. You are too solemn."

He remembered wanting Uncle Jackson to laugh like that again, so he trotted out another serious statement to see if it also seemed funny. "I keep my room neat."

This sobered his uncle. He leaned both hands on the car hood and stared into Jack's eyes. "Understand this one big thing, Jackie. I love you messy or neat. When you're good and when you're bad, especially when you say 'No' and 'I won't', your uncle always loves you."

Jack was puzzled, but he hugged his uncle. He remembered hopping off the hood, a happy kid, and waving goodbye as his uncle screeched out of the driveway. He'd gone inside to find his father in the basement throwing camping gear into a pack.

"Where you going, Dad?"

"Got a job to do for your grandmother. I'm climbing Mount Rainier – by myself, it seems."

"What for?"

"She wanted me to deliver this jar up there."

Jack didn't let on that he knew those were grandmother's ashes in that ceramic jar.

He also knew that Grandpa was sad and not well since Grandma died, so he offered to go up Mount Rainier with his father, but Dad said he was still too young for that beast. He'd added that there were others who should go, but they were too yellow to face it.

Days later, Jackson brought Dad home from the mountain, a really sick man. But, from that time until his mother came into the hospital room tonight, Jack was pretty sure his uncle and his dad had success-fully steered clear of a face-to-face for eight years.

His mother took off her coat and swung it over the visitor's chair. She glanced at Mr. and Mrs. Peterson and then moved to the window side of Jack's bed for more privacy.

"Come on, Mom. What's Jackson doing with Dad all of a sudden?"

"I think," she said slowly, "your uncle is attempting to teach your father the value of golf as a game and a challenge."

"Golf? Why?"

She shrugged. "Because your uncle is an optimist?" A tired smile flitted across her face, but didn't light it up.

Optimist – golf? None of it made sense. And from experience, Jack knew it probably never would make sense. His family always talked about Jackson in riddles. But tonight there was one story he was certain she would tell him.

"Did last night's gallery opening go all right?"

All at once, she became more animated. "That Kristi is a genius. She brought your friends and their parents. Parents buy paintings."

"So, I have to visit your paintings at my friends' homes?"

"Seems like it, Jackie."

He let her get away with his early nickname. She'd earned it by sleeping in a chair for several nights. As they talked, Mom stretched her arms and then began loosening her neck. She was pretty stressed these days, he guessed – stressed about him as well as her work.

"I've got the neighborhood park design almost finished," she said, "the one near Gantenbein Street. Next week it goes before the review board." She straightened suddenly and checked his empty bedside table.

"The nurse said you ate more tonight," Mom said. "I'm sorry you had to eat alone."

"Did you eat with Dad?"

"No. He and Jackson were done eating when I arrived. They'd got to discussing pretty hot and heavy by the time I went by the house."

Maybe it was a good sign that Dad and Jackson had eaten together. Probably only peanut butter sandwiches, but that was something. You had to offer to make a sandwich, and you didn't offer if you wanted to get rid of the other person.

"Mom, haul over that chair and let's play cards or something."

She actually looked relieved, like she'd been waiting to be invited to sit down, like this was his territory and she was the guest. The feeling was weird. While she arranged the visitor's chair on the side away from the Petersons' quiet conversation, he pulled open the drawer, searching for the deck of cards Berto had brought him. Mr. Peterson glanced at him and winked.

"Gonna lose to your mother tonight, eh?"

"Never. At home, I've cleaned out her penny jar."

"He certainly has," Mom said. "Luck and strategy are on Jack's side."

Mr. Peterson smiled at her. "A true mother. Keeps coming back even if the kid wins."

Mrs. Peterson poked her husband's arm. "She's probably the one taught him how to win in the first place."

"That's the truth," Peterson said, grinning at Jack. Then he turned back to concentrate on his wife.

Jack's mother leaned back, smiling. "Want to play cribbage or rummy?"

They played cribbage. By the time they had played ten minutes, Jack was no longer able to see the combinations that added up to fifteen. He could hardly hold up the cards, much less think.

"You need to fold, Honey?" his mother asked.

"Fold nothing," he whispered, "I've caved in." He was disgusted with himself. Only weeks ago, he'd been able to climb the Pillars of Hercules, and then Crown Point with no trouble – well, almost no trouble.

"It's not going to be fixed over night, Jack. We've got to get the right combination of medicines."

"I'm taking the pills Dr. Ambrose sends. But between trips to the can, down the hall a few times, and to the therapy pool, I can barely sit up." He fought down tears. It was bad enough to be so weak. He didn't want to be a three-handkerchief sob story.

His mother stood and put her arms around his shoulders, kissing his forehead. Baby that he was, he turned his head toward her arm and let hot tears roll down his face and onto her sleeve.

"It's all right, Jack. You've got every reason to be angry and scared."

"It isn't working," he whispered. "It isn't fair."

"Disease isn't fair. It just is. You got in the way of something we don't understand yet."

"I should have known sooner. I should have known the rash wasn't fiber glass."

She pulled back to look at him with a puzzled frown. "Why would you have known that?"

"I was certain I hadn't taken my gloves off. But then I got the rash. I was so tired from the night cramps that I thought I just didn't remember everything the way it really was."

She frowned. "Night cramps. What do you mean?"

"You know, the heavy covers, and stuff would make me get a charlie-horse or a foot cramp, and then it would be an hour before I could get it to stop so I could try to sleep."

While he explained, Mom's eyes widened as if she were alarmed. "Oh, Jack, I should have been more alert."

It was the first he realized she didn't know about all those nights. "I guess Dad didn't want you worrying."

Her gaze became narrow, concentrated darkness. "Your father knew you had these cramps at night?"

Her voice chilled him. He wanted to take it back, make his father as heavy a sleeper as she had been. But she wasn't stupid. All he could do now was make it seem unimportant.

"A couple of times he woke up when I was getting some aspirin."

"Oh, right," she said. Her voice dripped disbelief. "For *a couple of times*, read *several*. And for *didn't want you to worry*, read, *didn't want you hauling Jack off to the doctor*. God, do you have to imitate your father's worst side?"

"Mom, it didn't seem like that big a deal."

"Oh, certainly!" she spat out. "Doctor Ambrose says it started last spring before that hurdle race and has been getting worse ever since. However, you are a Huntington, so it is 'Not that big a deal' until it nearly gets you both killed." Her voice had turned acid with sarcasm. And her anger struck him as if he'd been backhanded. He sank into the pillow, guilt tearing at him.

"What is it, Jack?"

He stopped a sob in his throat, but the anguish he'd held inside rushed out. "He might have died," he confessed. "I almost killed him. I nearly threw him off that slab above the chimney section of the climb." His voice had grown thin, but his heart forced him to push out the last of his guilt. "He was already cold through to the skin, but I grabbed him. I yelled at him. And even then he . . . he gave me his own wool cap."

She leaned back, a look of horror on her face. "You fought each other on that mountain?"

He raised his chin. The pain of seeing her revulsion tightened his throat, cutting off his voice. All he could do was nod.

"Dear God," she whispered.

And then she became extremely busy. "You have had enough," she announced. "I'm getting some Jell-O for you to eat and then you will go to sleep."

He blinked, trying to understand what she meant to do, but she was already straightening his covers and not looking at him. He tried to rise up.

"I'm sorry," he said.

"Never," she hissed. "You will not be sorry for this. You are not responsible."

Not responsible. He was impulsive, stupid, dangerous – and not responsible.

"Mom," he said, wanting desperately for her to hear him out. Then he realized he was trying to justify what he'd done on the mountain. There was no justification.

She stood upright and marched out the door. He sank into the bed, a stone.

"Jack," Mr. Peterson said, his voice seeming to hover over Jack's name. "I think you misunderstand your mama."

Jack glanced at the older couple. Mrs. Peterson gazed at Jack, sympathy softening her face. Mr. Peterson put his hand on the table between their beds, as if he wanted to touch Jack, but couldn't reach.

"What she says, son, is exactly what she means. It wasn't your responsibility."

Jack blinked at him. Peterson didn't know the truth. If he told him everything, Peterson would be disgusted, same as Mom and Dad.

Moments later, Mom was back with dark cherry Jell-O and whipped-cream topping. "Evening snack," she said in forced cheer.

The rock in his throat kept him from swallowing, but he glanced at the flame of anger reddening her throat and he reached for the spoon.

She held onto it. "Nope," she said, dipping into the Jell-O. "I saw your arm shaking. Mom gets to feed her kid one more time. Open wide and watch the Jell-O fly in." She was trying to make him laugh, talking the way she did when he was in the high chair.

After two bites she asked, "Do you want me to bring you something? A book?" She waited for his answer, spoon poised with the next bite. While feeling ugly inside, he couldn't face the sugar sweetness of Jell-O. He had to think of something to ask for.

"How about my journal of Patrick Gass?"

The spoon lowered. "Who?"

"Patrick Gass." He spoke fast, pretending this was really important. "He was this guy, a carpenter. He went with Lewis and Clark across the whole country. I think the book's on the shelf above my desk."

"The carpenter wrote a journal, too?"

Jack saw the spoon rest on the bowl. If he kept her talking she'd forget about shoveling sugar, doing what she thought a mother should do.

"Five or six guys on the expedition wrote journals," he said. He swallowed hard before he could go on. "It's weird," he said. "You read each journal and you see what each guy thought was important. Like Lewis – he was big into the geography, and plants and animals, and Clark will tell you exactly by name which guys bagged a deer or trapped a beaver. That Gass, though, he hardly ever mentions the other guys, but he can tell you the specific kinds of trees they've passed that day. It's like they were each on a separate trip."

His mother sat for a moment, then she raised the spoon toward her own mouth. "We don't any of us make the same trip through life," she said. "You think you know someone, love someone even, and then you discover they are someone else."

She meant him.

"Oh!" she said. "I've been eating your snack."

"I can't eat," he said, lamely.

She stood, and he heard her drop the spoon into the glass dish with a vehemence that betrayed her feelings. She yanked the blanket over his shoulders and said, "Now sleep. And stop beating yourself up about the past. I want you to get well. You hear me?"

He opened his eyes to find her leaning over him, her head cocked to one side and all her bright hair falling over one raised eyebrow. He didn't have the energy to say anything but, "I hear."

She gave his blanket one more efficient tug, kissed him quickly on the forehead and lifted the tray, grabbing her coat and purse with her other hand as she left.

Staring at the empty doorway, he imagined her going home to greet his father. She would give Dad an extra long hug because she realized she'd almost lost him on Mount Tecumseh.

CHAPTER 26

Jack awoke with a start as the bell chimed for the hospital's evening prayer. Sister Kathleen Marie came on the crackling intercom as she had each evening. Jack wondered if God paid attention – if there was a God. He had a few things to lay at the feet of any god who cared.

"In Jesus' name, we pray . . .achoo . . ." Sister Kathleen Marie sneezed, and then she sneezed a second time. "Excuse me, Lord. I meant 'Amen'."

Jack opened his eyes.

"Good night to all of you in our care." She sneezed a third time.

The sneezes proved she prayed live each evening. Sister Kathleen Marie really believed there was a God, and that He listened. Now Jack imagined her getting up from her knees, crossing herself on the way out of the intercom room, and then going to a little cell in a nunnery attached to the hospital. Maybe on the way back she looked in on the patients in intensive care. Maybe, just maybe, she would come to the Cardiac Care Unit and tell Jack Huntington he wasn't a total jerk.

Mr. Peterson folded the Arts and Entertainment supplement and slapped it down on his bedside table. "Sounds like the good Sister has had a long day."

"Probably ought to be home in bed, instead of on her knees in this cold building," Jack said.

"Maybe she has a load of 'ought-to's' she's trying to live up to."

"What do you mean?"

Peterson pretended to wave his accusing pointer finger at the Sister in the intercom speaker. "You ought to take care of others, Sister Kathleen. You ought to pray first and then go to bed. You ought never to be sick. And you ought to do what other people expect you to do."

Peterson wasn't very subtle. Jack knew what he was getting at. Jack should drop the 'ought-to' list, stop doing what Dad expected, and hope Dad would get with the new program – help him get well.

"All right, All right," Jack said. "I will fling away my load." He didn't think he could dump Dad's expectations overnight, but he could start.

Peterson saluted him. "Good for you, Jack Huntington."

"It won't be easy," Jack said, "but I've inherited stubborn genes."

Mr. Peterson started to chuckle. But his voice caught as if he choked on something. Peterson coughed again, exhaling loudly. His exhale became a wheeze. Peterson pulled his left arm close to his chest, folding in on himself. Sweat beaded on his forehead. He never inhaled.

Jack rose from his pillow, yanking back his covers. He shoved his bedside table out of the way and swung his legs toward the floor. "Breathe," he said, keeping his voice as steady as he could. Peterson's eyes grew large with fear. And fear tightened Jack's chest.

Jack's left leg wouldn't follow his right, so he grabbed it with his hand, jerking it out of the bed. "Nurse," he yelled as he threw himself across the chasm to Peterson's bed "Nurse. Help! Anybody!"

He reached across Peterson and grasped the call-button on the far rail of Peterson's bed. He pumped the orange dot at its end. It was crusted with the dried sugars and salt of the Reverend's soup.

While he yelled, Jack's legs crashed out from under him. From beneath the bed, he saw that the plug for Peterson's heart monitor once had been duct taped to the wall. The plug had fallen part of the way out. The nurse probably turned off the alarm up front, waiting for engineering to repair it.

Even if he were up there, he knew he could do Peterson no good, and his own call button was on the far side of his bed. So he used his arms for traction and wrenched his body out of the narrow space between the beds, head-butting the legs of his bedside table. Once past the table, he hollered as he propelled himself, crawling Marine-style toward the hall. He had to get someone to help.

Behind him, he heard a thump and then the sliding sound of paper against paper. Peterson's news hit the floor just as Jack reached the doorjamb. He turned to see Peterson slump and hit his head on the bedrail.

Jack yelled again. Yolanda ran down the hall toward him. He called, "Peterson, heart attack."

Yolanda turned and yelled back to the nurse's station, "Code Blue, room 553."

Jack knew he'd be in the way, so he whipped his forearms against the ground, pulling his body into the hall and to the far side of the door.

Three bells rang, a pause and then three bells again. Exhausted, Jack pushed his back against the cold plaster wall. Beyond his bare feet, he saw an on-rush of green and blue-clad hospital staff. He let his head drop to the floor and listened to the scruff of hospital booties and scrub uniforms as nurses and doctors ran into Peterson's room. Two of the staff hauled a machine on wheels. He heard them maneuver the cart through the door, banging it on the metal jamb, backing it out and turning it once before jerking it straight in.

"Kid, can you hear me?"

Jack opened his eyes. A big man with straight black hair and a thin mustache leaned over him. Off in the room, Jack heard tense voices and then the sudden whap of what he realized must be an electric shock. Jack's whole body jerked in sympathetic pain. They were trying to restart Peterson's heart.

The man prodded his shoulder with one finger. "You with us, kid?"

Jack tried to answer, but he couldn't seem to get his mind on the words, only on the second whap of electricity as they tried again.

The man glanced back over his shoulder, calling, "Somebody bring a gurney. This boy is going into shock."

I am nobody's boy, Jack thought. *I am nobody . . ..*

CHAPTER 27

In the night, Jack found himself mummy-wrapped in heated blankets, his feet propped up on a pillow. Remembering snatches of nurse talk, he realized they had been afraid for him, but he'd been too groggy to care. Now he wanted to find August Peterson – and what? He couldn't move. He tried to wiggle his toes but they felt as if they were encased in boots made of lambskin.

He heard someone settle in the squishy chair next to his bed. In the darkness, he made out the shape of his mother. In the other chair, at the foot of his bed, sat a shadow he hoped was his father. He dropped off to sleep.

And dreamed he was helping Mr. Peterson rappel down a steep cliff. The tight-mouthed fear on Peterson's face told Jack that everything depended on him. The least mistake would give his friend a heart attack.

"Don't let me down, Jack," Peterson whispered.

His father's voice broke into Jack's dream. "What do you mean, I let Jack down?" Dad's words were so close to Peterson's in the dream that Jack held his breath.

Nearby, Dad said, "I need you, Alison. Let me come home."

"I can't do that, Mallory. Not while you refuse to understand."

"Alison," Dad whispered, "sitting up all night, wearing yourself out will not help Jack."

Jack struggled to sit up, but fatigue and his dream nailed him to the mattress. Through narrowly opened eyelids he saw his father kneeling near his mother.

"Take me back," Dad said.

"Something is bothering him," his mother said. "You see how he moans."

Jack hadn't been aware of moaning, just of yelling inside, "Don't do this Mom!"

"It's that incision," his father said, "and the crawling on the floor. This damned hospital isn't safe."

"Dr. Ambrose says this noise is not pain," Mom said. "It's fear. But he doesn't talk about his fears."

His father scoffed. "Jack afraid? Before that woman doctor got hold of him, he feared nothing."

But I do fear. I'm afraid I'll drop August Peterson. I'm afraid because I'm a guy who scares his Dad on a narrow ledge. I'm afraid to lose you. Mom and Dad don't fight about me.

Jack tried to tell them all of this, but he couldn't move.

"He has the same fears as you, Mallory. And you both fear others will see your fear."

"You would like us to be afraid, but that doesn't make it so."

"Mallory," Mom said, "Stop being his coach and just love him."

"But Ali," Dad's voice rose, "I can't just let him lie there and die."

Jack waited, hoping to hear Mom's answer. But she just rose, kissed Jack on the cheek and walked out of the room.

Jack was stunned. Dad didn't move for at least twenty seconds. Then Jack felt a large hand take hold of his toes. Through all the covers and the lambskin, his father massaged his feet.

After a minute, Dad spoke softly, "I love you, son." And then his voice broke, "Get up, Jack. Please get up . . ."

But Jack couldn't budge. Pain medicine ran hot through his veins.

. . .

Next, he awoke into the haze of gray that signals dawn. Somewhere outside the expanse of brick hospital buildings, a robin chirruped. Mom and Dad were gone. He decided he must have dreamed their argument. Mom loved Dad.

He tried to sit up, but his arms were melted lead, his legs as sturdy as oozing motor oil. Asbestos fibers lined his eyelids. He felt like a toxic waste dump.

Beyond his head, he heard the blip of a heart monitor.

Peterson. They started him again!

He wrenched his head around, hoping to see the man's slicked-back gray and white waves and his deep brown eyes.

In the small lights from the hall, he saw that the bed was empty and stripped of sheets. He stared at the thick plastic that protected the gray and white striped mattress. Peterson was gone. Wiped out.

Pain grew and filled his chest. He shivered inside his heated blankets. Hot tears spilled from his eyes. His nose itched. Snot ran down his cheek. He couldn't break his arms free of the blankets.

Conscious again of the blip, blip, blip sound, he twisted his head farther back. Peering through the distortion of his tears, he found himself attached to the monitor the way he had been days ago when he first woke up. Peterson was gone and he, Jack Huntington, was a blipping thing.

. . .

Nurse Sawyer's squeaky shoes woke him. "The lab tech is busy and we need a blood sample." She unwound his warm blanket and took his hand to pull his arm out.

He gazed up at her, blinking to clear his vision.

"I understand you created quite a fuss last night when I was off duty." She swabbed his arm with an alcohol wipe.

"Peterson?" he asked.

She readied her syringe. "Peterson's in intensive cardiac care."

Jack's heart soared. *Peterson is alive. Hanging in there.* "How far away is intensive care?"

"Whooey, son." She glanced at him as she tapped for a usable vein. "It's too far for you. Besides, he is not talking much, and only family visits the ICU."

Laying the needle against his arm she added, "This will be a sharp prick."

He'd heard people say that so many times that he didn't even tense. Besides, he couldn't tense. But Peterson was alive. As Nurse Sawyer wrapped the cotton blanket over his arm again, he whispered "Tell Mrs. Peterson, I hope he gets well."

"She for certain knows you care, son."

Nurse Sawyer lifted her tray and squeaked on out of the room to the next blood-letting.

. . .

As the mid-morning sun woke him, Jack prayed. At least he thought he must be praying. Endlessly, he asked someone to take care of Peterson, someone other people called God or Allah.

When his mother sat in the exhaling chair next to his bed, he opened his eyes. She took hold of his hand and said, "Hello, Hero."

"Hero?"

"Don't you remember? You saved your roommate last night."

So that was how they explained it to her – made him sound brave and smart, when he'd wasted important time trying to do things he couldn't do. But it was partly true. He had brought the doctors to Peterson. Jack hoped Peterson wanted to live as much as he wanted him alive.

"I'm afraid I'll die before I find my youngest son."

What if I could contact that kid of Peterson's? Jack laughed at his own foolish thought. *How could I find him from Trinity Hospital? Motorize my bed?*

"Mom," he said. "Do you think there's a God?"

She stiffened. Jack realized she must think he planned to die.

"I want to know for Mr. Peterson."

Her shoulders relaxed. Her head drooped toward her hands which held his. Then she looked up at him. "You like that guy, Peterson, don't you."

He nodded.

She studied his face for a moment and then said, "I think there has to be some power that cares. The world is beautiful. Animals, plants, humans. I believe we were set in motion with artistic joy."

"But does the power, the God, care enough?"

"Honey. I wish I knew. All I know is what I see, and I don't see interference in the consequences of choices we make – smoking, not exercising, exercising too much – all those choices."

Jack nodded. What she said was true. Yet, in his mind he repeated his prayer. *Make him want to live.*

His mother thought a moment and then said, "I think the rules are there from the first – this gene works this way. That gene works that way. Some wear out. Others work well and survive. I don't think God, or whatever we call the first impulse, I don't think that creator reaches down to change the system. But we also have people who love us. Their love shows us how to work for each other, to make peace, to solve problems, to help each other get well."

Moments passed while Jack thought about how hard he had worked, how he was beginning to get well, and then in one burst of energy, he seemed to have used himself up. Maybe he needed some more love, too. He shivered.

His mother glanced at him. "Do you need another blanket?"

"Last night, Dad asked you to take him back. Back where?"

Her face went white. "B . . . back," she stuttered. "We are working on something, Jack. Until we get it right, Dad is not living at our house."

Another chill shook Jack's body. "Why did you do that?"

"Because I love him."

"But he . . ."

"It's our problem, son. Not for you to worry about. He'll be here to see you this afternoon."

. . .

Jack slept fitfully, waking only to fret over what split up his Mom and Dad, trying to figure out how to help them make peace. Hours later, he picked up the creak of the leather shoes he'd been hoping to hear. He opened his eyes and his heart thumped. Tiptoeing made his father look like a little boy working his way toward the cookie jar.

Drinking in the sight of his father, oddly quiet and careful, Jack nearly forgot about Mom's news. Dad laid his backpack on the visitor's chair, shucked his blue parka, just as Mom always shucked her suit coat – folded it neatly and laid it over the backrest. He glanced at Jack.

"Oh. Hi. Sorry I woke you."

"I got nothing to do but sleep."

"You lose that Nerf ball?"

He hadn't thought about the Nerf ball for two days. "I think it dropped on the floor the other night."

His dad bent to look under the beds. Then he stood, empty-handed. "Maybe you left it in the bathroom."

Jack had a vision of himself as his father must imagine him – Jack tosses the Nerf ball to himself everywhere he goes. Jack even tosses the ball and pushes the walker fast enough to rumble downfield and catch his own pass. Jack sits on the toilet and, by mistake, tosses the ball into the tank.

Flush the ball.

His father actually lifted the toilet lid to check. Jack swallowed hard and waited for his father to get back to reality. Dad shook his head as he exited the bathroom. Then he studied the route from the window-side bed to the bathroom. Jack saw him study the empty bed that until last night had been occupied by Peterson. Dad fiddled with the edge of Jack's blanket.

"I'm sorry you had to go through all that with Mr. Peterson last night," Dad said. "I wish I'd been here."

Swallowing with difficulty, Jack said, "Nurse Sawyer says he's not talking, so I can't go visit him."

"Of course, you can't," Dad said. "You can barely get yourself to the bathroom."

"I like him," Jack said. "I want to see him."

His father twisted the telephone cord. "They say you saved his life."

"I sure hope so," Jack said. "He's barely alive. He needs his son."

Dad stared at Jack a moment, as if trying to make sense of him. Then he sat down in the chair. "I'm proud of you," he said.

Jack glanced over at him, warmed. "Thanks, Dad."

"Hell of a night," Dad said.

"Dad, why aren't you living at our house?"

His father ducked as if dodging a fist. After a moment he answered. "Your mother says I've got to make it up with my brother. I don't know why, because Jackson has nothing to do with you and me."

"Where are you living?"

Dad laughed, a high craziness in his voice. "That's the best part. I'm over at your Uncle Jackson's house. A bigger old lady I hope to never meet."

Flashing anger heated Jack's body. "Uncle Jackson is great."

Dad's eyebrows rose. "Of course you want to like him. He's your uncle."

"Don't talk like that. You don't know him."

His father sat in stunned silence for several seconds. Red crept up his throat and into his cheeks. Jack expected an explosion. Nobody talked to his father like this. And no one talked about Jackson. But his father merely sat there, blinking. He stared at his hands, then at the walls, and finally focused on Jack's face. "I wish I did know him," he said.

Jack didn't understand, but something had changed. He decided to press on. "Mom loves you," he blurted.

Dad jerked. "Yeah? Does kicking me out look like love?"

"Do me a favor," Jack said. "While you're at Uncle Jackson's, look up the word *polymyositis* on the internet."

"I've done all that research," Dad started.

"But you haven't read about my disease."

"This is an injury. You can get over an injury."

Jack spoke as if to a deaf man. "I'm . . . not . . . looking . . . to . . . be . . . sick."

Dad winced. Then his jaw tightened. "The truth is, until the hypothermia, Bradley believed you'd developing a phobia about testing yourself."

Rage stopped thought.

His father's tense eyes softened. "You're too good at what you do, son. Don't give up."

Jack's fist slammed down on the bedside table. His books jumped. Dad jumped, too. Jack's anger came in a harsh whisper. "How could you let him talk like that? I wasn't even there to defend myself."

Dad put a hand on Jack's shoulder. "Just get the stitches in your chest healed and then get out there and do the thing you fear."

"My leg hurts." Spit came out of Jack's mouth, but he was too steamed to wipe it off. "My foot turns itself inside out. That's not a phobia."

"Doctor Bradley is a trained . . ."

"So!" Jack shouted, "The truth is out. You want me to be assertive, be a leader, speak my mind. But not when I disagree with you. And not when one of your good-old-boys says I'm crazy."

His outburst surprised even Jack, but he kept his gaze on his father's face. After a long moment, Dad took a deep breath.

Dad stood up swiftly. "This is no disease. This is a short term deal – muscles can be built up and . . ."

"Look up the word, Dad. Do it if you love me."

Dad stopped moving. "If I love . . . How can you think . . .?" He stared at Jack. Jack stared back without blinking, even though tears threatened.

Dad sat suddenly, fished in his pants pocket and dragged out Dr. Ambrose' card. "How do you spell it?"

Jack told him, and then added, "The Mayo clinic site is good. So's the John's Hopkins site."

His father wrote that information, sat silently, staring at the card, and then said. "You need some sleep, Big Guy. You've been through heck in the last twenty-four hours."

Jack nodded. Sleep was one suggestion of his father's that made sense. As Jack closed his wet eyes, he heard Peterson's voice. "What is your father afraid of?"

. . .

During that fitful nap, Jack dreamt he was back in Big Meadow at the base of Mount Tecumseh, where the nanny goat watched him crawl across alpine grass and flowers. She came closer, curiosity overcoming her wariness. The bell around her neck rang a silvery note as she lowered her head to push him along.

Behind her, the billy nipped to get her away from the strange body of the boy. She kicked out at the billy, sent him flying backward. She returned calmly to rolling Jack's body toward the rescue helicopter.

The billy pawed the ground and lowered his head, ready to butt something, anything that moved.

CHAPTER 28

At noon, Yolanda, brought the lunch cart. She gave him a broad grin. "Nurse Sawyer says you fine."

"Fine," he said. "All wired up to monitors again."

"You see. After lunch."

He did see. Sleep had made him stronger. He could sit up. He could use the spoon. He hadn't lost as much ground as he'd thought. But emptiness had settled deep inside of him. He refused to look at Mr. Peterson's bed. And every time an image of his father came into his mind, he worried about his mother's sanity. He couldn't figure what she thought to accomplish by sending his father away. Did she think she could force Dad to admit Jack was no longer the old Jack? It would never work. His father couldn't even make himself read about his son's disease.

Maybe Mom was cracking from being worried. He had to make himself look better for her.

After Jack downed his soup and crackers, Yolanda whisked away the tray. Nurse Sawyer arrived and unhooked Jack from the monitor.

"With a recovery like this," Sawyer said, "you should be back in therapy and get out of here soon."

"I wish. I mean I like you and all that, but . . ."

She chuckled. "We'd be proud to see the back of you, too, young man."

After Nurse Sawyer left, Yolanda returned with his wheelchair. "You have a ride," she said.

He didn't want to be whipping around the halls in his pajamas. "Could I use my robe?"

"I get it for you."

"How come you're taking me, today?"

"Is my break time. I ask permission."

"Asked," he said, and could have bitten his tongue for sounding like his grammar-correcting mother.

"Past tense," she nodded. "Asked. Thank you."

"De nada," he said, using the only Spanish phrase he could remember. He liked discovering this thoughtful older-sister-nursing student, who cared enough to take him somewhere away from the empty bed in his room.

Ten minutes later, he was sitting outside the Intensive Care Unit with Mrs. Peterson. Yolanda sat on a nearby chair, looking proud of herself.

Mrs. Peterson had not let go of Jack's hand since he rolled up to her.

"I will tell him you came," she said. "I will tell him you are all right."

She seemed as tall and elegant today as she had before, but now he also could see how drawn and weary she was. He knew she had many worries – not only her husband's heart, which threatened to quit, but also their son, Malcolm.

"August asks about you," she said. "In his sleep, he says, 'Jack's on the floor. He fell on the floor.' Of course, that's the last he remembers – you sliding off the bed. He doesn't know anything about after that, what you did. You are such a good boy."

Jack wished there was something he could do to make things

better for her.

A nurse poked her head out of Intensive Care. "Your husband is awake. Come on in."

Mrs. Peterson's hand jumped from Jack's and covered her mouth. She glanced at him, breaking into a quiver of hopeful smile.

He nodded. "Tell him 'Hi' from me."

"I will. Oh yes, I will." She rose and strode toward the nurse.

Yolanda jumped up and said, "Give him our love."

Jack jerked his head toward her. He felt his eyebrows rise into his hair. Yolanda, his quiet nursing student, was getting bold.

As the door swung shut behind Mrs. Peterson, Yolanda faced him, her hands on her hips. "You love him much." Her jaw jutted, defying him to contradict her.

He smiled. She was right. He did love August Peterson. Two days, two arguments and one bad time they'd shared – and the laughter. "Yes, I love him. How about you?" he asked.

She sniffed and bustled over to grab the handles on his wheelchair. "Sí. Me also. He is a good man."

"Let me push this thing," he said, "I've got to get stronger."

"You're daddy will be proud of you," she said.

Jack glanced up at her, but he couldn't tell if she was teasing him. So, he just reached for the right wheel. Despite the pulling pain in his chest, he turned his chair down the hall toward the elevator.

Dad would walk the other way if he saw me pushing myself in a wheel chair.

But then Jack shrugged. *Can't please all the people all the time. And with any speed slower than four minutes a mile, you can't please Dad.*

. . .

His cracked sternum ached. The skin on his chest felt stretched and rug-burned. He'd navigated two long hallways, and in and out of the elevator. His biceps glowed with heat. He had to do this more often.

As he and Yolanda turned the last corner to his room, Kristi and Berto walked toward them. Berto flung out his arms and sang in a low voice, "Te amo, Yolanda. Yolanda, mi amor."

Yolanda snorted. "I have so many years, I might be your *tía*."

"Ah, but what an Auntie," Berto said, kissing his fingertips. "My favorite."

"You're embarrassing her," Kristi said, thrusting a finger into Berto's shoulder.

Yolanda laughed. "Don't make him stop. He needs much practice with the courting."

Berto slapped his chest. "My heart. My broken heart."

Jack laughed, "It's obvious why Berto gets straight A's in drama."

Kristi laid her hand on Jack's shoulder. She whispered so all four of them could hear. "He got a straight F at yesterday's play practice."

"No way," Jack said.

"Way," Berto said, nodding. "I had to miss the first half of practice because I couldn't show progress on our group paper. I forgot to bring my part to class."

"Oh, admit it," Kristi said. "There wasn't much progress to show."

"I need your help, old buddy," Berto confessed.

Yolanda held up a hand. "I must to attend nurses' class."

Jack waved at her. "Thanks for the trip."

After Yolanda disappeared, Kristi pushed his wheelchair toward the room. "I thought I saw you propelling this thing," she said.

"I near wore holes in my palms." He held his hands up for them to see the blisters forming.

As they rounded the corner into his room, he glanced at the sheetless bed next to his own and tried not to think about last night. Or about Dad and Mom. He felt as if he'd wandered into a time when if you touched something, it came apart in your hands.

"Where's Mr. Peterson?" Kristi asked.

Berto answered. "He's in Intensive Care."

That surprised Jack. Berto really kept track of people.

"How's Mrs. Peterson?" Kristi asked.

"Old." The word popped out before Jack could stop it. "Suddenly, she's old."

All three of them were silent. In front of Jack, Kristi wilted, and then looked away from them. "She's strong," Kristi said. "She is calm and strong."

He remembered Kristi staring at Mrs. Peterson on that first night when the Peterson's arrived. "She is still that way, Kris," he said. "She is worried and tired. But she is still strong."

Kristi's hands slapped her jeans-covered thighs. She stood up. "Where's Intensive Care? I'm going to see her."

"Third floor. If she's not in the lounge, then she's visiting Peterson, and she'll be out in a few minutes."

Kristi swiped at her eyes. "I'll be right back."

"Take your time," Berto said. "I'm gonna pick Jack's brain for our paper."

Jack watched her leave. Then he glanced at Berto and saw his friend's gaze following Kristi as well. Berto's eyebrows were pulled down with worry.

"What's up?" Jack said.

"Her damned dad's doing nothing. Says a hospital never did her mom any good before. Why would it this time?"

"The drinking is worse, huh?"

Berto stared at his fingers, twisted together in his lap. "Worse than ever."

"We've got to get her some help," Jack said.

"I bet your mom could talk to her."

Jack shook his head. "My mom's tripping out. My dad's living with Uncle Jackson."

Berto sat up straighter. "You know."

"Wait a minute," Jack said. "You mean you knew this and weren't going to tell me?"

"Well, yes. Our moms are best friends, Jack. But who told you?"

"Dad. This morning. He's ticked off at the doctors, at Mom, at Jackson."

"Go figure," Berto said with crackling disgust. "Pissed at everyone but himself. There's justice."

Offended at Berto's tone, Jack said, "My dad's just uncomfortable in hospitals."

Berto's eyes opened wide. "You believe that crud?"

"It's hard to live with a sick person." Jack's voice came out louder than he'd intended. "Old people like Dad can't turn a one-eighty overnight."

Berto snorted. "Either your dad cares enough to make some changes, or he doesn't. It looks like your mom wants to know which it's going to be."

"My dad cares," Jack said. "That's what makes him act like a coach all the time. He cares that I get well, and I'm not well."

"He wants you the way you were."

"Right," Jack said. And when Berto merely shrugged, Jack said, "Right," again, louder.

Berto didn't reply. Instead, he yanked his backpack onto his lap and unzipped it. Jack could see several books – a DeVoto edition of The Lewis and Clark Journals, a Biddle edition, and two volumes of the Moulton edition that had cost Jack seventy dollars each – Christmas and birthday money for two years. His favorite books in Berto's raggedy bag. If he'd still been hooked up, Jack figured his heart monitor would have gone wild.

"I had to use these at your house until today. Your mom said as long as I was bringing them to you, it was okay."

"You've been doing research at my house?"

Berto glared. "I'm not a complete Eff-up."

"Didn't say you were." Jack realized he was itching for a fight, but

Berto wouldn't give it to him.

"I found that kid, George Shannon," Berto said. "The one you said was on the expedition. Did you know that when one of the sergeants was sick, they made Shannon a back-up sergeant to lead that crew? Clark wrote that in his journal."

Jack relaxed. "I wish I'd been on that trip."

"That came through pretty clear the first time I saw your library. But I didn't know you painted, too."

"You been fishing through my art files?"

"Sure. I changed a couple paintings to make them more realistic."

Jack nearly upset his wheelchair. "You what?"

"I dabbed a little blood on the muzzle of the grizzly bear."

"No!"

"And in that one of the keel boat, I added a guy peeing over the side."

"You scuzzbag."

Berto sang out, "Clear across the wide Missouri . . ."

And then Jack burst out laughing. "You joker!"

Berto grinned and raised his innocent hands. "Never touched a hair on the grizzly's face. Honest."

"Stay out of my stuff, you hear."

"So, can we use your painting of the keelboat?"

"Sheees! No."

"And there's a cool one of your iron-framed boat."

"Berto, my pictures will not be part of this paper."

"Pretty hot stuff," Berto said. "Especially the one of Kristi in climbing tights. So can we use the boats?"

Jack's face flushed. "No way," he said. "And don't try blackmailing me. There are way better paintings in these books."

"You're afraid." Berto said.

"Of what?"

"If they see you're a sensitive artist, all the girls will be after you."

"I'm afraid they'll puke."

"Suit yourself." Berto hauled out three printed pages and a rubber-banded stack of five-by-eight cards with notes written all over them. "Lots of ideas and no clue how to use them," he said.

An hour later, Berto had a rough outline. His note cards of facts were arranged and numbered in the order he wanted to use them, and he had an opening and closing paragraph written.

"Pretty good work for a dweeb," Jack said, leaning back.

"Yeah, well, really it was your mom who helped me figure out this card method. How come nobody teaches this stuff about how to do research?"

Jack snorted. "Numb Brain, Mr. Crandall taught that last year. But you were mostly staring at Angela di Cieli. Ask her out, then pay attention in class."

Berto stood up. "You're the expert? You don't talk to Kristi about what you want from her."

"Why should I? The only time I tried, she put me on my rear end."

Berto snickered. "Give me a break. You were both twelve."

"How do you know?"

"She told me. Said she wished she'd understood you weren't offering to wrestle."

"Why would she tell you that?" he asked.

"You were unconscious," Berto shrugged. "Women regret things when they think you're dying."

CHAPTER 29

Kristi poked her head around the corner. "You still in that wheel chair?" she asked.

"Sure am," Jack said. *Amazing. I didn't even think about getting in bed.* Talking with Berto, he'd barely felt any pain.

Berto waved his backpack toward Kristi. "I'm on my way to a good paper here."

"Kid me." Kristi said as she sat on the side of Jack's bed.

Berto slumped. "Geez. No confidence." Animated again, he added, "I'm doing my section like I'm that kid, George Shannon. Like 'Here's how it feels to suffer from malaria, and eat prairie dog while sweating your way up the Missouri River.'"

Kristi rolled her eyes. "Sounds swell. Let's be sure to re-enact it next summer."

Jack thought, *I'm going to do just that..* Then he glanced down at his worthless legs. *Well, I'm going to do it anyway.*

Kristi put her hand on top of his book stack. "These journals by men on the trip?"

He nodded. "The carpenter, the three sergeants, even a short journal by the one fellow who died." Jack studied her face as he answered. He couldn't figure out what was different about her since she came back from ICU. She seemed taller, more quiet and certain.

"How's Mrs. Peterson?" he asked.

"She's in Mr. Peterson's room five minutes of every hour. He hasn't talked to her for the last couple of visits."

"Is anybody there with her?" Berto asked.

Kristi nodded. "Her oldest son came. He said something about not finding his brother, yet, but I think she hopes he'll show up soon."

Jack thought about the missing brother, Malcolm, and Mr. Peterson's fear.

At that moment, Yolanda arrived with a tray carrying three bowls of glistening red Jell-O topped with whipped cream. She took a quick look at Jack and said, "Still in your chair? You become stronger."

He did feel stronger, suddenly – maybe because Kristi and Yolanda noticed.

Yolanda set down the tray. "These for all of you," she said.

"Boy are you a great nurse," Berto said.

She laughed and winked at Kristi before striding back to her job. Berto passed out the bowls and whooshed into the green chair to enjoy.

Kristi glanced at Jack's books while she ate. "Too bad Sacagawea couldn't write," she said, and swallowed a big batch of whipped cream.

Jack blinked. *What if Kristi had been Sacagawea?* He imagined how Sacagawea's mind would have drunk in the sight of stunning cliffs and rocky rivers. She had endured starvation, snow, rain and the heat of the deserts, along with all the men. She had courage and stamina, like Kristi. Jack watched Kristi take another bite of Jell-O.

"Since Sacagawea didn't write," she said around the cream, "maybe she told the story to her women friends, and they told it to their daughters."

"And to her baby boy," Jack said.

He watched Kristi take another bite, then scrape the bowl. Famished. Where did she eat? Kristi set the bowl down. He gazed at her tanned hand resting on the book and thought – Sacagawea.

"Eat mine, too," he said. "I'm full."

She chuckled. "Full of baloney. I'll get something downtown."

"Why are you going downtown?" The question popped out of his mouth.

She eyed him. "Why do you think?"

His face heated. There'd been too much secrecy, so out spilled his fears. "I think this Swede guy has got you into something nutso."

"You think I'd let some boy talk me into doing whatever?"

"I think you're desperate to get away from your mom."

Jack looked quickly at Kristi, waiting for her to blow up. She fiddled with the spoon in her empty bowl. After a moment, she tilted her head to one side, then the other, as if she were loosening tension in her neck. She spoke in a dangerously soft voice.

"You guys have never understood, but I'll try to tell you. My mother loves me. She's sick – alcohol leaves her wanting more alcohol. Sometimes, she's been able to stay off of it for weeks and weeks. And those are the most . . . well those are the weeks when I know that if this wine stuff didn't have a grip on her, she would be the best mom ever."

Jack had never heard this from her. It left him stunned. And at last he could see how it kept Kristi in chains. Because of a few rare weeks, Kristi could not leave. Only one person could free her and that person was slave to a bottle.

"And now," Kristi said, "Mom's asked to go to a hospital to dry out, but my father says, 'Why bother? The cure works for a while, and then she's right back in the booze.'"

"So," Jack heard the sarcasm in his voice, but he couldn't stop himself. "Why does all this love and concern send you out on the streets with Swede?"

She glared at him and stood up. "You assume if I'm sick at home that I'm drinking. You assume if I'm not at home, I'm out selling myself."

She was gone in no time, while Jack reeled back in shock. What a stupid jerk he was!

Berto was up and out the door, calling her. He ducked back into the room. "She's gone, down the stairs or something."

"Catch her."

"She'll be going to the square. I'm out of bus tickets."

Frantic, Jack scanned the room, as if to conjure tickets. His gaze fell on his clothes locker, still open since Yolanda got out his robe. "My jacket. Bus tickets in my pockets."

Berto grabbed the jacket, pulled the pocket contents out on Jack's bed, including a row of bus tickets. "Two," he said, waving them. "And let's hope there's nobody with a wheelchair waiting at the bus stop. Loading them in takes forever." He ran from the room.

Jack stared at the mess on his bed. Four more bus tickets poked out of the pile of pocket debris and fuzz. *Maybe Jack should escape from this asylum and take to the streets with her.*

He thought about Berto's parting remark. "Loading them in takes forever." He scooped up the mess and stuffed it back into his coat pocket. Then, without warning, his head drooped toward his chest. He was tired, confused, angry, scared and guilty.

Into his mind popped the images of all the people he loved – Mom, alone in their big house, Kristi alone on the streets, Berto trying to patch together a destroyed friendship, Dad exiled to Uncle Jackson's. He bet Jackson was about to choke on that situation.

He needed to pee – or shit. Jack wheeled away from the locker side of his bed and headed toward the bathroom. He spent raging minutes banging around in his wheelchair, trying to force it through the door and toward the toilet. Once in the bathroom, he attempted to stand long enough to get from the chair to the throne. As he pushed his body up with his arms, his legs began to give out.

He refused to fall on the floor again. Grabbing at the toilet seat on the way down, his arms hit the porcelain, a rock-hard smack that jolted his left arm up into his chest. His right foot caught under his left, twisting painfully. He barely managed to pull himself up over the toilet. Staring down into the water, he thought he might as well puke.

Not much came out. But his chest hurt. A lot. He yanked the neck of the pajama top and found he'd pulled apart three half-inch sections of the thin skin that had formed over his incision. He stared at his bleeding chest and the scar where it disappeared into the bandages. *I'm a kid, but I had a heart operation.*

Jack gazed out of the bathroom at Mr. Peterson's bed – nearly the view he'd had two nights ago. The bathroom floor wasn't any warmer than the floor in the hall.

I saved Mr. Peterson. He's hanging onto life.

Good.

Hanging by a thin thread.

Not good.

And Peterson's son, Malcolm.

Still gone. Like Kristi. On the streets – dangerous for a girl who looks like Kris. Scary.

Dad lives with his brother. Out of heaven into – what? Not hell.

Why didn't Dad just take himself to a motel? He certainly could have afforded it.

He wanted to ask his mother what he could do to make it up to Kristi. But Mom kicked Dad out.

Her advice is as good as dog drool.

And here sprawled her favorite son, the brilliant and scrawny Jack, drumming up energy to pull himself back into the wheelchair. He guessed that was a positive step. He wanted to get well so he could fix the mess for Kristi, and for Mom and Dad.

Maybe Dad was right – the doctors were on the wrong track. Exercise always worked before. Why not now?

Exercise number one – get up: Jack pulled his feet under him. With his hands, he placed his soles flat on the tile floor. He could get a little traction from his calluses – what calluses he had left. He yanked the wheelchair directly in front of him and set the brake on the wheel he could reach.

Jack tried to turn the chair to give him access to the other brake, but it was too far and too hard. He raised his arms and grabbed both armrests. He pulled himself upward, working to push the wheel chair solidly into the floor, keeping it stationary. He wasn't sure what he'd do if he succeeded. He tried to imagine traveling with his chest in the chair seat and his face against the backrest. Not likely to get far.

Heck! He'd figure something out.

The far wheel, where the brake wasn't set, began to roll. In slow motion, the chair pivoted away from him. His feet held their place on the floor, but his body stretched to keep up with the chair. As he fell, he glanced down and saw the metal foot rests coming toward his face. In a last burst of energy, he pushed against the chair arms, thrusting his body backward, away from the footrests. The chair continued to wheel in a circle as he fell. He dropped his hands to keep his head from landing on the tile. He folded, protecting his incision with one hand and his head with the other, like a gymnast – tuck and roll.

Big jagged pain, but . . . no broken bones.

Not giving up! he promised himself.

The chair made a half circle and whapped him in the knee. His eyes gave him a wild light show, the colors of his own agony.

"Jack?" That voice was Bill Martin. "What the hell?" Bill's face appeared at the edge of the bathroom door. "Hey guy, that's no way to take a dump."

Suddenly, Jack couldn't stop laughing. It hurt his chest, his head, the shoulder he'd landed on. It even hurt the knee that probably had permanent tire tracks on it, but he couldn't stop. The whole situation was too whacko.

Bill knelt down beside him, grinning. Yet his quick actions and knitted brow told Jack Bill was worried. "You must have been desperate to get somewhere," he said, testing for cuts on Jack's head and then down his chest.

"Oh," Bill discovered the blood and opened the pajama top to find the small tears in the incision. He reached over Jack's head and pulled the nurses' call button.

"Jack, you've got to learn to ask for what you need." He pumped the button again. "Damn, get in here somebody."

Jack, stifling the last of his laughter, stared up at the button. He'd never even noticed it.

"For Peterson . . . should have . . . used that."

Bill glanced at him, then at the button. "Instead of the gummed up button on Peterson's bed? Huh-uh! You were closer to the hall than the bathroom."

Yeah, Jack thought. I did the right thing. *Peterson is still alive.*

"Bill," he asked. "Could you just put me on the toilet for a minute?"

Bill looked startled. "Sure."

"And call off the cavalry. I'm going to get back in bed and start getting well."

"It's a deal," Bill said. "Except that by hospital regulations, I've got to have somebody check you out."

"So check me out after I pee."

"Done," Bill said, and lifted him onto the toilet seat.

Fifteen minutes later, Jack leaned against his pillow feeling groggy as Dr. Ambrose' heels clicked into the room.

"You always come when I can't visit." Jack said. He knew it sounded silly. He figured they'd put meds in his IV to make him sleepy.

"I hear you've been a tough guy too many times this week," she said, taking a look at his pupils.

He liked the perfume she had on. "You got a date?"

"I would have if my patients stayed in bed." She felt his pulse. "Yolanda tells me your arms are strong but your legs are mush."

"Steamed noodles."

She laughed. It was a nice, soft laugh. He thought he smiled, but he was so sleepy he wasn't sure. And she probably didn't see the smile anyway. She checked out the rips in his incision.

"Jack," she said, "we're trying to get you back on track here. Not running, but at least upright and gaining weight."

"When does it start working?" He closed his eyes. Maybe he could just listen and save his strength.

"First, you've got to start leading a quieter life. With all this activity, your CPK numbers have shot up. And that was before today's incident in the bathroom."

"Big numbers?"

"A huge leap." She took the stethoscope from her neck. "Dr. Crescent and I were almost ready to send you home before the night you had to crawl to the hall."

"How is Mr. Peterson this afternoon?" It seemed long ago since Yolanda wheeled him up to Intensive Care.

Dr. Ambrose was silent while she listened to his heart. Then she folded her stethoscope and said, "Mr. Peterson? Doctor Crescent is also his heart doctor. She says he's a bull. He'll fight to live."

"Good," Jack said. Then, because he wasn't sure she heard, he said it again, louder. "Thass good."

"You're still in working order, but you seem to be fading, so I'll tell you this again tomorrow. I've called your mom about putting you on an intravenous medicine. It will help bring down that CPK number."

"Why?"

"Methotrexate is stronger than the medicine you've been taking. And it works sometimes when the other fails."

"Is that what's making me groggy?"

"No. That's pain medicine. And you've just thrown yourself at the can. You're tired."

"When do we start this new junk?"

"We'd start that tonight, but there's a little glitch to get over first."

Glitch, he thought. One little glitch between me and big-time medicine taking. He didn't even want to ask how long a guy had to keep taking the stuff. "Intravenous," he said, "Thass needles and tubes."

"Yes, it is."

"Can't exercise with tubes."

"You want to lay off exercising for a while, anyway."

"Want to get well, though."

"I want you well, too. Go to sleep. I'll talk to you about this tomorrow."

"You smell nice. Your date wait for you?"

She chuckled. "My husband is reading in the lobby. Good night, Jack."

He drifted toward sleep while her heels clicked out of his room. It wasn't until she was gone that he realized he had lots to do before anybody hooked him up to machines again. He'd have to wake himself up and get started.

CHAPTER 30

During the night, Jack smelled Mom's special perfume – paint pigment. Her hand covered his. He ought to feel guilty for making her spend another night awake and watchful. After all, it was his own anger that had put him on the bathroom floor. He should wake up and send her home. Instead, he touched her fingertips with his thumb to thank her before he slept.

But he couldn't sleep, because Dad started whispering.

"Ali, don't let them put that medicine in him," Dad said. "The list of side effects would make you vomit."

"I've seen that list, too. I think we need to discuss it with Jack."

Jack opened his eyes just wide enough to watch his father frown at Mom.

"He's a kid," Dad said.

"A kid who makes decisions about risk every time he climbs," Mom said.

His father stuffed his hands in his pockets. He rolled his head from side to side as if ridding his neck of tension. He did it just like Kristi did. "So okay," Dad said, "we talk with Jack. When is that lady doctor available?"

"Her name is Dr. Ambrose. She'll be here tomorrow noon."

"Tomorrow noon, then," his father said. "Now you need to get some rest. He's finally sleeping quietly."

"In a while," Mom said. "You go tell Jackson. He and Samara are worried about Jack, too."

"No," he said. "I'm not letting you walk to that parking lot alone. I want to know you're safe."

Her head drooped a moment. Then she slipped her hand from Jack's and stood up. "Thank you for worrying. I'll walk out with you."

She leaned over and kissed Jack on the forehead, whispering, "We do love you, Jack. We do love."

We do love what?

Their conversation wasn't meant for him, so Jack said nothing as she kissed him. A moment later, he felt a hand on his hair. There was something funny about the way it lay there – an odd angle and a heavy weight. When he opened his eyes to see what it was, his parents were heading toward the door, stiffly apart, their hands in their pockets.

Maybe that was Dad's hand. No way. He never does stuff like that. Then Jack remembered Dad rubbing his feet the other night – was that yesterday? A week ago?

. . .

Jack shifted in his bed as sunrise hit his face. A voice in the hall had awakened him – not a loud voice, but a voice that touched his memory, and made him struggle to become alert.

A short, round lady bustled in. Her navy blue suit was creased in places where the cleaners never crease suits. The collar of her starched white blouse lay half in and half out of her jacket lapels. At the edges of her pixie face, her white hair curled with no apparent plan, but her stride looked determined. Her black leather shoes were the kind that tied high on her arch – the toughest footwear he'd seen this side of hiking boots.

"You're Jack Huntington?" she asked – or maybe announced – he wasn't certain which. He tried to rise to greet her, but she waved him down again.

"Bill Martin's worried about you," she said. That surprised Jack.

She held out her hand. "I'm Sister Kathleen Marie."

"Oh," he said, feeling awkward. "You're the prayer lady."

The nightly intercom voice in shit-kicker footwear; there went his freshman-English image of Chaucer's dainty nun.

She smiled as she sat on the chair to his left. "You feel like talking about Mr. Peterson?"

Wham!

She came with bad news. He looked away. "I don't want him to die."

"He's alive. He's as well as when you were there yesterday afternoon with Miss Garcia."

"Garcia?"

"Yolanda."

Oh yes, he remembered. "Has she seen him today?"

Sister Kathleen shook her head. "This is her day off, but I went by Intensive Care."

"Has he talked yet?"

"A few phrases during the first night. Then quiet. Sometimes such deep quiet means the patient is reserving strength to fight for recovery."

"How can you tell?"

"You can't," she said. "You just pray and hope."

"That's why they hire you, huh?"

She smiled again. "Dr. Ambrose says your folks are having a hard time with this hospital stuff."

Jack felt his eyebrows rise in surprise. "Geez! You dive right for the finish line, don't you?"

She nodded. "No point avoiding hard things."

Avoiding. Not talking. That's what his family was good at.

"They were here last night," he said. She didn't need to know they didn't go home to the same house.

"Yes," she said. "I saw them walk out about two in the morning."

"You mean you say those ten o'clock prayers and then you don't go to bed?"

She chuckled, her small button of a nose wrinkling. "I prowl the halls most nights."

"Finding germs and demons to exorcise?"

Sister Kathleen Marie studied him. "Sometimes," she said, "it's the demons in our heart that keep us from getting well."

No demons here. He moved his gaze away from hers. *Nothing a guy can't handle.*

He tried to think of something to say, to get her off the subject of demons. "That Yolanda's a great nurse," he said, attempting to sound as if the thought just occurred to him. "She used her lunch hour to take me up to Mrs. Peterson.

Sister Kathleen nodded. As she talked, she straightened the things on his night stand – books, water bottle, a roll of bandage tape the nurses must have left when they fixed his chest last night. "Yes," she said, "Yolanda will be very good. She tells me you and your Dad are having a tough time."

He jerked as if she'd hit him. "Why does she think that?"

"We've both sat in the lounge with your parents," she said. "Have you talked to your father about that day on the mountain?"

Twisting to one side, Jack eased his tired back muscles into a new position making it impossible to look Sister Kathleen Marie in the eye.

"Dad wants Dr. Ambrose to stop my medicine. I guess that's why Mom told Dad to take a hike."

Behind him, she sat in silence. He wished he hadn't mentioned Mom kicking out Dad. Sister Kathleen Marie was sitting back there either shocked or disapproving.

Long moments passed with no comment from her. He thought he must have left her speechless. But after a while she said, "Jack, you nearly died."

The memory of the night his sternum was cracked open flooded his chest with renewed pain. He barely heard what she said next.

"Now that you're with us again, there's something I hope you'll do for yourself."

"From this bed?" He hadn't meant to sound so harsh.

"Best place. In bed we can't escape thinking."

He waited.

"Do the thing you would regret not doing," she said.

He opened his mouth to ask what the heck she meant, but she spoke first.

"And now, the prayer lady would like to pray with you."

He had to see if she was laughing at him, so he rolled to his back. She had her eyes closed. Her chin leaned into her clasped hands.

"Dear Lord," she said, "thank you for Jack's growing health." Her tone made him think she talked to the Almighty over turkey sandwiches at lunch. "Please give Jack your support as he faces his greatest fear."

Jack bristled. What was she talking about?

"And now, Lord, please help this old woman totter back to her office."

Jack glanced at her again.

"Amen," she said.

He studied her round face, wrinkled by a lifetime of smiling. Bright-eyed. Sure-footed. Old, yes, but no way was she tottering. She raised her head. Her face radiated warmth and care for him.

"Good morning, Jack. I'm glad you're alive and ready."

"Good morning, Sister Kathleen Marie." Without thinking, he reached out a hand. She held it in hers, not a shake, but a clasp, offering strength.

She nodded to him, and whispered, "God be with you." And then she walked out his door.

He lay back, feeling the weight of her charge. "Do the thing you would regret not doing."

He allowed his thoughts to skitter into images of his father, upright and hearty, but smiling at someone else, someone taller than a wheelchair. There followed images of himself hulking across an empty room, awkwardly tangling his legs with a pair of heavy crutches; images of his mother, coming home from work and tossing her brief-case on the dining chair before calling out a greeting to her aging son. There was no one else to come home to.

The heaviness in Jack's chest congealed into a single boulder of granite. He tried not to put a name to the problem. Jack swallowed. Tears oozed from his eyes as he told himself he had to face the facts. His father could not change, could not understand or love him this way.

But he had to make one last effort to talk to him. He had to be certain before accepting Dad's withdrawal. That was the thing Sister Kathleen would have him do. It was what Peterson had said, too.

CHAPTER 31

By the baking smells, Jack figured it was about eight in the morning – time for breakfast delivery on the cardiac ward. He started to stretch his arms when his hand ran into something hard on top of his covers – one of his books.

Groping about, he found that someone had left a narrow card between the pages. He slipped it out. The script on the bookmark shone a glossy purple. *Patience, Perseverance, Prayer.*

Sister Kathleen, he thought, and smiled to himself.

A rustle of fabric caught his attention. When he turned his head, he discovered his father standing at the window, staring out at the one tree and the smokestack of the hospital energy plant. He hadn't expected to see Dad before noon.

Jack watched as Dad fiddled with the shade cord, then reached into his pocket for his old Hand Spring electronic calendar. He tapped on the digital screen and left a message for a colleague, or maybe a reminder for himself. He re-pocketed the tool and fished his pen from his shirt, unscrewed the barrel, emptied the cartridge and spring onto his hand, and then put the whole thing back together.

No wonder he climbs mountains, Jack thought.

"Hey, Dad," Jack's voice came out too loud. His father whipped about, every muscle on alert as if he'd been attacked in an alley.

Jack laughed. "Sheesss! Lay off the Starbucks, Pop. You're a nervous wreck."

His father's smile was slow coming. He tilted his head – his equivalent of a shrug. "Jack, you look great."

A bald lie. Jack saw intent wariness tinged with calculation as his father's gaze moved down Jack's legs. "You must be feeling one hundred percent," Dad said.

There it was – the ever-optimistic assessment. "One hundred percent better than yesterday," he agreed. He couldn't face this expectation every day – the idea that some easy solution would magically make Jack normal overnight. The son of Mallory Huntington suddenly becomes an athlete again.

His father smacked his palms together and then gave them a friction rub in preparation for action. "They got all that crud cleaned out of your system."

"What crud?"

"The steroids and all that."

"What about the new medicine the doctors think we ought to use?"

"I told them 'No'."

Jack shoved up on his elbow. The tightness of fresh bandages reminded him of his adventures with the toilet, but he braced himself to have his say about medicine. His hand bumped into the book. The purple bookmark glinted up at him.

"Patience, perseverance, prayer."

He took a deep breath for patience, and asked, "Why did you say 'No'?"

"I did look up Polymyositis. That doctor . . . None of these docs know much about this disease. It's pretty rare. They're guessing."

Patience be damned.

"Dr. Ambrose is not guessing. Who told you that?"

"Bradley. And the websites. I've done a lot of reading."

Bradley again. "Bradley's your friend, right?" Jack deliberately stared at his father's nose, not his eyes.

"Of course."

"And I'm your son."

"What the hell are you getting at?" Dad moved slightly, obviously trying to get eye contact and stare Jack down. Jack kept his gaze on Dad's nose.

"Your son," he said slowly, "wants you to talk to his doctor. You got that? My doctor, not your friend."

"What difference does it make?"

Now, he had enough courage – and anger – to look Dad in the eye and tell him. "You say nobody knows about this disease," Jack said. "Yet you did some research on the Internet. So you know Dr. Ambrose's name. She's quoted everywhere. If anybody understands this disease, it's her."

"I know its name and I know her name, but there is a lot of controversy about how to deal with it."

"I have a disease. Dr. Ambrose is the national expert. Other docs come to her, write to her, call her. So I want her advice about what I should be doing – not Dr. Bradley's."

Dad's jaw worked. Jack waited, gaze not wavering. His neck was getting tired of holding his head up, but he couldn't back down now.

"Your friend, Doctor Bradley, told you I have a phobia about testing myself. So you decide to believe him, right?"

"He believes you . . ."

"Your friend is a lousy doctor who doesn't want to admit he missed the diagnosis. And you are the kind of dad who would rather think his kid is nuts than admit his kid has a disease, right?"

"Not nuts, just unready to . . ."

"That's a shitload of excuses for your own fear, Dad."

"My fear?" Dad forced thin laughter.

"Okay, I messed up on the mountain," Jack said. "Okay, I've got next to no working muscles in my legs, but my arms are still functioning. Can you be glad about that?"

"So, you give up and play wheelchair basketball the rest of your life?"

"What would be wrong with that?" Jack asked.

"Mere weeks ago you were climbing mountains. Are you going to settle for less?"

"And if I settle – if I haven't any choice, where will you be?"

His father slammed his fist on the bedside table. The roll of forgotten bandage tape jumped. "By God, they've got you, don't they? Convinced you to give up." The impact of his fist rattled the whole table. Most of Jack's books fell off, smacking the floor. The tape rolled toward the edge.

"Who's got me?" Jack asked, ignoring the books.

Dad glared at him. "Your mom. That doctor. I'll bet even that numbskull Jackson has been in here talking to you."

Jack's heart stopped beating, and then it whammed into action so hard it made his head roar. Now he had the answer to his question – an answer he wished he'd never figured out.

If he couldn't climb, he'd be crossed off Dad's list – no more a part of Dad's life than Uncle Jackson. His chest ached. Without thinking beyond the next minute he spat out the forbidden question. "How did Jackson manage to piss you off so good?"

Dad glowered. The muscles in his neck tightened and his nostrils flared. "That is strictly between Jackson and me."

"No, it isn't. It's between you and Mom."

His father blinked and jerked back. "You haul yourself out of my business."

"Fine, Dad. You haul yourself out of my business. Go climb a mountain."

Dad reeled back against the door jamb, stared at Jack a moment then turned and left the room.

. . .

A half hour of regret and second thoughts made Jack realize he could not get through to his dad. He would have to face life disappointing the man. Loneliness invaded his body. He closed his eyes and lay back against his pillows.

Jack's hand landed on the book. Bernard de Voto, *Journals* . . .

On that trip, Captain Clark handed out lashes for plenty of mistakes. But with Shannon, he never mentioned either apology or punishment. He'd said merely, "We were greatly relieved to find our missing man sitting on the river bank."

Why couldn't Dad be greatly relieved to have his son alive, whether he was well or flat on his back?

Jack stared at the plastic cover on Mr. Peterson's mattress. *I'm afraid I'll die before I find my youngest son. As soon as I said those things, I wanted to take them back. I don't want it to end this way.*

Jack whispered, "Don't end this way."

He stared at the door and thought about his view from this room – a narrow view of the backs of people who came to see him for a few minutes each day: Mom and Dad, stiff and apart; Yolanda carrying an empty tray; Nurse Edna Sawyer, her shoes squeaking as she whipped around corners; Dr. Ambrose, who must think he had a screw loose after all those comments about how nice she smelled; Bill Martin, off to help another patient build muscle; Uncle Jackson, quiet, calm, sure; Sister Kathleen, caring and direct.

And then, Berto trying to catch up with Kristi who ran from Jack's questions and his assumptions, to hide on the hard streets.

I don't want it to end this way, he thought. And then an idea flashed into his misery.

He yanked open the drawer to his nightstand and pulled out his watch. *Nine o'clock in the morning.*

"Dang," he muttered. "At noon, everybody comes in here to decide whether I get hooked up to those IV medicines. After they do that – If they do that –I'm stuck here for who knows how long.

"It's not going to end that way," he said.

CHAPTER 32

Pulling the roll of bandaging tape from the edge of his bedside table, Jack stuffed it under his pillow, out of sight. Out of the table drawer, he pulled his Buck all-purpose knife and hid it under the pillow with the bandages. Holding tightly to the bed rail, he reached for the walker, still folded against the Naugahyde chair.

He dragged the lightweight metal toward himself, and pulled it into his lap. He leaned back into his pillow and pulled the walker across himself to the window side of his bed. Unfolded, and firmly set down on the floor, it provided a frame on which to lean. He lowered his feet to that side of the bed. Next, he pulled his rear end off the bed and put all his weight on the walker.

His chest gave him little knife-point stabs where the skin had pulled apart the night before, but he saw it wasn't opening any further. He couldn't believe how mushy his legs felt. They forced nearly all his weight onto his arms. Pushing the walker and then lurching after it, he crossed the two feet to his closet. He leaned heavily, bent down, twisted his head to one side and grabbed the door handle with his teeth. Two tries and he yanked the door open, only to have it bang on the frame of the walker and ricochet shut again.

After jerking the walker a few inches away from the closet front, he had to bend even further to get a grip with his teeth. His feet began to slide out from under him, but he held tight to the walker bar, pulled at the door with his teeth and got the closet open again. At last, his clothes were revealed.

Mom had buttoned every button on his shirts and jacket. Maddening neatness. There was no way he could stand here long enough to unbutton everything. He had to pull the hangers out.

Jack centered his left hand in the walker bar, then, shifting his weight to that arm, he reached inside and pulled up on the shirt hanger. It lifted from the bar. He dropped the shirt over the front of the walker and grabbed the metal walker to steady himself.

A moment later, he lifted his jacket hanger. Another grab of the walker, another steadying and he was ready to deal with the jeans – neatly folded and draped over the round clothes bar. As he pulled up on the jeans, he realized that one of the belt loops had caught in a neighboring hanger. He had to yank extra hard to pull that hanger off the clothes bar and free the belt loop. The momentum of his pull sent him staggering backward. One leg tangled in the walker. The hanger, suddenly freed, flew into the window, creating a loud whap. Jack landed in a heap on the sunny side of the bed. The walker, with its burden of clothes, folded and fell in front of him.

Leaning back against the metal bed frame, he took a deep breath. The floor was becoming way too familiar. His rear end wouldn't hurt so much if either he or the floor had more padding. After shaking out his arms and testing his legs for breaks, he decided he wasn't in bad shape, considering. And he decided to use the time to get dressed.

Exchanging the pajama shirt for his plaid flannel proved easy. The pajama pants came off with little trouble, but the jeans going on was entirely different. His feet tangled in the loose threads of the hems where he'd constantly walked on them. Wishing he'd listened to his mother about not getting such long pants, he pulled his big toe out of the threads.

His chest hurt. Just the incision, he thought. Can't lean over like that. It pulls the skin. He looked down at his chest, unbuttoning the shirt to see what damage he'd done.

No blood. Good.

He decided to make a last effort on the pants and pulled them over his calves and up onto his thighs. But things got rough after that. He had to lie on his back and wiggle the jeans up and up. This would have been easy if he'd been able to push his hips off the floor, but he had little help from his legs. The pants had to go on one inch at a time.

At last, he snapped and zipped the blamed things. Then he had to rest against the cool floor and start to figure out how to pull himself back into the bed. As he lay there, he noticed that during his argument with Dad his books had fallen open under the bed. Stretching out his arm, he snagged the hard cover of one volume. He heard the squeak of Nurse Edna Sawyer's shoes.

"Jack?"

Might as well pretend this was intentional. "Yo. Under here," he said.

"Not again!"

"Just trying to retrieve a book I dropped."

Her face appeared under the opposite side of the bed frame. "Looks like you dropped the lot of them." She began gathering books that were closer to her.

"Sure did," he said, "Table went left. Books went right." Gathering in his volume, he glanced at the open page. Captain Lewis had just spotted a lone man on horseback. He hoped the man was Shoshone and would sell him horses.

Maybe I can buy a horse myself, Jack thought. Any transportation would improve on this walker.

"Mrs. Sawyer," he said. "Could you bring me a wheel chair?"

"Doesn't look like you've even had breakfast yet."

"I always get meals last. I'm way out in the wilderness at the end of this hallway. As soon as I've eaten, I'd like to take myself a ride. See the sights in the hospital."

She stood. He couldn't see her face any more, but he could hear her smoothing down her uniform skirt. "Why are you dressed?"

He had to think fast. "I want to look good for Mom," he said. "She's seen that old pair of pajamas way too much."

Nurse Sawyer studied his shirt. "If you learn to button that shirt straight, she'll like what she sees. You clean up pretty good for a back-woods mountain climber."

He looked at his buttons – all kitty-wampus. Jack chuckled and started on the buttons again, thinking, *She buys it. I might make this story work after all.*

"Will someone come to push you?" she asked.

Will she never stop finding the holes in my story?

"I'm thinking Mom will be here sometime before noon, but I want to see if I can get myself up and down the hall a little bit first – kind of surprise her."

Suddenly, Mrs. Sawyer stood near his head. "I'll be kind of surprised if you don't need help getting in bed again." She had her hands on her hips, but an indulgent smile in her normally unreadable face.

"A little help into the wheel chair would be accepted."

She shook her head as if exasperated with his floor explorations. But then she waved her hand to indicate he could have *whatever*.

"First let me take this useless walker out of the way." She bent over him, flipped his jacket onto his chest, and then pulled the walker up and over him as if she were dead-lifting his barbell. He ducked.

"Coward," she said. When he glanced up at her face, she was actually grinning. "I lift patients and mattresses and all kinds of things heavier than this piece of scrap-metal."

"The Olympic committee is looking for you."

"They are thirty years too late," she said. "I'll be right back."

Within half an hour, with the help of Nurse Sawyer and a new aide, Jack had eaten his breakfast, had his shoes tied on him and sat in a wheel chair with his feet up on the footrests. When Nurse Sawyer began to fuss with his bed, Jack decided to distract her. Didn't want her to find the knife, the tape and the bandage roll he'd hidden under the pillow. He started making sculpture out of the metal hangers that once held his clothes. First to appear was a crude crescent moon.

She stopped bed straightening and glanced at his sculptures. "Your mom will like that one." She picked up his breakfast tray and headed out the door.

After Nurse Sawyer left, he fished in his jacket pocket and found what he needed – a folded up string of four bus tickets. He had more than enough for what he wanted to do. He reached under his pillow for the knife.

Using the can-opening blade, he cut part of the third hanger and twisted it into two eyes and a frowning eyebrow for the face on one of his hanger sculptures. He wrapped the metal of the two wobbly sculptures to the upper armatures at the back of his wheel chair. The face on one side, and the moon on the other hung slightly above his head.

He fished the bandaging tape out of his bed pillow and bound the sculptures to the wheelchair handles. Then he took out the paper and paints his mother had brought and made two signs. He was thankful she'd bought water-color paint instead of oil. It dried completely in minutes.

As soon as the signs were ready, he tucked them inside the cover of a book that he stashed next to him in the wheelchair seat. He stuffed the rest of the tape in one jacket pocket, the bus tickets in the other. Ready at last, he rolled himself out into the hallway.

The doorway to the hall was a lot easier negotiating than yesterday's trip to the bathroom.

Jack's arm muscles heated up as he rolled into the elevator. then another fellow in a wheelchair moved into the small box. The man pushed himself backwards into the small space, then grimaced as their wheels locked. They each adjusted so that Jack was packed into one corner and the other guy sat near the control buttons.

"Lobby?" the guy asked.

"Yeah," Jack said. "Where's the bus stop to downtown?"

"Lovejoy Street. Right outside the big double doors."

The door opened two more times, but people waved their elevator on, willing to wait for the next trip rather than chance getting tangled with their spokes.

As they left the elevator and moved toward the front doors, no one seemed to pay attention to Jack. He realized that dressed in street clothes, he looked like any other out-patient on wheels. As he and his elevator companion headed onto the entry walk, Jack felt like an entrant in a new form of roller derby.

Once outside, the fellow in the other wheel chair turned left, saying over his shoulder, "Luck with the bus." Then he whizzed away. The first bus stop hovered too close to the hospital entrance for Jack to feel he'd safely escaped. By the time he pushed himself three blocks further and out of sight of the hospital doors, his arms were rags. He let them hang for a couple of minutes before he looked up at the bus signs.

CHAPTER 33

Berto was correct. Passengers didn't like waiting for a wheel chair to load onto the bus. Two people arrived at Jack's stop. They were surprised to find a wheelchair rider three blocks from the hospital. The two glanced at his chair, at each other, and soon walked away. After the others left, he sweated alone in the October heat of a Chinook wind, listening as the red and yellow tree leaves hushed against each other. The bus finally lumbered to the corner. Its door hissed open. The wheelchair lift clacked and squealed out and down until it rested on the sidewalk.

Jack believed everyone for miles heard the noise. At first, the driver assumed he'd been through the boarding routine, but when Jack had trouble pushing the chair onto the lift, the driver came down and helped lock it onto the elevator platform.

Inside the bus, Jack asked to be let off at Pioneer Courthouse Square. He noticed other passengers' curious glances. A couple nearby stopped kissing and watched the driver strap his chair into place.

The bus crossed Burnside Street and lumbered into downtown Portland.

At Pioneer Courthouse Square, the driver came back and unhooked the straps. Jack asked, "Where do I catch the bus to return to the hospital?"

"Over on Sixth Avenue." The guy's eyebrows pulled together, giving him a puzzled look. "You on the lam from Trinity Hospital?"

Jack decided to bluff it out. "Yeah. Runaway from the maternity ward."

"Sure!" the guy chuckled. "Escape from the nursery . . ."

"Yup. Crawled out of my incubator," Jack said as he moved down the aisle toward the door. "Left my twin behind. No sense of adventure."

Now the bus driver was laughing. "Was it you or the twin who created the hanger art?"

As Jack rolled onto the lift, he glanced at the frowning face over his left shoulder and the crescent moon on the right. "My twin did these. For his age, he's pretty good with his hands."

"Here you go," the fellow said, still smiling as he lowered the elevator to sidewalk level. "Catch the Number Seventeen across Sixth Avenue to return. Have a good time."

Now that he'd made the guy laugh, Jack felt less helpless. He twisted to the side and figured how to release his wheels from the elevator ramp. Rolling off the lift unassisted, he felt like he could do this thing he'd set out to accomplish. He could find Kristi.

Another wheelchair buzzed down the sidewalk toward him. The fellow in the chair was older. His cheeks and mouth were nearly hidden by a red and gold bush of a beard and a handlebar mustache. Jack watched how he maneuvered, not using his arms to push at all, because he had a motor. With his fingers, he toggled a switch on his chair arm to turn right and left. He could stop within inches of a pedestrian, but mostly he just moved forward and people opened a path for him. Driving as if he had the right of way, he whizzed past Jack, halted and then backed up.

"Where'd you get that antique?" he asked.

Startled, Jack said, "I borrowed this from Trinity Hospital."

"Yeah? That the best they could do?"

For some reason, Jack felt the need to defend his hospital. "This is my workout chair," he improvised. "Supposed to build my arm muscles. Physical therapy."

"Build up your arms. Tear down your back."

"I suppose."

"Kid, don't try going up that steep sidewalk in that chair. The cracks alone will give you sciatica."

"Where's the best path?"

"You looking to pick up chicks with all that art work?"

"I'm looking for two friends. I was hoping the hanger art would make them notice."

"Oh, they'll notice. Just drive down to the east end of the block, go straight onto the bricks and park in the center of the plaza. They'll find you."

"Thanks," Jack said.

"And next time, bring your physical therapist. I bet he never tried to negotiate this place in one of those old chairs. Idiot idea."

Jack chuckled. The fellow reached out his right hand. It looked as if, years ago, it had been fused into a crabbed fist.

"Name's Joe Parker," he said, watching Jack stare at his hand.

Jack reached and shook the tight claw. "Jack Huntington." The hand was warm, but so closed it was hard to find anything to grip.

"You'll get used to it, Jack – the wheelchair I mean."

Jack felt color flood his face. He had thought Joe was talking about getting used to shaking hands with him.

"I . . . I did figure out the bus lift," Jack said.

"Passengers give you a bad time about holding up progress?"

"No. Just left for other stops."

"Don't let the bastards wear you down. If pedestrians stare over your head, you stare at their belly button."

"Why?"

"Make 'em wonder if their fly is open."

Jack snorted.

"No kidding. You watch. Their hand goes to their belt buckle as they move out of your way."

"I'll do it."

"See you around, Jack."

He barely had time to say, "See you, Joe," before the fellow raced off. Jack watched Joe's progress across the street. He seemed to have no fear of being hit by busses. As soon as Jack rolled into the square, he felt conspicuous. Most people his age were hanging around the edges of the plaza near the bus stops and the street vendors. He checked out each cluster of kids, but didn't see Kristi, or anyone else he knew.

Of course, most kids he knew didn't live down here. They lived at home and went to school. He wanted to live at home too, but it would never be the same again. At that moment, he understood Kristi a little better. Her home, and her mom were more responsibility than she could handle. If he found her, he had nothing to offer but an apology, and maybe his mother – he knew Mom could help her.

Of course, Kristi would only be found if she wanted to be found. Sitting here in this chair wasn't going to convince her. So he reached into his jacket and pulled out his roll of bandage tape. From the book he kept beside him, he took his two painted signs. Twisting in his chair, he attached one sign to the frowning face sculpture. In big blue letters it said,

Kristi, I'm a jackass. I'm sorry.

It fluttered in the light wind, but hung as he'd hoped, stiff enough to be readable from a long distance.

Then he attached the other sign to the crescent moon. Its red letters spelled out,

Malcolm Peterson, your dad apologizes. Ask me.

He didn't really believe Malcolm Peterson might be here, he'd just thought he ought to give him a try.

Jack glanced around and saw that kids were looking at him, but pretending they weren't. Sidelong glances swooped away when he caught them staring. He heard them whispering to each other. A couple of kids sniggered and then made a hee-haw donkey voice at him. Well, he figured he deserved it. He had been a jackass with all his assumptions about what Kristi was doing down here.

Jack wheeled toward the middle of the plaza, pretending to be interested in the names on the bricks – Cliff and Willie Williams, James Williams, Linda Williams, Al and Trudie Williams. It looked like one very prolific family helped pay for the plaza when it was built. He'd never heard any mention of Huntington bricks down here. He raised his head and gazed over the space. This was a huge city block and these bricks covered most of it. If there were Huntington bricks he'd never find them.

Quite a while later, he'd decided that names beginning with Mc or Mac won the prize for civic support when this place was built. He couldn't pretend to care about names on bricks any more. And still there was no sign of Kristi.

He fried in the sun. Reflected heat from the bricks boiled his feet. A blister formed on the heel of each hand. He figured people who use wheelchairs all the time, must build up calluses, or wear heavy gloves.

Jack had begun to believe he'd never hear from Kristi or anyone who knew her. People seemed to avoid him and his signs. So, he wheeled himself into the shade of the one small building at the edge of the plaza. From this little patch of cool space he watched a few kids selling things to each other. The way they did it, any policeman had to know it was drugs, but nobody seemed to be around to care.

For a second, he feared Kristi had gotten into that stuff. Then he caught himself. It was that kind of thinking that made her angry with him the last time she came to the hospital.

Shoppers walked through the plaza, headed from Nordstroms to Meier and Frank department store. People scurried out of office buildings and purchased coffee at the shop on the upper, western end of the block. On the east side of the plaza, busses stopped on Sixth Avenue. They seemed to inhale and disgorge passengers all at once. Every six or seven minutes, the MAX light-rail train whipped past the south side of the square, then screeched into its turn-around block. Soon it squealed back downhill past the north side of the square and off across the Willamette River again.

Kristi, please come talk.

On the corner across Sixth Avenue, a stocky man hawked *Street Roots*, the newspaper of the homeless community. Heading up that same sidewalk, five guys in suits, walked abreast, oblivious to anyone else in their path. Red-bearded Joe's wheelchair appeared in front of their phalanx. Two guys in the middle of the group nearly fell over him before they opened a path around the chair.

And as they continued down the block, each of the five checked his belt buckle.

Jack laughed.

From the tall clock on the tower of a white stone building, Jack saw it was almost noon. There'd been no sign of Kris. No one had even asked about his signs. Maybe he could be more like Joe. Go after what he wanted.

He wheeled himself toward a group of young kids. *Geez!* he thought, as he got closer, *they aren't even high school age yet. Do they all live on the streets?*

"Hi," he said to the nearest girl. She yanked the hem of her small yellow tee-shirt, popped her gum and turned away, but he kept talking to her back. "I'm looking for a friend, a girl named Kristi. Do you know her?"

She glanced at him, but kept moving. One of the boys near her said, "Why don't you pick on someone your own age?"

That stung. He wasn't trying to pick up this baby. "Kristi is my age," he said. "If you know her, tell her Jack has news for her."

The kid snicked his sign like he was flicking goobers from his finger. "Kristi don't talk to jackasses." The whole group laughed and turned away from him.

The next knot of kids he approached closed their group to keep him out of their circle. He kept asking, though, speaking to their backs, hoping someone would tell her about the guy with the stupid sign. A third hour passed with Jack asking after her or wheeling himself out into the sun for a few minutes so that he could be seen from everywhere on the plaza. When he couldn't stand the heat, he moved to the shade for a few minutes and then came back out.

At the end of a fourth hour, he knew he'd have to give up soon. His vision was beginning to blur from the glare of sun on brick. He'd sweated a lot and hadn't thought to bring a water bottle. Worst of all, his chest stitches pulled every time he wheeled the chair to a new location. Blood now showed through his shirt.

He fished in his pocket for a return ticket to the hospital. As he pulled his hand out, the tickets dropped to the ground. He lunged for them. A foot covered them before he could grab. Jack nearly fell out of the wheelchair.

"You claim these tickets, pip-squeak?"

As he jerked himself back into the seat, Jack couldn't see the person. The sun was directly behind him. He could tell he was a thin kid with stringy, brown hair. The fellow's short body stood just out of reach.

"Those are my tickets."

"Maybe. Maybe not. I found them on the ground."

"I need them to get back to the hospital."

The guy leaned down and grinned at him. "They let you out the psycho ward?"

"Yeah. I'm a berserker. Dangerous when not medicated." Even as he played the fool to keep the kid nearby and talking, Jack believed he'd seen the last of the tickets. He was going to have to wheel himself the whole two miles to the hospital.

"You want these little scraps, you have to take them, Berserker Man." The kid started to saunter away, but his first step was straight into the chest of a bigger boy.

"Hand me those, Jersey," the boy said.

Jack still couldn't see either of them very well because of the angle of the sun.

"Come on, Pete," the kid said. "I was just funnin'."

At the name Pete, Jack sat up straight. "Are you Swedish Pete?"

"Some call me that." As he answered, Pete took the tickets from Jersey's hand and shooed the kid away. "Why do you want to know?"

"Last time I came here, you were the only person who admitted you knew Kristi."

Pete came closer. When he stepped out of the sun, Jack could see he was the kid he remembered Kristi talking to – tall, quiet, dark-skinned with a thick afro that had gotten longer in the weeks since.

Pete studied him as well. "I never talked to someone in a wheelchair."

"I wasn't in a wheelchair then."

Pete tilted his head, searching Jack's face. "Oh, yeah. That mountain kid. You haven't been here in a month. How come?"

"I've been in the hospital."

Pete reached out and strummed the spokes on Jack's chair. "Hella bad luck. You weren't even limping much back then."

Jack felt bitterness rise in his throat. He'd thought he was so cool before the climb – so cool, and yet this guy remembered him as not limping *much*.

"Do you still see Kristi?" Jack asked.

"I see her." Pete flipped the end of Jack's sign. "What'd you do that makes you such a jackass, kid?"

Jack forced himself to look at Pete. Even in a ragged T-shirt and baggy pants he'd probably found at the Goodwill, the guy seemed to be a leader on the plaza. Jack remembered how fast Jersey handed over the tickets and beat it.

Pete crossed one foot in front and propped his worn Reebok on its torn toe, waiting for his answer. Jack decided this guy was his only chance, so he'd best be honest. "I said some pretty nasty things to her."

"Such as . . ."

"Stuff I'm not telling anyone else. I don't want every jerk down here to talk to her that way."

"You think you All That?" Pete had stiffened, glaring at Jack. "Think you can make her run away just for some piddling thing you said?"

"Not just me. But I sure didn't help her."

"I saw that other kid come down here looking for her – that stubby little guy."

"That's my friend, Berto. He's worried about her, too."

"He down here with a bad conscience, like you?"

Jack took a deep breath. *Patience, perseverance, prayer.* "He's the one who knocked me upside the head about what I did." Jack sat there, not letting his eyes move away from Pete's face. He saw Pete's stiffness vanish, and realized Pete used every tool to intimidate him. He wanted the deeper truth for Kristi's sake. After a moment, Jack asked, "Have you hurt her?"

Pete glanced down at his hands. "I expect I have. Tried not, but she's fragile – breakable, you know."

Jack winced. Not expecting that kind of insight, he'd been ready to accuse Pete of hiding Kris, or using her. Jack remembered exactly how fragile Kris was. Then he said, "I hope she'll talk to my mom. Get some help. Could you tell her that?"

"When I see her. Now this other sign you got here – tell me, who is this Malcolm Peterson?"

"I don't know him. His dad was my roommate in Trinity Hospital."

Pete's face went stone still. "Was your roommate?"

"He had a heart attack. He's in Intensive Care. He's not doing too good."

"Too well," Pete said, but he wasn't looking at Jack. That automatic correction was so much like his mom, that Jack felt a pang. Pete's attention was off in the distance for a second, not really a part of their conversation anymore. And then he turned his black eyes fully on Jack.

"I'm going to need a couple of these bus tickets," Pete said. "Can we call that pay for rescuing them?"

The abrupt change in tone took Jack by surprise. "Sure," he said. He wanted to ask why, but instead asked, "Will you talk to Kristi?"

"I'll talk. She might listen. I don't have much time." He tore off two bus tickets and handed the rest to Jack.

It came to Jack at that moment, the reason Swedish Pete was a thoughtful guy, a guy who took care of people and worried about them. Jack studied him, imagining an older man with cinnamon-dark skin, white hair, a laughing mouth and a soft mustache.

"You better get over there quick, Malcolm Peterson," he said.

The guy blinked in surprise, then gave Jack a quick, sad smile. "I'll go. Thanks."

Malcolm walked off, crossing the plaza so fast Jack barely had time to recognize the new feeling he had – a worried-brother sort of feeling. "Hurry," he whispered, as if to Malcolm, Swede. "Take the next bus."

As he said it, Jack knew he wanted to see his own father – needed to try one more time.

Chapter 34

Jack started toward the bus stop, but realized for the first time just how sweaty his shirt was. He'd been in the sun most of the day, and it had netted him one find – Malcolm Peterson. His body was drained, but his heart was too full to pay attention.

He wished he could go home, sleep, hear his mom's voice, his father's footsteps. But his father wasn't home any more. In the shade, he shivered in his sweat-wet shirt, so he wheeled into the sun. Out of the corner of his eye he caught a wave of motion in the crowd around the bus stop. He glanced over in time to see the kids break ranks to let someone through.

Swedish Pete, Malcolm, ran for the bus. He climbed on, handing over a ticket. The bus door squealed closed, the motor hissed, and the lumbering vehicle pulled away from the curb.

The route name at the back of the bus read "Forest Park and Audubon."

"Hey," Jack yelled. "Wrong bus. Take the Number Seventeen, the hospital bus!"

But Malcolm never heard him. Then Jack realized that Malcolm hadn't even hesitated about which bus to catch; he was going to hide in Forest Park. Even the police might never find him in that huge sanctuary.

Shivering, Jack slumped against the back of the chair. All the wet clung to him, a chill sank into his chest. The sun was low, too low to dry his shirt. He pushed his chair toward the bus stop, but his arms were limp as wilted spinach. His left arm was weaker than his right, making the chair roll in a half circle.

As he tried to push up the incline to the sidewalk, a sudden sharp pain made him pull his hands off the tires. He shook his hand and the pain spread. Studying the heel of his hands, he realized that he'd opened the blisters formed early in the day. No telling what he was picking up from the tires – spit and bird shit. He rolled down his sleeves to use as gloves, but the fabric drooped into the spokes.

The sun dipped behind a building. His part of the plaza was suddenly in shadow. Cold. He was so cold. He focused on the bus stop. For the return trip, he'd have to cross Sixth Avenue and catch the bus on the other side. Pulling himself inch-by-inch uphill from the plaza bricks toward the sidewalk, he tried to put all else out of his mind – his failure with Kristi, his failure for Mr. Peterson. He had to get back to the hospital, if only for Mom.

Mom. Why hadn't he gone back in time for her? If the sun was setting, it was hours past time to meet with Dr. Ambrose. He'd been so determined he'd paid no attention to time. Mom would be frantic. He should have left a note.

When he tried to move faster, his shirt cuff button caught in the spoke of his left tire. The sleeve yanked down with the motion of the wheel. Searing pain sliced the length of his incision. The chair spun. His head spun.

"Ah!" he cried out. The edges of his vision clouded. Shivering came faster and faster until his teeth ground against each other with the force. He couldn't regain control of any part of his body, but sprawled half in and half out of the wheelchair, pinned in place by his button and his exhaustion.

"He's having a fit," some kid shouted.

"Don't touch him. He might bite you."

Jack couldn't see, couldn't open his eyes, but he knew they were coming closer. All these kids who turned their backs on him when he wanted information, they were willing to come around when he was helpless.

"God, who let him come down here?"

"He said something that scared Swede," a girl said.

"Well, he came down here looking for Swede's girl."

"You saw how Swede ran off."

"Get out of my way. Move."

This last voice was a man's. To Jack's surprise, the voice accompanied the clop of horse hooves and the creak of a saddle.

"Son, can you hear me?"

Jack tried to open his eyes. He barely made out the shadowed face of a man in a dark blue uniform, a brass badge, stiff collar – a policeman. The man's lids pinched with worry. Behind him stood a brown horse who eyed Jack with mild curiosity.

"I've called an ambulance," the man said. He touched Jack's shirt. "Great Jehosephat!" he said, and stood to unbutton his own coat. "Your sweat is freezing." He dropped the coat over Jack's chest and started to pull him up into the chair. Then he realized what the problem was. He turned to one of the onlookers.

"You! Can you get that button out of the spokes?" He held Jack in place while a boy came to the side of the chair and fumbled with the button. "Just pull it off the shirt," the policeman said. "Let's get him loose, somehow."

The boy pulled at the fabric until the button popped off. Jack's arm swung free. The whiz and wail of an ambulance sounded in the distance. The policeman lifted Jack more into the chair. He checked Jack's eyes, the way Dad did on the mountain, but Jack's shivering made it difficult to hold him still.

The man laid his fingers at Jack's throat, maybe looking for a pulse.

At that moment, the crowd beyond the horse opened and Jack saw what he desperately wanted. His father pushed toward him, hair wild in the wind, his eyes opened wide with fear.

"Dad," he managed. "Daaaa."

The policeman turned, his hand still on Jack's chest. "You his Dad?"

"Yes. Yes. We've been searching for him all afternoon."

Jack reached his free hand out and his father took it. The pain in the blisters was nothing.

"What's happened to him?" Dad asked.

"His sweat is cooling. There's blood on his chest."

Jack knew then that the policeman's coat was ruined. "Sorry," he tried to say, but the sound he made wasn't a word. Behind Dad, an ambulance scattered the crowd of gawkers. It pulled into the plaza and parked next to the taciturn horse.

. . .

For Jack, the ride in the ambulance blurred into the bustle of people at the hospital. He was in such pain and so exhausted that he retreated far inside and let all things happen to his body as if his real self had moved on. These worried people seemed to be fiddling over the body of a doll with sweaty hair – checking blood pressure, hooking the Jack doll to bags of liquid and monitors. It was all something he allowed to happen to the guy that was his shell. The person who lived in his mind watched for important people.

Dad rode in the ambulance, his eyes on Jack's face, his hand gripping Jack's numb fingers, his voice whispering, "Why? Why?"

Then at the ambulance entrance, there was Mom, who both cried and laughed hysterically while she pulled the blanket close around his chest to keep out the breeze. Dad hovered behind Mom, touching her shoulder, watching Jack's face.

And then Uncle Jackson appeared and Dad turned toward him, talked to him about something. Uncle Jackson's solemn face watched his father intently; he glanced at Jack and then back to Dad and nodded.

"I saw Berto and Kristi searching for him near the hospital," Jackson said, "Samara and I will find them."

Then Jack knew everyone in the family had been out hunting for him. And he knew that Kristi was safe. He'd put them all through hell. It was going to cost him, going AWOL from the hospital. At the least, it would take him a long time to get his legs working – if they ever worked again. At the worst . . . he couldn't think about the worst. His mother looked too frightened.

Minutes passed with nurses and doctors doing tests. And then Edna Sawyer strode into the emergency cubicle and watched over all the activity. A frown wrinkled her forehead. She asked the emergency nurse a question. The answer made her sigh. Jack read worry in her taut body and fear on her lined face.

She cared about him, but he'd probably put her reputation, maybe even her job in jeopardy by leaving the hospital during her watch.

After a moment, she sighed again, then started to take the empty wheel chair out of the cubicle. She stopped to study the signs on each handle, then took out a pocketknife to cut the hanger art from the chair.

. . .

The next time he woke, he was in the same room in Cardiac Care where he'd been before. While staring across the foot of his bed, he noticed changes on his white board. His hanger sculptures with their signs still attached were taped to the frame. On the white board someone had written CPK 24,000. Methotrexate and IVIG.

He remembered the word Methotrexate from Dr. Ambrose's articles – a medicine they used on cancer patients. So they had decided to do the intravenous treatment. Dad wasn't saying 'No' any longer. He wondered if they had started it already.

Later, he heard Kristi's voice out in the hall. "Can I see him?"

"No," Nurse Sawyer said. "He's asleep now."

"He was looking for me?"

Mom answered her. "That's what the signs say. And someone named Malcolm Peterson."

"Oh Lord," Kristi said. "I got to go upstairs."

"Where?"

"Intensive Care. That's where Mr. Peterson is. I hope he is."

"We'll be here." Mom sounded puzzled. Jack realized Mom had barely met August Peterson. All the worrying and sweating he'd done and his mother hadn't even known why.

It had done no good. By now, Malcolm was deep in Forest Park. *Please, Kris, bring good news about Mr. Peterson.*

. . .

The next morning, Jack thought he'd been transported back a whole day. There stood Dad, just like early yesterday morning. The sun shone through the window onto motes of dust that wafted in the wake of his father's constant jittering. His dad stared at the lone tree with its turning leaves and at the power plant chimney while he fiddled with the drapery cord. Then he glanced over at Jack.

"Hi." Dad dropped the cord and stepped to the side of the bed.

"Dad," he said, and was grateful he could say it. His voice seemed to be working again.

Dad looked across the bed at the IV tower and then above Jack's head at the heart monitor. "That was stupid yesterday," Dad said.

"Stupid, but I had to try."

Dad touched Jack's hand, then held Jack's fingers in his. "I don't understand," Dad said.

He took Dad's thumb in his fingers, the way he'd done as a little kid, grabbing Dad's hand for safety when they walked.

"I hurt Kristi – hurt her bad. I had to try to find her. And Mr. Peterson's son – I thought he would fight to live if his son came back."

"But you could have died out there." Dad sat heavily in the Naugahyde chair. He leaned an elbow on Jack's mattress, still holding Jack's hand. "I don't think you have any idea what it felt like for Mom – well, for me, too – because you up and disappeared."

"I'm sorry, Dad. I was afraid."

"Afraid? You go in a wheelchair, flying these signs and never leave us a note. You whip all the way to the Pioneer Square by yourself – but you're afraid? That makes no sense."

"I knew Dr. Ambrose would hook me up to some medicine," he explained.

"The IV made you afraid, too?" Dad asked. "It scared the shit out of me."

Jack glanced at his father. He hadn't told Jack it was silly to be afraid. He admitted his own fear. The change was so unexpected that all Jack's thoughts spilled out with no logical order.

"I was afraid because if I got hooked up, you were going to be gone all the time. I'd never be able to get out of bed. I had to do something because I only had about three hours left. Kristi had run away. I didn't know that Berto finally found her, so I thought maybe if I found her, I could tell her I was sorry. I hoped she'd talk to Mom and get some help."

"What about the other sign?" Dad asked, waving his arm toward where they hung over the white board.

"I hoped maybe Malcolm Peterson was down there, too, because a lot of street kids hang out there. And I did find him, but he took the bus to Forest Park. He's probably hidden in some camp up there, like he doesn't want to see his dad."

Dad held up his hands to stop the flow, "Whoa, Jack. Slow down."

Jack stopped altogether. Breathing hard, he realized he'd out-talked his oxygen supply.

Dad bit his lip, "Berto and Kristi were helping us look for you. I don't know Mr. Peterson's son, but Kris says he's upstairs talking to his father. And your trip triggered that somehow."

A startling warmth darted through Jack. "Mr. Peterson is talking?"

Dad tested a small smile. "Kristi says Mr. Peterson is getting better."

Jack lay there, stunned. *Peterson is better.* Elation made him want to shout, *Peterson is better!* Jack closed his eyes, thinking *Yes! Yes!*

Then he thought about Kris and Malcolm Peterson. "That Kristi . . ."

" . . . is great." Dad finished for him.

Jack looked at him, surprised.

"Something else happened yesterday, before anybody knew you were gone," Dad said.

Jack studied him and waited, his heart thumping with anxiety.

"Kristi Labbé took some advice from your mother. She went to her father's office. After they talked, he drove her over here. They planned to see how you were doing, and then they were going home to talk to her mother. As it turned out, Mr. Labbé helped in the search. He found the bus driver who remembered you."

That brought an unstoppable grin to Jack's face. "Mr. Labbé came here? Did they go home after you found me?"

"Yes, but I don't know what happened then. How come you never told me about the troubles Kristi faced at home?"

"She was afraid you would think she drank, too."

Dad shook his head in disbelief. "Why would I assume that?"

"I did once. I guess other people have, too. She wanted you to think she had no problems."

"What did Kris think I would do?"

Jack shrugged. "I guess she thought you would bug off when she had problems. That's what her dad did."

Dad fidgeted with Jack's bed covers. "Is that what you thought, too?"

"I . . . I wasn't sure. I guess I thought she might be right."

His father seemed to stare at his own elbow and the creases it made in the mattress. His jaw muscle bunched and released. At last, he spoke again.

"This morning, Jack. Well, I guess it was yesterday morning, but it seems real vivid in my mind . . .. Anyway, I remember telling you that Uncle Jackson and me, that wasn't any of your business."

Jack nodded. He could hardly breathe.

"Well, I guess it is your business."

Relief swept over Jack.

"I don't understand it," Dad said. "I just know your Mom believes it bugs you that I don't get along with him."

Jack said, "When we came back here in the ambulance, you guys were getting along."

"Yeah, well, we can work pretty well together when it's important."

Dad sat in silence for a moment and then he asked, "Is that what you need from me? You need me to get along with Jackson?"

"You crossed him out of your family."

He sat up, both hands gripping the mattress edge. "I think you know why. You know what he did on Nanda Devi?"

"Yeah," Jack said, angrily. "I know Uncle Jackson was in base camp, puking with altitude sickness, but Grandma climbed anyway."

His father jerked upright. "What are you saying?"

"She left him," Jack let his voice grow harsh. "Uncle Jackson was sick – bad sick, but his mother and father both left him so they could climb."

Jack's father stared at him a moment and then sank abruptly, leaning into the back of the chair. He stared out at the power-plant chimney and then up at the IV tower. His hand rose to his mouth and then moved up to cover his eyes. Jack watched in stunned silence as his father's mouth drew tight and his face took on the red darkness he'd seen only in those rare moments when Dad was angry. This wasn't anger. He was sure it wasn't.

"Dad?"

His father glanced at him. In the instant during which Jack recognized tears, his father stood up. He began pacing the room.

"I didn't think," he said, waving an arm at empty air. "I mean Jackson said he was sick that day, but I didn't think he meant really sick." His dad paced to the window. "They couldn't have known," he said. "They must have thought he was faking it."

A sudden flush of anger swept over Jack. "Sure," Jack said, "Uncle Jackson was up-chucking for show." Dad turned sharply toward him, but Jack couldn't stop his mouth running on. "Real heroes can't be sick," he said. "And, Huntingtons have to be real heroes."

His father sucked in a sharp breath. Jack expected him to storm out of the room, but he just stood there, hanging on to the window frame and staring at Jack. The air between them seemed to hold still. The fall leaves on the one tree stopped twisting. Even the motes of dust hung in the sunshine, waiting for some signal to float again. Finally his father straightened away from the wall and came closer to the bed.

"Jack, is that what's going on between us? You think I don't believe you're sick?"

A shadowy curtain seemed to have risen, allowing them to see each other clearly for the first time. Jack grew afraid of saying the wrong thing, but he had to say something in this rare moment. "At first you didn't believe me. Now, you can't help seeing how I am."

His father glanced at the heart monitor and then back to Jack's thin legs before he spoke. "What do you need?" he whispered.

An image and a warmth entered his memory – August Peterson's forthright answer about being afraid to die without finding his son. That honesty was what he needed from Dad. Jack knew he wouldn't deserve honesty if he didn't offer it, too.

So he said, "I need you to stop being afraid of me."

"Afraid of you?" His father stood there, his mouth open at the audacity. He fell into the chair. His glance raked the length of Jack's body. "How can you think I'm afraid of you? You're my son."

Jack said, "You keep trying to put me back the way I was. I'm not that way anymore."

"But you will be. We just need to start a program."

"No, Dad. I might get well. I might someday be like I was. But I need you to care about me now. When I am this way. If you can't do that, then it's just like a friend of mine said. You only love me if I make you look good."

"Who said that?"

"It doesn't matter. What I need to know is do you love me, or just the memory of how I used to be?"

"I love you. I want you to be well."

"Can you push a wheelchair filled with this emaciated body and still be glad I'm here?"

His father's hand swiped across his beard stubble. "God, how can you think I'm not glad to have you now?"

"Because you won't listen when I try to tell you how I feel."

"Okay, Buster, I'm listening. How do you feel?"

"I believe you think I'm the body of the son you used to have."

Dad's eyes widened. He blinked as if startled by sudden light. And just as suddenly, he leaned his head on the sheets near Jack and grabbed for Jack's hand. Jack could see the chords at the back of his neck tighten as air rushed from his throat in a low whine. For a moment, Jack didn't understand what was happening. He pushed up off his pillow, afraid this was Mr. Peterson again, a heart attack. But then the bed began to shake with the motion of Dad's crying. Silent sobs wracked his father's body.

Stunned, Jack put his hand on his father's head. Fingers tangling in the mess of curls, he leaned over and whispered in his father's ear, like a parent comforting his hurt child, "Dad. Oh Dad."

Dad's voice came, so muffled that for the first words, Jack could understand nothing. Then he began to make out phrases.

"I didn't know. . . how sick you were. Thought you were . . . giving up."

Jack put his hand on his father's shoulders. As he did, his father's head came up and his arms enfolded Jack. "You were so . . . so cold," Dad said between jerky gasps for air. "When I realized what I nearly did, I . . . I was so afraid for you. And mad at myself."

Jack buried his head in Dad's shoulder.

Later, his embarrassed father untangled their arms. He smiled, sniffed, and set to work straightening the things on the tray table. Then he stood and rearranged the flowers on Jack's windowsill.

Jack watched all the fidgeting. One vase of chrysanthemums was moved at least three times. He decided to try clearing his conscience at last. "Dad, I nearly killed you."

Dad glanced around at Jack. "Oh, you mean up on that slab on Mount Tecumseh?"

"When I grabbed your jacket. You made me so angry I even thought about taking you off the cliff with me. You saw it."

Dad's attempt at a laugh seemed forlorn. "You're pretty strong. Ought to get mad more often."

"What?"

Dad stopped moving things and faced him. "It wouldn't have worked, tossing me off. I was already hooked into the protection you'd put there. But the look on your face – that thought I saw there – that made me pay attention."

Something had happened since yesterday. His father actually talked about stuff. Jack decided to see how far he could go with it. "Dad, am I always gonna have to knock you around to get your attention?"

His father raised both shoulders. "Let's hope not. This week, between you and Mom, well . . . I hope I've got the message."

Dad reached a tentative hand to touch Jack's head, ruffled his already messy hair. "I do love you, Jack." He said it right out, without glancing away or fidgeting with anything. "I love you now, in bed, in the wheelchair – you can't guess how my heart stopped when I saw you shivering in that wheelchair in the wind."

Jack warmed. "Yeah," he answered. For a second it was the most he could get his voice to do. Then, after swallowing hard, he whispered, "Go talk to Mom."

His father mock-saluted. "Yes, sir. I'll try. I get it all wrong lately, but I'll try."

After he was gone, Jack realized that the other night, when Mom had kissed his forehead, it had been Dad's hand on his head – the angle, the weight. It had been Dad. He was certain.

CHAPTER 35

Jack flexed his fingers and found they still had strength. Under the bandages, the blisters on his palms stung. Just to see if he could, he retrieved his drawing pad from the drawer and tried drawing without bending his taped fingers. He had to use whole arm movements, but it worked. He sketched the bus stop. In the background, a policeman sat on a stolid horse. In Jack's mind, the colors of Portland in wet sunshine appeared, as if he'd already painted them – red brick plaza, white, gray and salmon-pink buildings, the metallic shine of Joe's wheelchair, Joe's red beard and hair, the primary colors of bus ads, and the tan and brown scruffy bark of Sycamore trees.

"Hey! Buzzard bait."

Kristi poked her head around the door. She had no spikes. Her hair lay in silky smoothness about her face.

"Hi." He waved his pencil. "I'm decent." He dropped the drawing pad on his blankets.

She smiled, charged into the room and picked up his bandaged hand. Startled, Jack jerked his fist, and her, toward his chest. She came willingly, even leaned over and kissed him on the mouth. Her lips were warm, soft. He didn't know what to do beyond straining upward. After a moment, he let his tongue touch the edge of her upper lip.

She jumped back, just as surprised as he was by what she had started.

He let his head drop into the pillow and smiled. "You can't put me on my back for that," he said. "I'm down already."

"Yeah? A few months from now you'll be up and strutting around. I'll get you then."

He chuckled. "Meanwhile, could we rerun the part before you give me the karate take-down?"

She tilted her head, as if to consider it. "Wasn't that first one perfect?"

Her smart self had placed him in a verbal mine field. "You were perfect," he said, carefully. "But I was surprised. I need practice."

She blushed. He congratulated himself on saying the right thing for once.

Under her knit coral shirt, she shrugged one slender shoulder. His breath caught. Her face turned toward that shoulder, her tongue curled toward her upper lip as if she were thinking, but the move served merely to heat him up.

"We have to get all the moves down," he whispered.

She colored a deeper tan. "Yeah . . . but I've got news to tell you first."

He'd always known she had some of Dad's problem with being in one place for long. Then he remembered that he had news, too.

"Malcolm . . ." he said.

"Swede . . ." They spoke at the same moment, stopped and then both went for it a second time.

Then Jack heard what Kristi was saying. "Swede was so scared, he hopped the wrong bus. As soon as it started up into the hills, he jumped off and ran to the hospital."

Jack imagined Malcom's worn Reeboks as rags after that dash.

Kristi fished in her jeans pocket and brought out two one dollar bills which she slapped on the table. "That's for the bus tickets. He says to tell you thanks."

Jack snorted. "Tell him he's twenty-five cents short."

"He's bumming that off his brother this afternoon."

"Of course," he laughed, and she joined him. She looked wonderful.

"Why Swedish Pete?" he asked.

"Ego," she said simply. "He said he figured no one would forget a black guy named Swede."

Jack chuckled as he brought her hand to his mouth. She watched him. He watched her watch him touch her fingertips with his thumb. Then he ran a finger over her palm – a ticklish move he'd dreamed about for weeks. She blinked and yanked her hand from his grasp, nearly jumping off the bed. She was nervous. He felt great.

"And Swede says I should tell you something else," Kristi said.

Jack watched her warily, afraid he didn't want to hear what Malcolm wanted her to say.

"He says I can tell you about the Sally Arrowsmith Shelter. I can't tell you where, but I can tell you what."

"What shelter?" he asked.

"You've seen those girls at the plaza – babies, some of them."

"Tough babies," he said, remembering.

"That tough act is how they survive," she said. "Some are down there because they like the excitement. Others though, they've got no safe place, not even home. I talk to them. After a while, when I can tell they're ready to get outta danger, I take them to the shelter."

"Are you living in that shelter too?"

"Sometimes I do intake there, or I'm the night duty assistant, but mostly I go to your house or I go home."

"And Malcolm, Swede?"

"He knew the shelter existed. He had a phone number but no address. He talked me into going there that first time I ran away."

"How'd he know about it?"

"He does the same volunteer work for a boy's shelter. That's what

he and his dad split over. Malcolm wouldn't give the police – his dad –
information about people he took to the shelter."

Jack thought how tough that must have been for both of them –
each one certain he was right.

Kristi dug into her backpack. "Tah dah!" she exclaimed and handed
him a thick report. Through the blue plastic cover, he could see a title
page, "Tools that Should Have Opened the West, (But Didn't)."

He laughed. "That's a new twist."

"We showed how people developed tools that served their purpose
well for a time."

"For a time . . . and then what?"

"And then they had to develop new tools to face situations they
never expected. Did you know the Shoshone taught Lewis and Clark
how to make better, more stable canoes for the rapids on the upper
Columbia River."

"True. Those guys had a lot of help the whole way – tribes showing
them how to live in new land."

"So, in our paper, we showed how failure pushes creativity and
cooperation."

Jack grinned. "So did we get a D or an F?"

"Turn the page."

He opened the report. On the title page, a large A-plus decorated
the right hand corner, accompanied by a note, "Great! You made us
all think about how we need to be flexible – ready to change when we
meet new situations and new people."

"Ooh! Flexible!" Jack said. "You're a genius, Kristi."

She grinned. "Yep. Berto, too. After we made our presentation, the
kids asked a lot of questions. Nobody could figure out why you picked on
that dumb boat until Berto got up to answer. He talked about how each
failure points the way to new trials. He got grand about how the iron-boat
was the first in a long line of river boats for shallow waters, boats that still
sail in the upper parts of the Missouri and Mississippi Rivers."

Jack's eyes widened. "What a great bluff."

She nodded. "A real showman."

"Showman! Geez, I forgot all about the *Sound of Music*. Was he a good Captain VonTrapp?"

"Big time good," she said. "Five curtain calls on opening night. Berto and Angela brought down the house with their *Edelweiss* duet."

"I missed everything."

"Nah! We bought tickets for you for two weekends from now because Dr. Ambrose says you're outta here as soon as that new medicine kicks in."

"Outta here? How can I get out when I'm such a wussy mess?"

She shrugged. "Actually, for a guy who spends his days panhandling in the plaza, you look pretty good."

He knew then. She loved him, skinny legs and all. It felt wonderful.

Rising, she messed his already scruffy hair. "Want me to braid that mop?"

He took advantage of her distraction and wrapped his arms around her waist. She leaned toward him, all softness and energy. Jack opened his mouth and captured hers before she had a chance to say anything. She tasted like blackberries – sugar, sweet juice and the promise of sharp thorns. Mystery, excitement, adventure.

One more taste, and she suddenly pushed up from his bed. "Nurse Sawyer will pick now to arrive," she whispered.

"Nurse Sawyer's shoes can be heard two doors away."

Kristi took his hands in hers and smiled. "My Dad is waiting. We're going to an Alanon meeting."

Jack must have looked puzzled. "It's for families of drinkers," she explained. "Mom's in a thirty-day rehab – a nice place."

"Great," he said. "That's great." Now he knew why she seemed so bold and so free. Her dad had finally come back to be in charge. She beamed, nodded and pursed her lips as if she were afraid she might cry.

She started to say something else, but couldn't seem to get it out, so she just nodded again.

"Come back soon," he whispered.

"I will." Her voice rasped, then cleared up. "I already signed on to drive you to some of your therapy visits with Bill. As soon as you're home, you have two workouts a week."

"How do you know that?"

"I was at the family planning meeting last night. Your doctors, your dad and mom, Jackson, Samara, me and your little brother, Berto."

"Where was I?"

"Asleep. Zonked. Snoring."

"Was not."

"We had to close your door so the nurses could think."

He laughed.

"Oh, I forgot one more thing," she said, jumping off the bed and lifted her backpack, preparing to exit. "At your mom's gallery opening all her paintings sold in two days – all except the herons."

"Herons was a great painting," he said. "Why didn't that sell?" Jack was already talking to Kristi's back as she headed toward the door.

"Your mom kept it for your bedroom." Kristi looped her pack over one shoulder. "Berto had to hang it for her because, of course, she would cry and get the watercolors all wet."

As she strode into the hallway, Jack fell back into his pillow and took one long inhale. He felt exhausted by all the excitement and nervous energy that was Kristi on a happy day. He hadn't seen her this way for a long time.

He had to get better. Had to, just to keep up with her.

CHAPTER 36

Afternoon. Hot sun streamed in. His father and Uncle Jackson bumped into each other as they arrived at Jack's door. Jack expected them to lock antlers and start snorting, but his uncle merely laughed and said, "I'll come back later."

"No way," Dad said. "Grab an extra chair from the hall and come on in."

Jack blinked. Maybe Dad hoped with Uncle Jackson around, Jack wouldn't ask how it went with Mom. While he tried to figure out what made his father tick, Dad strode into the room and propped a large flat package against the closet door. Jack figured it must be the galleys of his father's Denali-Mount McKinley book.

Uncle Jackson set a chair at the foot of the bed. Jack's father whooshed into the Naugahyde, loosened his shoulders and then gestured toward the IV tower.

"Now that you're more stable, Dr. Ambrose will come start that Methotrexate and IV steroids," he said.

Jack was surprised. Dr. Ambrose usually talked to him about what she intended to do.

Uncle Jackson coughed. His father glanced at Jackson and then back at Jack. "Oh, yeah. She says to tell you she's going to come explain the side effects and all that to you before the medicine arrives."

"Steroids. I thought you hated steroids." Jack said.

"We all do," Dad said. "But you're in bad shape, big guy, and your doctor convinced us that we need them to get your inflamed muscles to cool off – give you a chance to get over the worst."

"How long do I have to be on the IVs?" he asked.

"Well, that's why I came. Looks like it will be four or five hours each time. And maybe once a week. So I, uhm . . . I thought maybe you'd like me to read something to you. Maybe when my voice dries out, old Jackson here can read while I get us coffee or something."

Jack stared at him. He'd never seen his father willingly sit still for longer than thirty seconds. His father glanced away from Jack's close scrutiny.

"Of course, if you get too tired," Dad said, "I could also shut up."

"But stay here," Jack said, with such emphasis it surprised even him.

After a moment, his father had digested that challenge, and evidently decided to gloss over it by changing topics.

"I brought a couple of books." He fished a paperback out of each coat pocket. Jack noticed a mountain peak on the cover of one and a startled deer in the cross-hairs of a rifle on the cover of the other.

"Can I choose?"

"Shit, yes!" Dad said. "I mean 'shoot'." He held out both books for Jack to study. Jack knew without taking them that they were both wilderness adventures. Probably books he would like, but at the moment, he was into testing these new waters to see how deep they were.

"I'd like to hear parts of the *Journals*." He pointed to the stack on his nightstand.

"Lewis and Clark? Haven't you read those about six times already?"

"They're good stuff," he said.

His father picked up the Biddle edition, weighing its five hundred pages in his hand. "Kind of a slog through muddy waters, isn't it?"

Jack pretended to misunderstand. "Every day. Mud. Floating logs. Mosquitoes. And a lot of the time they had to get out and pull the boat around and over sand bars."

Jack forced himself not to look at his uncle. Jackson would know what a test he was putting before Dad. His father took a deep breath, sighed and then let the book fall open. "Where do you want to start?"

Without hesitation, he answered. "August 26, 1804."

His father found the place and began reading. George Shannon had just killed a bull elk. By the time his father got into the reading, Shannon had been sent to find two missing horses, and gotten himself lost from the expedition. Clark, worried about him. He sent the tracker, John Coulter, in search of Shannon. Even Coulter couldn't find him. After the expedition had several encounters with the rambunctious and proud Yankton Sioux, they still had not found Shannon and were concerned he'd fallen afoul of the tribe. Nearly sixteen days after he disappeared, they polled around a bend in the river and Shannon sat there on the river bank. In their journals that night, the captains wrote of their deep relief.

"What the heck was he doing all that time?" Dad asked.

"Trying to catch up with people who were actually behind him." Jack said.

His father looked at him with narrowed eyes, then glanced at Uncle Jackson, who shrugged.

"You know what was so cool about that?" Jack asked. "Shannon over-estimated the speed of the rest of the expedition, but he finally figured out where he had gone wrong, doubled back and met them."

"Pretty good thinking," Dad said.

"He found the horses, too," Jack said.

"Only one," Dad countered. "It says he met them with one horse."

"Some think he ate the other one," Jack said.

Dad closed his eyes, then glanced at Uncle Jackson again.

"Mallory," Uncle Jackson said. "It's okay to be behind, sometimes. The important thing is to meet somewhere and go on together."

Jack tensed for Dad's reaction. Instead of biting Jackson's head off, his dad set the book aside and reached for the package beside the closet. "Your mom sent this," he said, laying the brown paper package on Jack's legs.

Jack hefted it. Almost no weight for its size. Maybe about fourteen by eighteen inches and two inches deep, he estimated. For a moment, he thought it might be the heron painting, but Kristi had said that was hanging in his room.

"Open it," Dad urged.

From the shape and sturdiness, he figured if it wasn't the Herons, then Mom had sent him matte board and a frame for a painting – kind of her way of telling him to start producing since he couldn't climb mountains. He stared at the brown wrapping, not certain he wanted that message.

Uncle Jackson stood up, leaning on the back of his chair to get a better view as Jack opened the package.

Well, Jack thought, maybe Mom is right. He should start framing his stuff. He hoped he'd be strong enough to use a saw and hammer soon. He ripped the paper off. And there in his hands, already matted and framed, lay his own painting of the iron boat, the one Berto had wanted to use for their report. The matte was a perfect dark burnt sienna, playing up the rust on the iron.

"Your mom and I framed it," Dad said. "She chose the matt."

Jack stared at it – a derelict boat, beached on an island in the middle of a sluggish river. The elk-skin covering seemed worn. One piece of leather flapped in the imagined breeze coming in from the cold, unexplored mountains in the background to the west.

He glanced up at Dad and noticed that Uncle Jackson watched Dad as well.

"You've sure got a slew of paintings stored in that file drawer," Dad said. "I never saw most of them before this morning. You pick real different subjects, but you're getting to be as good as your mother."

Jack fingered the oak of the frame, carefully mitred and joined. Its strong grain and weathered color focused attention on the iron skeleton, the worn leather, and the forlorn air of defeat and uselessness in the image of the boat.

Mom and Dad had framed it together. At least they were at home long enough to do that. He didn't know what to say, so he whispered, "Thanks, Dad."

When there was no answer, he glanced up. His father sat, elbows resting on the arms of the Naugahyde chair, his head leaning on one hand, one finger covering his upper lip, his whole attention on Jack. After an awkward moment, his father brushed that finger across the end of his nose, sniffed, and then leaned forward to look at the painting again. Dad didn't notice that behind him, Mom had come to the doorway.

Dad took the painting, studying it. "That's the boat you've been building, right?"

"Yeah," Jack said. "Nobody knows for sure what it looked like. This is based on descriptions of it."

"Whatever happened to the real thing?"

"When they put it together, it worked great. Lewis wrote that it floated like a cork. But when a storm blew up, the caulking on the seams failed. They had to hide the boat on an island and leave it."

"They couldn't caulk again?"

"The caulk they had was no good. And they were already late – pushing toward autumn — and they had no idea how far they would have to go on foot to cross the Rocky Mountains."

"Not good planning," Dad said.

Jack nodded, "Except how could they plan? They were in a new place. Uncharted territory. Nothing was what they expected."

Dad pointed at the books. "At least we know they made it all the way."

"They made it because other people, the tribes, along the way helped them."

"That so?" Dad looked up, surprise in his raised eyebrows.

Jack nodded. "On their own, they would have died."

Dad sat back, staring at the painting again, and that was when Mom stepped into the room. Jack's father glanced up and smiled at her.

"Alison, you know what I think?" he asked, raising the painting toward her in salute. Dad pointed at the boat. "Next summer, when Jack gets a little stronger, I think we should make an expedition to this place. All of us." He waved Uncle Jackson into his invitation. "We'll rent however many canoes it takes. Berto, Kristi and Samara, too. We should rescue this poor old boat."

Mom chuckled. "I bet all kinds of people have been looking for it during the last two hundred years."

Uncle Jackson said, "All that iron . . . the latches on one hundred barns in northern Montana. Probably the hinges on every garden gate for miles around."

Dad grinned up at Uncle Jackson. "Old iron in every weather vane within shouting distance of the Missouri headwaters," he said. "But I still want to see the pieces."

"Me, too," Mom said.

Dad leaned his head against her wild hair where it touched his cheek. "What do you say, Jack?" he asked. "We can search for what's left of it. Follow the river for as long as we hold out."

"What?" Mom asked in mock horror. "Not climb every peak in the Rockies, just to keep it exciting?"

"Some year, maybe, when Jack wants to climb," Dad said. "But next summer, we'll study the world from a new angle – from a canoe and a wheelchair."

"Sounds good to me," Jack said, and he waved in Dr. Ambrose who had been waiting in the doorway while his family planned their future.

Book Group and Classroom discussion questions for *Uncharted Territory*

Jack's Story

1) Author Rae Richen wanted to write a story with no villains, where everyone is doing the best they know and yet there are huge obstacles for the hero to overcome. Did the author succeed in this goal?

2) Jack has pressures on him to succeed. What are the sources of those pressures? To what extent does Jack finally succeed because of these pressures? How do these pressures hinder him?

3) Jack's particular interests (his friends, the track team, mountain climbing, painting) are encouraged, made possible and are colored by his family's interest. How do family interests, sometimes support and sometimes stifle the young people you have known?

4) There are taboo topics in Jack's family. What are they? Why do they remain taboo for so long? Do you know families with topics that cannot be discussed? What might happen if one family member forced those topics into the open?

5) Jack's admiration for the members of the Lewis and Clark Expedition is a major part of his character. How does this play into Jack's approach to any obstacle?

6) Discuss the relationship between Jack's mom and dad. What are its strengths? Its weaknesses?

7) Toward the end of the book, Mom takes a stand on Dad's attitude. How do you feel about what she did? Was there potential for disaster for all of them in her position?

8) Two key scenes in the book take place in Portland's Pioneer Courthouse Square. Portlanders refer to this downtown square as "Portland's Living Room." It frequently hosts community concerts, live theater, summer movies on a big screen, protest rallies and holiday celebrations. Yet, it is also a gathering place for young people, some of whom live on the streets. Are there community living rooms in your town? How do they function for the variety of people in your community?

9) Jack Huntington's family is clearly upper-middle class. Does their relative affluence have any influence on Jack's potential for solving his family problems? His health problem? What if Kristi were the young person with this disease (polymyositis). How might her family's options be different from Jack's?

10) Jack is a mentor for some of his fellow students. How do we imagine this quality playing out in his future?

11) What about life and family does Jack learn from his father? From his mother?

12) How do Jack's friends, Berto and Kristi, force the issues in Jack's life to the forefront? How do Kristi's problems change Jack?

13) What role does Uncle Jackson play in Jack's life? How would Jack be different if he never had known Uncle Jackson?

14) August Petersen is in Jack's room for forty-eight hours. Discuss

your mentors, however brief their moment in your life.

15) Are there avenues for each of us to become a mentor for others? How are some of these workable for us? Not workable?

16) What makes Jack unique? In what ways is Jack an Everyman?

Style and Craft

a) Dialogue and interior monologue play a major role in the style of *Uncharted Territory*. What effect did this style choice play in your feeling about the story and its characters?

b) The author chose to write *Uncharted Territory* entirely in the point of view of Jack. Thus, we have to guess the thoughts of Dad, Mom and everyone else only from what Jack observes. How does this story-telling choice control our understanding of every person in Jack's life? Is there someone you wanted to know more about?

c) Portland, Oregon, the Columbia River and Cascade Mountains are characters in the story as well. What does the author's use of the city, river and mountains show about Jack, his friends and family? How does geography, including both rural and urban setting, affect the people in your region?

d) Have you looked up Mount Tecumseh on maps or the Internet? This is the one location the author created. It is plunked from her mind onto a map location that is presently a crater. Mount Tecumseh is a composite of climbing problems the author and her husband have met in several different Cascade Mountain areas, including meeting families of semi-wild goats. The features of Mount Tecumseh are created to provide the kind of obstacles that test and forever change Jack and Mallory's relationship. How does discovering that this is a fictionalized location affect your understanding of the book? Are you disappointed that you won't be able to climb Mount Tecumseh?

e) The author would like to hear from you about your reactions to *Uncharted Territory* and any ideas you have about the characters and topics raised in the book. You can write to her by visiting her website and blog at www.raerichen.com.

Rae Richen's short stories and articles have appeared in anthologies, newspapers and in handbooks for writers and teachers. She has taught junior high, high school students and adults and has always been impressed with the wide-ranging curiosity and the persistent search for answers among her students.

Uncharted Territory includes questions for book groups and classroom discussion. The questions deal with story content and also with style and storytelling choices of the author. They are appropriate for students studying fiction writing as well as reading and comprehension.

The author is available for classroom presentations and discussions of this book. She also enjoys leading workshops for any age group on the writing of fiction in general. Contact her at:

Lloyd Court Press
P.O. Box 12262,
Portland, OR 97212-4039

Books available at Amazon, Nook, Kobo, IBooks and Ingram